Run From The Black Dawn

by

A. Stephen Rutter

Order this book online at www.trafford.com
or email orders@trafford.com

Most Trafford titles are also available at major online book retailers.

Note for Librarians: A cataloguing record for this book is available from Library and Archives Canada at www.collectionscanada.ca/amicus/index-e.html

Printed in Victoria, BC, Canada.

ISBN: 978-1-4251-7349-4 (sc)

ISBN: 978-1-4251-7350-0 (e-book)

We at Trafford believe that it is the responsibility of us all, as both individuals and corporations, to make choices that are environmentally and socially sound. You, in turn, are supporting this responsible conduct each time you purchase a Trafford book, or make use of our publishing services. To find out how you are helping, please visit www.trafford.com/responsiblepublishing.html

Our mission is to efficiently provide the world's finest, most comprehensive book publishing service, enabling every author to experience success. To find out how to publish your book, your way, and have it available worldwide, visit us online at www.trafford.com

Trafford rev. 6/12/2009

Trafford PUBLISHING® www.trafford.com

North America & international
toll-free: 1 888 232 4444 (USA & Canada)
phone: 250 383 6864 • fax: 250 383 6804 • email: info@trafford.com

The United Kingdom & Europe
phone: +44 (0)1865 487 395 • local rate: 0845 230 9601
facsimile: +44 (0)1865 481 507 • email: info.uk@trafford.com

Special thanks to Joanne Thauli for her assistance in editing and improving the manuscript – and to my brother, Stan, for his work on the cover.

A

Getting to know Africa...........

When a newcomer sees a fly land in his beer, he pushes the glass away and orders a fresh one.

On his second tour of duty, he flicks the fly out of his glass and carries on drinking.

Thereafter, he wrings it dry so that he won't miss a single drop.........

PROLOGUE

Gordon Blake pulled his chair a little closer to the fire and poured himself some more brandy from the decanter. It was one of the few pleasures he had left now, apart from his memories, which would remain sharp and clear for what few years remained to him. It had been a full, eventful and, for the most part, exciting life, crammed with experiences of which most men can only dream.

Since the death of his wife shortly after their retirement, Gordon had been lonely, listless and frustratingly bored. He had even thought, seriously for a while, of writing his memoirs as most generals do. But then he wasn't a general, at least not in the military sense, although in his day he had probably wielded more power than most rule-ridden military leaders. Gordon had risen to the position of Managing Director and Chief Executive Officer of the Combined Africa Company Limited. Chief Executive Officers, however, unlike real generals, retain neither their rank nor their prestige after retirement.

Gordon had never been one for keeping a record of his involvements. Besides which, who really cares about the kind of wars which use mergers instead of cannons, dividends instead of medals, and dull, routine office procedures instead of the excitement of battle?

The wind curled and howled around the cottage, knocking on the doors and windows and blowing a fanfare of admiration for the cold, damp English January. How very different from those bright, hot days of his younger years, days which would be brought back to life in all their colour and sparkle during the next few hours. Not that his part in the incident was a particularly significant one, except as an advisor and powerless spectator.

He picked up the book and scanned the cover for the hundredth time.

"Biting The Hand – A Nation Off The Leash", by Derek Scott. It was originally supposed to be an exposé of The Kumanga Affair, but Derek had soon realised that he didn't have enough material to sustain interest. So he let his imagination run wild, and turned it into a work of fiction.

Although Gordon was familiar with most of the context of what he was about to read, he had been looking forward to this moment for many months, ever since Derek had told him that the book was finished and ready for publication. Gordon had made a few suggestions and straightened out some points of administration, so he felt that he was a part of it. It was Derek's story, though, and Gordon didn't want either to steal any of the glory or detract from the enjoyment of reading the finished product. Strange that it had taken Derek twenty years to write it. Well, to be precise, three years actually to write it since he retired, and the previous seventeen to think about it. Gordon was glad that the Good Lord had spared him long enough to be able to read what to most people would be just another adventure story, little realising the elements of truth behind it.

He lit a cigar, another luxury which he had denied himself for so many years. Marjorie had been adamant against smoking since she learned that it was associated with the promotion of cancer. It was ironic that it was she, Marjorie, who had succumbed to the dreaded disease and not himself. Gordon didn't really care now. He kept telling himself that he should derive as much pleasure as he possibly could from what time was left to him.

1

The bedroom door burst open as a heavy boot smashed into it. Derek never locked it, and had never bothered doing so, unlike some of his neighbours whose experiences with night prowlers had been unpleasant. Derek argued that if a burglar wanted to enter, no simple domestic lock would deter him. A slight touch of the doorknob would have gained entry, but the Africans' flair for the dramatic insisted that it must be kicked in. This was undoubtedly a direct influence of the second-rate police films which were filling the screens and minds of those who could afford television - or those brazen enough to secure an unauthorised vantage point. Television was a creeping menace - unstoppable, irresistible and naive, yet welcomed as a necessary leap of progress, another measure of sophistication.

Derek sat up in bed, instantly alert, as the mosquito net was ripped aside by a sneering policeman.

"What the hell . . . "

"Shut up you mouth. Get up. You under arrest."

Derek saw that he was surrounded by half a dozen leering black faces. Four rifles were pointing at his head, and two pairs of arms dragged him roughly to his feet.

"Take your hands off me; get out of here. What the hell d'you think you're . ."

His protest was silenced as a rifle butt smashed against his jaw, filling his mouth with blood and sending him reeling into the arms of his captors.

"Take him," commanded the sergeant.

Derek was dragged outside into the warm, damp air of the early African morning, and pushed roughly into the back of a Land Rover. Eager but gentle hands lifted him from the floor and helped him into a sitting position.

A chorus of voices greeted him as he slumped back, his jaw on fire from the impact.

"Are you all right, old chap?"

"I say, this is a frightful mess."

“There’ll be some explaining to do.........”

"Keep still, will you...... I’m trying to wipe off some of the blood."

"All right," Derek mumbled, trying to focus his eyes on the faces around him.

"What . . . Have they gone mad?"

"They’ve gone completely bloody berserk, if you ask me. I imagine we’ll soon find out, though. It looks as though they’re taking us to Central. You're apparently the last for this trip."

Derek recognised this last voice, quiet but firm, calm but full of authority. In the dim and changing light of what few street lamps were still functioning, he could make out the features of James Barrett who, as always, was trying to look dignified, even under these impossible circumstances. His wrinkled, bloodstained pyjamas did little to enhance the image.

James P. Barrett was the regional manager of the International Bank of Asia and Africa, Colonial Division. Headquartered in London, it was by far the most influential bank on three continents. Over the decades, I.B.A.A. had built up a rapport with European and Asian governments which could, if put to the test, have a dramatic influence on the economy of emerging countries such as Kumanga. There was considerable pressure to change the "colonial" part to "commonwealth" in accordance with the current political climate, but it would be a while yet before "A. & A. Col." became anything else.

The rugged vehicle bumped and clattered its way through the narrow streets of the town, jarring the pain in Derek's face to an excruciating degree.

Now that he had some voices to help with identification, the faces became more recognisable. Derek focussed on Alan Rushton, his assistant, whose face was half covered by the blood seeping from a cut on his forehead. Derek pointed.

"You . . . "

"Just a scratch, old man. You should see the mess I made on the doorstep. Going to have to put in an R362 for it."

He was trying to be flippant, as usual. An R362 was the form requesting urgent repair authorization to a Company-owned residence. It was inappropriate and tasteless comments like this which got Alan into more trouble than was necessary. Alan was clad only in a pair of running shorts.

He followed Derek's quizzical gaze, anticipating the next question.

"First thing I could grab," he gabbled in a sheepish tone. "Don't usually wear anything. Never have done."

He gave a sly glance towards Jean, who was sitting next to him, and she turned her head away with a scowl.

Derek saw Jeremy Wilson, 26 years old and a talented engineer in charge of the province's electrical generators. Jeremy kept himself to his own circle of acquaintances and Derek knew very little about him. There was also Henri Gaudet, French and fat. Henri was the general manager of La Compagnie Française des Transports de L'Ouest Africaine, usually referred to simply as "C.F.T." Henri was a staunch supporter of the small but active French club, and outside the infrequent visits he made to that establishment, Derek's only real contact with Henri was of a strictly business nature. Both Henri and Jeremy were fully dressed.

And there was Jean.

Jean was wearing, not unexpectedly, a low-necked nightgown, partially covered by an unfastened dressing gown which had been hastily thrown on. She showed no signs of having been ill-treated or handled roughly, and despite the lack of make-up, her complexion was flawless. She evidently has some magical influence over the marauding, power-crazed African police patrols as well as most of the town's expatriate males.

They bumped along the familiar road which led through the market, a route which Derek had used twice each day going to and from his office. Amid the buzz of murmuring and whisperings going on around him, he tried to work out how many times he had travelled this route since his posting to Ugbeshu. His mind was not up to it, and he gave up out of sheer confusion after the first two miles. An odd thought came to his mind. He had never before made the journey in the back of a vehicle, since it was always his practise when touring to sit next to his driver. It was an ironic twist that this, the first time, would be as someone's prisoner instead of being the one in control.

Derek tried to speculate why he and five other people had been dragged from their beds in the early hours of the morning, but the motive for this apparent insanity escaped him. He could only conclude that everything would be straightened out when they reached their destination.

They came to a halt outside Central Police Station. The concrete exterior used to be kept a gleaming white, but Derek had noticed over recent months that in company with many other official buildings, the ever-present laterite had been allowed to creep up the walls.

Laterite. Derek knew of no other place on earth which had a ground cover quite like West Africa's laterite. It was a fine, red powder, so fine that a mere footstep could send a choking cloud upwards to stifle the nostrils, settle on the tongue and irritate the eyes. A short walk in a pair of light-coloured slacks would turn them to a bright, brick-red hue from the knees down. Little wonder, then, that most buildings were in constant need of washing or repainting. Laterite covered the base of every exterior wall, fading and lightening until the original but faded paint colour appeared high up, high enough to be out of cloud range. During the rainy season the consistency changed dramatically. The fine powder mixed with the water to form an even paste, heavy enough to cling to shoes and tires like cellulose glue, making one's feet, after a few short paces, almost twice their weight. It was a grim sense of humour which had bestowed laterite on West Africa's coastal regions.

The rear door of the vehicle opened and they were pushed into the Charge Room, where an officious-looking sergeant holding a clipboard demanded to know their names. James Barrett slammed his fist down hard on the sergeant's table, making everyone jump, the Africans in particular.

"This is an outrage," he roared. "What is the meaning of this idiocy? I demand to see Superintendent Symons. What do you people think you are doing?"

The outburst surprised everyone. James P. Barrett, the banker, the gentleman, always correct in everything he did, had never before been known to raise his voice, let alone lose his control.

The sergeant looked nervously over his shoulder to where a greying inspector was watching the scene from a chair in the corner. Without a word the inspector inclined his head towards a dimly-lit passage at the end of the room, and the sergeant put down his clipboard.

"Of course we really know what your names are, so you will please come with me."

"Like hell, I will." This was Alan Rushton, prepared to resist the request. He changed his mind when the muzzle of a Lee Enfield rifle appeared against his nose. They were all ushered along the passage, not without loud but futile protests, as two armed policemen prodded them from behind. They were directed into a large, unpleasant-smelling cell which was usually the overnight resting place for vagrants, drunks and other assorted petty villains. There was no-one else in that night; it was as though it had purposely been left vacant for the occasion. The sergeant made a great show of locking the cell door behind them.

They all started talking at once.

"What's happening?"

"Why?"

"What have we done?"

Or, more likely, what are they pretending we've done? What's all this madness about, and who's responsible for it? Above all, where's that pompous idiot Reg Symons, and why isn't he controlling his men?

No one had any answers, and after the initial outbursts they fell silent. Except for James Barrett, who again demanded to see the Chief Superintendent.

"Chief see you only when he ready, not before," a young constable yelled back in a tone he had never before dared to use when addressing a white man.

Half an hour went by, during which time they muttered, protested, threatened and even pleaded to be released. Their cries went unheeded, echoing around the bare walls of the cell block. Then footsteps were heard along the passage, and the cell door was suddenly flung open. A tall, well-built black figure walked in, and became recognisable in the gloom of the cell as Inspector Ovremwe, one of the rising hopefuls of the Kumanga Police. He was wearing a well-pressed khaki uniform and a gleaming Sam Browne belt.

Ovremwe had earned his stars the hard way, having joined what was then the Moresia Police sixteen years ago after his discharge from the Royal West Africa Rifles with a creditable record of active service in Burma. Any sophistication he possessed was a rub-off from European fellow officers during the five years in which he had held the Queen's Commission.

He stood in silence as though waiting for a reaction. When none came, he spoke sharply and with impatience.

"You will stand when an officer of the Kumanga Police enters."

He had picked this up from his brief contact with the Japanese.

"Like hell, I will," said Alan once again. "Especially when it's you. Who do you think you….?" His words were choked off as Ovremwe, without showing any signs of anger, lifted his ceremonial cane and struck Alan lightly across the face. Alan looked up in surprise. No-one had ever done that to him before. With a snarl of rage he leapt forwards and grabbed Ovremwe by the throat.

"You jumped-up, black bastard. I'll teach you where your place is, you......"

His words were choked off as the butt of a rifle crashed down on his head, sending him to the floor in a flurry of blood. Both Derek and James lunged at Alan's attacker, but were each met with a rifle in the chest. Jean cradled Alan's head and tried to stop the blood with a piece of material torn from her nightgown.

Ovremwe coughed, then spluttered.

"Enough of this. I came here with the intention of explaining the situation and perhaps arranging to make your stay more comfortable. But if that's your attitude, you can rot here forever, as far as I'm concerned."

He nodded to the constables and prepared to leave.

"Just a minute," Barrett said with a puzzled frown on his face. "Where is Mr. Symons?"

Ovremwe had regained his composure by this time.

"Mr. Symons is now just that - a mere 'Mr'. And by now," he glanced at his watch, "should be somewhere over the Sahara, thankful to have got away unscathed."

With his cane he tapped the arrangement of crowns and stars on his epaulettes.

"By the way, in case you hadn't noticed - I am now in charge around here, and no longer do you demand anything."

He walked out of the cell.

Henri Gaudet voiced the question which was on everyone's lips.

"But what have we done that makes you bring us here and lock us up, so, like common criminals? It is my wish to talk to the French Consul."

Ovremwe turned with a smile on his face as the cell door began to close.

"That will not be possible. He has had the wisdom to leave the country. Under diplomatic immunity, of course." His sarcasm lay heavily on the last sentence.

Ovremwe's tone hardened.

"You are all under arrest, but I do not have the authority to say why. The orders came from the top, and you will be spoken to very soon by the District Commissioner, or whatever he now calls himself."

"You must have some idea, being now in such high authority."

Barrett was pandering to Ovremwe's obvious air of self importance, and the ruse worked.

"All I can say is that you are not alone in this. You will be joined shortly by others. It might be of interest to know that this is happening all over the country. At the same time, all expatriates of no political or commercial value are being rounded up and expelled. Those who try to resist will be arrested for treason. That is, if they are not shot while trying to escape."

His words hung heavily in the air, accompanied only by the ponderous footsteps of the captors as they retreated from the cell block.

"This is treachery," yelled Alan, who could think of nothing more significant to say as he swam back into consciousness. At that moment he realised that his head was still being cradled and appeared to lose all interest in anything else.

James shook his head.

"No, it isn't. It's their country now, remember. Something like this was bound to happen sooner or later. Whatever it is."

He glanced sharply at the constable outside the cell who had begun to nod his head vigorously. The officer had obviously been planted there to listen and report on what was said, since his presence as a guard was quite unnecessary. Derek followed Jim's glance and lowered his voice.

"I think the least said at the moment the better."

They fell into a brooding silence. Derek's mind began to race. He was at a complete loss to comprehend this sudden, violent change in attitude by the Africans. He supposed that it must have something to do with the recent events in world affairs, but couldn't for the life of him tie the two together.

The cell was hot and clammy. Although he had been pulled rudely from a deep sleep, Derek no longer felt any trace of tiredness. His thoughts began to wander back over the past few months, to the slowly changing political climate, back to Independence, back further to that day twelve months ago when Debbie had taken the children to England and safety; back even to the circumstances which had brought him, young and eager, to the shores of Africa.........

2

Derek closed his eyes. His muscles yielded to the irresistible comfort of the garden chair. Before the ecstasy of sleep had been given chance to overtake him he heard the soft pad of bare feet along the length of the veranda.

"Yi hakuri, sah."

Silence.

Derek knew from past experience that if it were something important Hassan would speak again. If not, he would go away and tell the world that his master was sleeping.

"S'cuse me, sah. Important."

"Yes, Hassan. Menene ka?"

"Telephone, sah. De G.M.."

"Damn," Derek muttered to himself. "Na gode, Hassan. Tell him I'm coming small time."

When the khaki-clad figure had padded away, Derek, with a supreme effort, pulled himself away from the comfort of his chair and walked slowly from the humid shade of the veranda into the cool shadows of the house.

"Why does he think everyone else wants to work on Sundays just because he has nothing else to do?", he mumbled to himself as he approached the telephone.

"Hello, Gordon," he reluctantly breathed.

The phone crackled into life.

"Afternoon, Derek. I hope you weren't trying to sleep."

Derek snorted to himself.

"No," he lied.

"I presume that you weren't able to get through to me this morning."

That's because I didn't try very hard, Derek thought.

"And since I didn't hear from you I also presume Debbie and the children got away alright."

"Yes, Gordon. The plane was only an hour late in arriving, so I suppose you would say that they were away more-or-less on time."

"For this place I'd say that it was damned good. Pity in a way it's a direct flight. I would have loved to have seen them on their way through."

"Well, as I told you the other day, Gordon...."

"Yes, yes, I know. It would have delayed them for several hours and involved a change of planes. I'm not complaining. Just like to keep in touch with my family, that's all. Now, if you have a moment, I'd like to go through a couple of points regarding your special merchandise requisition, the one you sent last week."

Derek sighed audibly this time and sat down at the small table which served as his desk, drawing his briefcase towards him. Today would be no different from any other Sunday. When your boss is also your father-in-law he has a double reason for disturbing what would otherwise be known as a day of rest.

Derek Scott was 34 years old. The whiteness of his papers contrasted sharply with his bronzed skin. He was medium height, medium build, medium everything. So mediocre was he, in fact, that it came as a complete surprise to everyone, himself included, when he was appointed District Manager of Ugbeshu area within the framework of the prestigious Combined Africa Company Limited. But after all, as some were quick to point out, he **did** marry the General Manager's daughter. Not that this really had any direct bearing on his promotion, but in a highly critical and gossip-ridden society typical of expatriate communities, such circumstances do not go unobserved.

Derek's father had been a welder in one of those big, ugly steel factories which sprawl across Britain's industrial midlands. He had worked hard to bring up his three sons in this working-class environment, determined to give them the chance of enough education to lift themselves into the "professional" world. He would have been proud of his family, had cancer not taken him while Derek was still in his teens. The elder brothers were lawyers, having survived the horrors of World War Two with distinguished service records. Their ambition had been to form a family law firm, with Derek included, and set up practice in the labour-oriented midlands and, to use words which Derek could picture his father saying, "help the working man in his fight against money-grabbing, profit-worshipping capitalist employers".

Derek was among that small number of people for whom the end of the war came too soon. He was summoned for duty at the start of 1945, but by the time he had been through enough training to earn his commission, they all decided to call off the fight and dispense with his services. Along with several thousand others, that is.

Being both unwilling and financially unable to direct his

energies towards university, despite the encouragement of his brothers, Derek drifted for a while from menial job to menial job, as did countless others for whom His Majesty's Armed Forces had no further use. He was young, carefree, independent and relatively intelligent; his attitude was that "someday, something interesting will come along."

Something eventually did come along. He replied to an advertisement in the Daily Telegraph which offered the prestige of management coupled with the excitement of travel overseas. Having just been denied the prospect of going abroad when the war ended, Derek saw this as an opportunity, and grabbed it enthusiastically. It wasn't everyday that someone else offers to pay the cost of an exotic journey. He didn't know much about West Africa, apart from what he could recall from his school geography class. He knew that the left hand bump on the continent was the west side, but other than that, his knowledge was as dark as the description "dark continent" could imply.

After three interviews, the last of which involved his being fired from the most recent employment when references were taken up, Derek had found himself accepted as an overseas recruit by Combined Africa Company. The job offer promised the prospects of "a fulfilling career, exciting travel opportunities and retirement on full pension after only 25 years' service." It sounded almost too good to be true, but there was nothing to lose by trying. Especially since he was recently out of work, as a result of the Combined Africa Company's energetic background follow-up.

Armed only with his brief experience as an Army Officer, an unquestionable quickness of mind and an obvious willingness to learn, Derek embarked on a disciplined and intensive training program. It was a program designed to mould him into a competent manager of the Company's affairs, and an ambassador of his country in one of the West African colonies. It came as a mild shock to discover that beads and trinkets were no longer in demand, and that the so-called "colonies" were on the brink of blossoming into substantial importers of sophisticated merchandise, as well as being suppliers of enormous and varied amounts of raw materials. Furthermore, some of them were also talking about independence, a spectre which the British government would not be able to avoid for too much longer.

His brothers were pleased for him, if disappointed that their dreams of a full family business would remain incomplete. His mother was happy to see young Derek finally settled in something, even if she couldn't fathom out exactly what. Anything was better than drifting from job to job with no idea what he wanted to do. Dad would have been happy, too, and proud that all of their sons had now come out from under the working-class burden.

There was a brief but bewildering introduction to the complexities of CAC's enormous commercial empire, after which Derek and six other successful candidates settled to a routine of learning, assimilating and absorbing the theories of merchandising as applied to under-developed countries. The book knowledge was richly supplemented by periods of up to six weeks at a time working in the offices and factories of the manufacturers whose products they would be selling and distributing when they eventually reached their West Africa destinations.

After 18 months of this he became noticeably impatient, and he assumed, like most newly-trained and keen young recruits, that he already knew everything necessary to turn around the fortunes of his company and the world. A re-shuffling of vacation schedules made it apparent that he would shortly be on his way to "the Coast", and he waited almost breathlessly to see where he would be sent. He hoped that it would be one of the more progressive countries such as Nigeria or the Gold Coast, and not a backwater like Gambia. He was overjoyed when they told him that he was to go to Moresia, and spent a few days avidly reading and absorbing all the available literature. Finally, the day he had been waiting for, training for, at last arrived. He boarded the Stratocruiser at Heathrow airport with scarcely a backward glance. He anticipated a culture shock, since he had been warned, but he was still not completely prepared for the total difference in life style which he found.

The Colony and Protectorate of Moresia, named after the explorer, exploiter and, later, first Governor Sir Clifford Mores, was looking forward to a long period of post-war prosperity. In accordance with Britain's blue-print for the self-government of her colonies, Moresia was expecting at least a decade of economic growth, after which would come independence and full nationhood. The name "Kumanga" had already been chosen by the local power faction who would form the first government. This was a reversal to the original reference of centuries earlier, when the area had been described by the first Portuguese explorers as a rich source of "ebonie, cacao and humanes". The future promised a rich and fast development as a result of the seemingly unlimited deposits of oil found just off the Atlantic seaboard. Shell and B.P. had already invested several millions of pounds in the drilling and refining procedures which more-or-less guaranteed automatic acceptance in world economic circles.

CAC's plan for increasing its manpower came at exactly the right time for Derek. He progressed along with the Protectorate's fortunes, through the stages of assistant manager, department manager, to branch manager and finally to his present position as district manager in charge of a whole province. There was still a chance that sometime in the not-too distant future he might attain the dizzy heights of general manager, except that the looming and uncertain prospects of independence could well result in a severe cut-back in expatriate personnel.

His life's experiences so far had left Derek with a deep sense of satisfaction. He had overcome the disadvantage of having been born to a family whose economic circumstances were, to say the least, a struggle. He had seen his parents go without holidays, without luxuries, without any of the pleasures he now enjoyed and took for granted. He had worked his way against social odds to a position of status and importance, capable of holding his own not only with his peers, but also with those referred to as his superiors. He had even managed to lose most of his Brummie accent, although he tended to slip back into it on the rare occasions when he became agitated. Not bad for a welder's son from Walsall.

Those around him knew him in a variety of different ways. To his staff he symbolised the British Empire - firm but impartial, wise but compassionate, arrogant but condescending, and he could usually be relied on to make the right decision within the realms of his authority. To his friends, colleagues and acquaintances, both black and white, he was a stolid, dependable person. A little aloof, perhaps, especially with strangers, but popular and always ready to throw his full weight behind anything which had his approval and conviction. To his wife and family, he was a rock of respectability, thoughtful, caring and loving, always there to help and encourage, a model of gentleness and understanding, keeping the petty irritations of family life under control.

Derek rarely showed his emotions. He had his moods, as does everyone under the right conditions, and his wife had come to appreciate that under the seemingly unfeeling mask which hid his countenance was a genuinely sensitive and deep-thinking ideologist. He was far from perfect, despite the first impressions which made the casual acquaintance wary of him, and it was this combination of traditional solidarity and elusive fallibility which had made him a popular dinner guest. Debbie knew that while he gave the impression of being capable of dealing with almost any crisis, somewhere deep down there was something stronger. She couldn't discern exactly what, but it seemed to hint at unfulfillment. It was something which some day, somehow, would come out and complete the mental composure which he tried so hard to perfect.

Derek had befriended and eventually fallen for Gordon Blake's daughter during her many visits to the country. It had not been by any means a conventional courtship. Derek was then only a department manager, subject to immediate and unquestioned moves as the Company required. Debbie spent most of her vacation time in Ivebje, the capital, where her father held a commanding position. Derek and Debbie saw each other only occasionally, but Derek knew that out of the overwhelming amount of bachelor attention Debbie received, she held him in some sort of special regard.

Derek proposed to Debbie by mail, and to his surprise, delight and trepidation she accepted instantly, with her father's unhesitating and eager approval. The wedding was sumptuously, if hastily, prepared. To the ladies of Ivebje it was a Godsend. Their monotonous lives were enriched by a touch of romance, a touch of excitement and even a touch of home. They did their utmost, even to the inevitable maternalistic squabbling, to make it an occasion which would be talked about for many years to come. To the Africans it was wonderment in the extreme. Most of them had never experienced a real, true-life European wedding on their soil, and both Church and reception alike were overflowing with laughing, admiring and highly effusive uninvited guests.

That had been eight years ago. Since their two children were now at an age where formal education could not be put off any longer, Debbie had taken them back to England to find a suitable school. This, at least, was the reason to which they had all as they parted that morning. Everyone knew, though, that in reality it had become expedient to send wives and families back home in case the mounting nationalistic fervour, depressingly anti-white, should go out of control.

This was the pretext on which Gordon Blake had phoned, knowing full well that had there been any serious delay he would have been among the first to be told.

Formalities completed for the day, Derek settled back in his chair once more, a cold beer at his elbow. He picked up the novel he had started to read several weeks ago.

Reading would probably become a major leisure activity again, now that he was on his own.

Hassan sat on the back door step, well out of the way of the sun's undiscriminating glare. He liked Sunday - Lahadi. Lahadi was the cook's day off, the day when he, Hassan, was the undisputed head of domestic routine, when he was allowed to demonstrate his doubtful skills in the culinary arts. Lahadi was the day when he was justifiably in charge of the kitchen and could without conscience leave all the menial work to Mustapha, his small boy protégée, in the excuse that he was fully occupied in preparing meals. The pressure would ease considerably now that madam had gone, especially since mai-gida would frequently eat out at the Club or someone else's house, like he used to do before when he was still a bachelor. On such occasions he could expect the host steward to recruit his help at the table. It was not uncommon for guests at a dinner party to be waited on by their own stewards on a reciprocating help arrangement.

Hassan was quite happy. He had been with Mistah Scott for over ten years, having joined him when mai-gida was in the Northern Province. This was almost a record in African domestic circles, since the appearance of a new madam in a regimented bachelor household usually brought conflict and dissatisfaction. An expatriate bachelor rarely interfered in the running of the household, but when a woman comes - kai!! - what a palaver she is! It usually results in a mutual parting of the ways, and having to find another bachelor to join. Debbie, though, had been in West Africa often enough to appreciate that she would never be completely in control of domestic affairs. Apart from one or two disagreements, which resulted in the hiring of a cook and a small boy, she had come to terms with Hassan regarding mai-gida's well-being.

Hassan was a little concerned about all the talk he was hearing in the Sabon Gari market of something called "independence". He wasn't quite sure what it meant, except that his country would no longer be controlled by white men. Seemed a little odd, since the baturis had been in charge of just about everything for as long as he could remember. As long as his fathers could remember, too, and the oldest one in his family was 62. But it was said that the baturis would all go to that mysterious place they call "home", and that this black man's country would be run by black men. He wasn't convinced that it would all be as good as some of his fellow countrymen promised. He was at least employed right now, unlike many of his family and friends. If all the baturi people went "home", as many were threatening to do, there would be a lot more of his people out of work. Himself, for one. He couldn't see himself working as a gidan-boyi for an African. He had tried that, once, and it wasn't a very happy experience.

All told, life was good for him at present. He had an arrangement with Pious, the cook, that whatever was left over from the kitchen would be equitably shared by Pious, himself, Mustapha, Samson and the mai-gardi; in that order, of course, according to importance. Hassan had saved enough money to be able to support a son in mission school back in the north, and his wife was a very frugal housekeeper. Mai-gida had bought him a bicycle to use for going to the market, and he had a large stock of cast-off clothing which the family had given him over the years. What he couldn't use he could sell or barter. He paid no rent or electricity, as little tax as he could get away with, and water was readily available - a very important bonus in Africa where some people have to walk miles to get it. His biggest advantage, though, was the prestige of being "steward to the District Manager", the most important man in the biggest Company. What more could a barely literate village boy hope to achieve? Pray to Allah that it wouldn't all be taken away just so that some political men could take over and get rich.

His daydreaming was interrupted as the telephone jangled into life once again. He jumped up swiftly and willingly. He knew what this call would be. Hadn't his friend Isaac already told him this morning that Alan and Nancy Rushton were planning to invite mai-gida to dinner that evening? He smiled knowingly to himself as he took the message, and padded back to the verandah.

"S'cuse me, sah. Not much important, but I tell you whatever."

Derek brought his thoughts back into focus and stared menacingly at Hassan, wondering what sort of "not much important" message would justify having to disturb him once again.

"Missez Rooston say you come chop today. Karfe takwas. I orready tell am O.K.."

Derek grunted.

"Madalla. May as well close, then."

Hassan grinned his approval and nodded.

"Yes, sah. Na gode, sah. Sai gobe, sah."

It still amused Derek, even after all these years, that whatever time of day or night his staff were dismissed, they would always bid him a "goodnight". It was well meaning, of course, but still a little - well, odd - to be wished a “goodnight” just after breakfast.

Hassan didn't need telling twice, and raced to lock the back door and reach the sanctity of his quarters in case mai-gida should change his mind.

Derek closed his eyes again. If the phone should ring again, from now on he would ignore it. He wondered what life would be like as a bachelor, so to speak, once again. He didn't altogether relish the thoughts of the months ahead, since it would be the first time that he and Debbie had been apart for any length of time in their 8 years of marriage. This was excluding the occasions when his duties took him on a trek into the bush, but this was never for more than 3 or 4 days at a time. During the first couple of years Debbie would go with him, a welcome companion in those remote areas where there was nothing to do in the evening but follow the time-honoured routine of "sit and think and read and drink".

He remembered his early days as a bachelor when his head was filled with lecherous thoughts as he travelled from village to village, bolstered by tales proudly related by his peers of how they never had to spend a night alone when they were in the bush. Derek could never quite find the courage to accept the many offers which were made to him. At the risk of offending his native hosts he could not bring himself to take in one of the local beauties, chief's daughter or not. It was probably his strict, working-class upbringing which was urging him to remember the moral values impressed on him in his youth. Not that he was a total prude, and had in the past enjoyed relationships with females of his own kind, but to do it in the bush with someone he didn't know and would probably never see again just didn't seem right. During the next few months, though, there would no question of these or similar thoughts being entertained. He was a responsible, married man, and although this didn't seem to deter some of his counterparts, the desire to go off the rails right now was absent.

He drifted into an uneasy sleep, which was dominated by irrational and illogical dreams.

His subconscious was already troubled by the twin conflicts which were on the minds of most expatriates in Moresia. One was the looming independence of one of Britain's oldest and most promising colonies. On the surface all looked well. There would be a continuing two-way trade concession, as there had been for decades, with London still exerting tremendous influence in both economic and political spheres. It was hoped that Moresia, or Kumanga as it would then be called, would fulfil Britain's aspirations as a fully-fledged member of the Commonwealth. But memories of India still lingered like a bad dream in the minds of Whitehall bureaucrats, darkened this time by the anxious desires of the Soviet Union who were openly hammering on the door of all emerging nations. The cry of "white man go home" was already being heard, spread by a very vocal few whose following was increasing rapidly each day.

More significant was the row shaping up on the international scene between the Soviet Union and the Western World. It was known that Cuba had embraced Russia with open arms, dangerously close to America's back door, and that a show-down was inevitable sooner or later. The effects of this could be catastrophic, making the white man's troubles in Moresia/Kumanga seem pale in comparison. Derek smiled to himself. That wasn't intended as a pun.

Derek dreamed that he was being chased through the jungle by a black bear. He was wearing nothing more than a Union Jack; then he found himself at the water's edge, trying desperately to climb aboard an American ship from which the hand of Debbie was extended in an effort to pull him to safety. Before he knew whether he would make it or not, he awoke with a start, confused and depressed. There was no Debbie, no ship and, thankfully, no bear. He smiled to himself as he shifted position, and fell back into contemplation. This time his wide-awake dream was much more real. He re-lived being asked to serve on the Independence Day Celebrations Committee. It was no magnanimous gesture, nor was it a prestige appointment. The stark truth was that he, as the District Manager of the town's major trading organisation, had the authority to put at the Committee's disposal any "damaged" materials which their plans might require.

The tropical sun had started its descent when Derek returned to full consciousness, lengthening almost imperceptibly the shadows of the trees which had been permitted to remain when the compound was cleared by forgotten predecessors in CAC's early days. The garden was ablaze with colour, awaiting the evening ritual watering by Samson, the garden boy. Samson was small, ragged and ageless in appearance. He was totally illiterate, loyal to a humiliating degree and the complete master of all the garden's activities.

Samson had been with the house for as long as anyone around could remember. He would wait with endless patience for the full fury of a tropical storm to abate so that he could complete, according to his custom, his twice-daily task of watering the sodden flowerbeds. He scorned Nature's warning that she could fight off his puny efforts, and humbly admitted that "his" garden was the best in the reservation. Derek had once indicated, in a slightly intoxicated and joking manner, that a certain uninteresting patch of earth would be very much improved by the addition of some colour. He was astounded to see the very next day an established, healthy flowerbed in full glory. He did not dare to ask how the plants had appeared so suddenly, although there was a nasty rumour going around the Club that someone had had the audacity to raid and plunder the grounds of the Residency. In the eyes of the Administration, this almost amounted to treason.

Derek reluctantly prised himself out of the chair and trudged indoors to prepare for his dinner engagement. Obviously, the Rushtons were concerned that he should not have to spend his first evening without the family in brooding solitude. Alan had been a contemporary during those London training days, but had not shown any great promise or aptitude, and now looked upon Derek as his immediate superior. That was for Company purposes only, since outside the office they were still the best of friends. Alan was the manager of the Hardware Department, and unless something drastic happened in the near future, (which he hoped it would) he was likely to remain so for the rest of his career.

"Bicycles, pots and pans and golf. That's my station in life, old boy."

This was Alan's regular and monotonous theory on life, knowing very well that if things became really tight, he could well be one of the first to be replaced under the Company's Africanisation program. Nancy and their daughter Sharon were due to go home next week on the eve of Independence, leaving Alan alone and in the same situation as Derek.

"Then we'll split a few beers for old times' sake, eh?"

At that moment Derek could not bring himself to think about splitting a few beers, or anything else for that matter, old times' sake or not. But it was a thoughtful gesture, he mused, as he turned on the shower.

Derek found that he was not the only guest invited to the Rushtons' final dinner party of the tour. He should have known, he thought, that Alan would use this as a good excuse to indulge in a full-scale show-off event.

He was the last to arrive and realised that he was being treated as a sort of unofficial guest of honour. He wondered how much of the proceedings would be presented to him in the near future as a bill for "Company entertaining expenses", and what plausible reason would accompany the claim. He was soon to find out.

Derek settled himself back with his customary Pernod and soda aperitif and glanced around the assembled company of five other guests. There was Jean - he couldn't remember her other name. In fact he couldn't remember ever knowing it. All he knew about her was pure hearsay. He had heard that she was from a good, English county family and had come to Moresia three years ago as Assistant Matron of the Ugbeshu Native Authority Hospital. Which meant that she was adequately trained as a nurse in her home country, but in the Colonies she was well above required minimum for a supervisory position.

Jean was ambitious, carefree, efficient but sympathetic, and was filled with a joie de vivre which made her an instant success with the hospital staff and European peer group alike. She had recently been promoted to Matron, and it was said that already she had begun to set the hospital on its ear with the changes and improvements she had made to the level of efficiency. She had acquired a certain reputation as being free with her favours, but Derek had yet to meet any of the town's bachelors who had actually scored.

Jean was in earnest conversation with Barry Finch, who headed up the local branch of the Income Tax department. Next to him was Tony Agamoru, no doubt invited as Alan's gesture of impartiality and goodwill to the indigenous people. Chief Agamoru had assumed the role of District Officer, previously held by a white man, and was a very influential protagonist of the upper class black community. Tony was trying to avoid the attentions of Mrs. Finch, shrill and bird-like, who had him in captive range of her incessant whining. She was trying to draw Tony out with her opinion of appointing Africans to the Magistrates' Bench. Tony was not biting, though, since he was himself involved in appointing local magistrates.

Derek was introduced to a fresh-faced, fair-haired young man who was trying, in faltering English, to explain that he was on a "Cook's tour" of West Africa on behalf of a German manufacturer of domestic hardware.

"That's it," said Derek to himself. "That's the excuse for the party. That's what justifies the occasion. That's what the expense account will cover."

Derek had seen the young man, Hans von-something, around the office during the past couple of days, and knew that Alan had some interest in promoting certain lines of cheap ironware which he, Derek, would eventually have to sanction as new merchandise imports.

It was all very normal, very commonplace, but Derek couldn't help wondering just how long this atmosphere of cordiality would continue once the notion of independence became a reality. It could be completely destroyed and replaced with a totally alien social life. He glanced at his watch, wondering where Debbie would be at this time, and hoping that dinner would not be too far away. Debbie always teased him about his habit of "watch-watching", as she called it. Even when they were going together he always seemed, to her at least, to be looking at his watch. He tried to explain it away by claiming that his life had always been run on the clock, and anyway he didn't want to be in Mr. Blake's bad books by keeping his daughter out too late! Not that it would really have been a problem – Debbie was no longer a child, and was quite capable of taking care of herself.

At that moment, as if by some remotely triggered impulse, Isaac appeared in the doorway to break the tedium and announce the news for which everyone had been waiting.

"Chop ready, Madam."

3

After a few weeks of his resumed but unaccustomed bachelorhood, Derek had slipped into a routine. He worked longer hours at the office, partly from necessity as the approaching independence brought an unparalleled surge in business, and partly to keep him away from the temptations of the Club. The Club was just about the only form of recreation to which a single white male could turn in small-to-medium sized West African stations.

But that situation was changing, changing rapidly along with the rest of the country's traditional institutions. The Ugbeshu Club was small compared with some, but reflected what was happening everywhere in the country. It was hard to imagine, looking around now, that until five years ago no black man had ever set foot in what was then called the Ugbeshu European Club, except as a staff member or tradesman. And there still hadn't been any black women signed in, even as guests. It was a place where Africans had felt awed and uncomfortable, with the exception of a small number whose sophistication and sense of equality had been acquired outside of the country. The Africans preferred the company of their own kind in the Highlife Club, built and maintained by funds from CAC's Staff Social Trust, or one of the many noisy, crowded and smelly bars in the town. Occasionally, some Europeans did visit these bars, but it was usually as a courtesy to an African associate, and far from being a matter of preference. Or it was a self-indulgent and often brief desire to experience the culture, usually by back-packing students hoping to absorb "the local scene".

The township bars were also frequented by members of the Peace Corps, when they could afford it. They were a group of zealous and intense young adults, mostly American, whose mission in life seemed to be to expand the global village of humanity, to point underdeveloped peoples in what they were convinced was the "right" direction, to share the benefits of civilisation, to show the less fortunate where they had been led astray. In other words, however well meaning, to undo a century of European influence, attitudes, progress and ideals. It wasn't that their motives were questionable; they were sincerely dedicated to the task at hand. Rather, it was the means by which they went about this proposed reformation, this revelation. They tried desperately to identify with the African peasants, even to the point of "living bush" and attempting to emulate the culture. Their efforts were thwarted at every turn, since the African peasants, for the most part, looked upon them with suspicion and, sometimes, amusement. The spectacle of a group of white men and women living with and like the villagers was totally foreign to their understanding, and even regarded by some as a cruel mockery. For the most part, the intended message was either scorned or met with a mixture of indifference and disbelief. After a harrowing and extremely frustrating period of time, most of these social evangelists gave up trying to save the peasant from himself and others, and went back to university in the USA, deflated and disillusioned.

The Club's polished oak tables had gone, and been replaced by the more sanitary but less characteristic chrome and Formica. Inappropriate pictures of smiling local politicians now joined the dignified portraits of the Queen and Duke on the walls of the dining room and lounge, and the new national colours occupied the centre slot in the shield of five flags over the decorative but useless fireplace. The new curtains were gaudy. Derek vaguely remembered seeing the same material adorning a prominent chief, and also the wife of the Volkswagen dealership manager. The textiles department played no favourites. It was as though it had dawned on the Africans that the Club seemed typically English because in the past only the English had ever done anything about the décor. They set about changing this situation.

There had been decades of happy times at the Club, and yet still would be, Derek supposed. But the atmosphere was different. Many of the people were different – not just different individuals, as can be expected in such a transient community, but a different type of people, a different class.

These were the new colonials. These were the so-called technical experts sent from all corners of the world to try to pull Africa closer to the age of technology, now that the work of the colonial administrators was done. They were for the most part brash, young, unsophisticated and uneducated in anything other than their own specific field of expertise. They knew little or nothing about Euro-African relations, nor did they care. Those who spoke English (and many didn't) disgorged embarrassing dialects, used vulgar expressions and defied the long-standing traditions of gentlemanly conduct and genteel behaviour. They drank beer from the can and stayed in the Club after seven pm in their shorts. They sat wherever they wanted, without regard for custom and propriety, and fraternised with the African staff. In the words of their predecessors, they were definitely not officer material.

These newcomers, in turn, made fun of what the Club used to represent, of old-fashioned chivalry and upper-class English stuffiness. They still, though, had the natural distrust of and dislike for foreigners with skins of a different colour, a dislike which they didn't ***think*** they had when they first arrived but discovered that they did after a while. In this respect they did not differ from their predecessors, and they still shared the desire to be looked up to while abroad. It also seemed as though they had a slight twinge of disappointment that they had been unable to inherit the Empire which they had always used to regard as a purely ruling-class institution.

They wouldn't, of course, have the psychological intelligence to understand the implications of their attitude, and would deny that which they didn't understand. To the Africans, though, it was very plain. The newcomers were still the white managers, still ruling, directing and dictating in their own specific fields of influence, regardless of their social background.

Derek caught up with much of the bush touring around his district, which he tended to neglect a little when his family was with him. For the most part, his life was busy but unexciting, apart from the general aura of chaos surrounding everything which in any way concerned preparations for the country's coming of age. Derek was obliged to attend the many Celebrations Committee meetings which were called every time a minor problem loomed. As Independence Day came closer, Derek found himself being called upon more and more to assist in his own exclusive way.

"More cement is needed. Would Mr. Scott be in a position to make available another 50 bags?"

"Could the D.M. see his way clear to providing five bales of cloth to decorate the Highlife Club?"

"Would it be possible to let us have another six drums of paint for the sports stadium?"

And so the list went on, seemingly endlessly. Derek knew that he was being asked to overstep his authority, and yet the Company would not dare refuse to grant such politically-motivated favours.

Derek could have made himself a lot of money if he had been of such a mind. Many people were doing so, black and white alike, in the general confusion of the "lost" merchandise which was being chalked up to unofficial but unavoidable "dashie". It wasn't that he was morally against a little on the side, even if it did involve some petty larceny. What dictated his behaviour was the prospect and consequences of being found out, and it wasn't worth the risk.

The committee ordered bunting, festoons and flags. Some of these were sewn upside-down, and had to be replaced by a second batch, to the delight of the merchants involved. Posters, photographs and slogans were randomly placed so that even the least literate of the populace should be fully informed as to the identity of their proposed new leaders. To most of the masses the word "independence" was not fully clear, except that from now on the White Masters in London would no longer be controlling them.

Parades were arranged and the police band was rehearsed in selected pieces where mistakes were least likely to occur. The route which the Lieutenant-Governor's entourage would take was guiltily cleaned up. New buildings were repainted along with the old, some of which had not seen a coat of paint since the day they were thrown together. All the seedy-looking unsightly spots along the route were carefully screened off, and even the town's clean-up crews were issued with new uniforms. Many of these were worn to church on the first available Sunday as an indication of official status. The police were given extra hours of training, and senior officers braced themselves to cope not only with chaotic traffic conditions, but also a heaven-sent opportunity for all the pick-pockets, thieves and petty crooks around who might want to cash in on the action.

CAC's stores and offices hummed with activity as provisions of every kind were laid in for the three-day national holiday. The chartered banks prepared for the biggest ever onslaught on their reserves as record cash withdrawals gathered momentum. Hotels, clubs and bars hired extra staff in anticipation of the biggest binge the town had ever seen - bigger even than that which followed the soccer game of five years ago, when the local team defeated the tired and travel-weary first reserves of an obscure English Third Division club at the end of its African tour.

The main festivities were, of course, to be held in Ivebje, which was two hundred miles away by air and over three hundred and fifty miles by tortuous, grit-laden roads. It was in Ivebje's Government Square, now renamed Independence Square, that the actual handing over of constitutional rights by the Queen's representative would take place. Provided, of course, that all went according to the over-intricate and ambitious plans. Independence Square would see the official supposedly tear-jerking lowering of the Union Jack and the unfurling for the first time ever of Kumanga's blue-white-blue with a palm tree on it. Independence Square was where the songs of victory would be sung the loudest, and where the new national anthem (composed by an English lady in Berkshire) would first be sung in public by the combined choirs of nearby girls' schools.

Derek was always fascinated by the groups of girls he saw, especially those on excursions from their schoolrooms. This was not in any way sexual, but rather a kind of wonderment. They wore identical cotton print dresses, their hair done in almost identical masses of small, stiff, spiky plaits, and all wore brightly coloured beads around their necks. This latter adornment was not an official part of the school uniform, but might just as well have been. They had the shy, apprehensive look of timid gazelles, as though ready to bound away to safety at the slightest threatening sound. Their plump limbs and high breasts straining beneath tight bodices gave them the appearance of ripe fruit ready for matrimonial plucking. Despite their timidity, they had an air of worldly maturity, and it saddened Derek to think how quickly the bloom on these graceful young creatures would fade as they grew into farm and household drudges. As young girls, African females can be quite sensuous and lovely. As old women, they portray the wisdom and characteristics of weather-beaten old trees. In between these extremes, however, they sink into ungraceful mediocrity, which to the European eyes appears as an absolute waste of femininity.

Derek sensed the reflected enthusiasm in the words of Dr. Akparu, the country's first president-elect, as he prepared to accept the symbols of authority from the Governor-General. He seemed to think he had heard most of them before, from the White House lawn. Those expatriates not normally stationed in Ivebje, especially those still in government service, were instructed to remain at their serving locations, in an effort to make the rest of the country feel that they were involved - that this was truly a national fiesta and not just for the capital city. However, such is the Africans' capacity for fun and enjoyment that they didn't need the prompting of their colonial masters in this, of all things, to throw themselves wholeheartedly into the great event, wherever they happened to live.

To a pessimistic few, mainly Europeans, it would be a "bloody miracle if one quarter of what they had planned came off without a foul-up at every turn". To the optimistic and excited majority, however, it was to be the greatest moment in their history, and they were determined to enjoy it to the full. There were a few sour notes, though, such as the issue of the invitations to the celebrity garden party in the grounds of the Residency. An internal quarrel almost turned to violence when the local native dignitaries found out who had or had not been invited. The fact that all Europeans were automatically on the guest list didn't help. Many minor chiefs and not-so-influential stalwarts of the community found themselves excluded, and were not at all pleased with their apparent low standing. The moments of frustration passed, however, when it was realised that all the security in world wouldn't be able to stop them from gate-crashing. Most of them were determined to be there, invited or not.

The scene was thus set. The preparations were finally if frantically concluded, and it was with a sigh of relief that Derek closed his office on the eve of what Alan Rushton had glibly dubbed "take-over day - the beginning of the end". Derek's first official function was a private cocktail party for his managers and a few selected government officials, black and white. With Debbie away he had had to leave all the arrangements to his boys - sorry, he corrected himself, - his "domestic staff", as they were now to be called. He hoped to high heaven that they wouldn't let him down.

Well, things were going to be very different from now on. This was the beginning of a new era, in all of its originality. Derek had already sensed a change in attitude around the office. There was nothing he could really put his finger on, just an underlying uneasiness accompanying the way his staff had looked at him and spoken to him of late. This was particularly noticeable among the senior clerks whose far-reaching ambitions were undoubtedly slanted towards the new concept of self-government. He prayed that he been able, over the years, to instil enough Company pride and loyalty to overcome the antagonistic attitudes which certain of the country's radical elements were blatantly advocating. Time alone will tell, he kept reminding himself.

In the dying moments of Moresia everything came to a standstill. The Royal Princess, cousin of the Queen, declared Her Majesty's pleasure at being privileged to give the viable, economically-sound and rosy-futured country back to its native-born peoples.

"Probably bloody glad to get rid of it. If at all she knows where it is," was Alan's opinion.

There were hopes for a successful future, welcome to the Commonwealth, continued friendship, and so on. At one minute to midnight the Union Jack was lowered for the final time, and President Akparu ordered the hoisting of the new Kumanga flag. At the stroke of midnight precisely, according to the clock on Ivebje city hall, (which was known to have been more than a few minutes out since the day it was unveiled) the Republic of Kumanga was declared. The crowds went wild.

For newly-independent Kumanga it had all begun. For the British expatriates in Moresia it had all ended; they saw it as another nail in the coffin of the once-mighty Empire.

The following three days were an energetic blur. For Derek and his colleagues it was a busy round of official ceremonies and social functions, peppered with congratulations, hopes for the future, and, amongst themselves, regrets for the passing of an era. The Africans were, for the most part, delirious as the propaganda speeches told them that they were now citizens of a free country and that from this time on everyone was equal under the flag. Public reaction varied from rank disbelief on the part of older and wiser patriarchs, who could see that there was no place for equality in their traditional tribal systems, to a blatant arrogance from the young, educated opportunists. The majority of the population lay somewhere in between, with a desire to see the new order work, mixed with cautious apprehension about trusting their own leaders to do the right thing. It was felt, on the whole, that the whites could now be tolerated for as long as necessary, for as long as it took them to train suitable Africans to take over their jobs. The key word from now on would be "equality". Some, of course, would remain more "equal" than others.

When the official holiday ended it was not easy to settle back into anything approaching a normal work routine. The country's feeling of euphoria gradually faded when it dawned on the populace that nothing had really changed. Nothing at the workers' level, at least. Oh, yes, there were different names on the government stationery and office doors, but nothing to benefit the common folks. As the weeks went by, a feeling of helpless disappointment grew. The people were still no richer at the end of the day, which their new government had promised they would be. The White Man was still giving the orders, which their new government said he wouldn't be. What was worse, those of their fellow-countrymen who had attained positions of authority by whatever means, were for the most part far more demanding to work for than their European predecessors had been.

The Governor-General had given way to a President, and Her Majesty's top representative had his status reduced to that of High Commissioner. The Resident became the District Commissioner, and the traditional colonial post of District Officer was simply known as Local Administrator. Both of these rungs on the colonial ladder immediately became open to Africans, appointed by the Federal Department of Internal Affairs instead of London, and jobs were handed out according to favour and influence. And, of course, to tribal affiliations. Behind every important, highly-placed African there was still a European advisor, who would remain until the new appointee was sufficiently versed in his responsibilities or replaced by someone who was better qualified.

Multi-nationals corporations such as CAC still retained their firm grip on the economy, and continued to be run by their existing management forces. The pressure was on, however, to "Africanise", and management vacancies caused by resignations, vacations and transfers were being filled by hastily-promoted chief clerks, senior salesmen and technical assistants. Usually the first action on reaching management was to establish their new importance by purchasing a car on the same company credit terms as their white predecessors.

Derek lost only one of his managers during the first flush of nationalism. Charlie Woods was a veteran of some thirty years' coast service, having joined the company when, as he put it, "going on trek was exactly that." Charlie was tough, fearless and blunt, with an active, agile brain and a ruthless manner towards the Africans which they had grown to expect and enjoy. There was no doubt that he commanded the respect and affection of his staff and customers despite his pseudo-tyrannical attitude. It was Charlie's crude, boisterous and frequently offensive air towards his superiors which had kept him at the department manager level for all these years. That and his undisguised scorn for the "toffee-nosed twits" who came from Head Office these days; he had no desire to move at their level. Charlie was happy with his bungalow, his houseboys (who had been with him for 20 years or more), his black mistress and his insatiable capacity for Scotch whisky. Times were changing, however, and the new, modern Africa was no longer the paradise to which he had been accustomed. He wanted no part of it, and elected to take the retirement package which he had steadfastly resisted for the past few years.

Charlie was replaced by Felix Abusa, a young, intelligent African from one of the coastal tribes. Felix had a nimble mind and quick grasp of business situations, and in the three years he had been with CAC had made a rapid rise from shop floor to storekeeper, then sales, and finally to the supervisor's desk.

Educated at the Methodist Mission School and then provincial grammar school, Felix was the automatic choice when Derek was forced by government pressures to elevate a "suitable" candidate to management level immediately. The only misgivings Derek had were that Felix was actively involved in local politics; so far this had not affected his work, but his new-found authority as a manager could open up a whole new vista of possibilities. Otherwise he was loyal to the Company and extracted maximum effort from those under his charge. In this he was something of a rarity among his fellow promotees, whose motives were usually more self-indulgent than Company oriented. Derek considered himself fortunate to have such a valuable and reliable employee within his jurisdiction, and could foresee a career path to the very top for the ambitious and diligent Felix. If – an important "if" right at the moment – he backed the right political horse.

In government circles similar changes were taking place as the months rolled by, but at a more rapid pace. The new masters of Kumanga seemed determined to sever as many colonial ties as possible without jeopardising the economic balance. Where a suitable alternative to British involvement could be found, it would be called in as a substitute without any apparent trial or test case period. Africans replaced Europeans in not only administrative jobs in the Civil Service, but also those positions requiring a high degree of technical expertise. Where no suitably trained natives were available, the Kumangan government was turning to Japan, China, Egypt, other African states and, of course, to the Soviet Bloc. The effects of this too rapid a move were increasingly evident. Sometimes inadequate, sometimes comical, and sometimes disastrous, all avenues were being explored.

The telephone and telegraph services, never very reliable at the best of times, became hopelessly ineffective. Hospitals ran short of essential supplies as the over-worked and under-trained staff became more incapable of coping with the demand. Transport facilities fell apart through lack of adequate maintenance; buses and trains failed to meet schedules, or, sometimes without warning, didn't run at all.

There were some episodes of comic relief which brought smiles to many of the inhabitants, black and white alike. The government was deeply concerned that so far none of the Kumanga Airways planes had been piloted by a native son, and in fact it seemed as though it would be a long time yet before a Kumangan pilot would be sufficiently trained to take over a command. Orders were issued that the training had to be intensified, and that within three months a proud Kumangan would wear captain's bars on his epaulettes. With a mischievous grin, the British manager of the Kumanga Air assigned his most promising trainee African crewmen to a forthcoming special diplomatic flight which was to convey several of the country's top ministers to an all-African conference in a neighbouring country. As soon as it was learned that one of their brothers was to be at the controls, the ministers and diplomats booked on the flight hurriedly made excuses to change their travel schedules. Self-preservation was a much keener instinct than national self-confidence. The orders were withdrawn, "in the interests of air safety", pending further flight crew training.

There were several other instances where a personnel vacuum could not be filled by African substitutes, by virtue of their lack of readiness. In such cases the politicians began to enlist the support of some white men who spoke an unintelligible language and had strange-sounding names such as "Chernikov", " Borovski" and "Gorodin". The Russian revolution of Africa was well under way.

Within nine or ten months the exodus of Europeans, especially the British, was in full swing. Not by expulsion, as the fledgling government had frequently promised, but by the voluntary repatriation of those for whom the new regime was becoming intolerable. At first it was wives and children, leaving noticeable holes in the social life of each and every station. These were followed by several long-service employees who chose to take a premature retirement, since they were unable and unwilling, like Charlie Woods, to adapt to the new structure being forced on them.

They left by the planeload and the boatload, carrying with them the treasures they had gathered over the years. To most people, these were the mementoes of a lifetime of service to a seemingly ungrateful nation.

After a year there were very few Europeans left in government circles. All that remained of the London-based administration were the top advisors, and their departure was just a matter of time. The Africans were now being guided at all levels by Soviet experts, whose brand of colonialism was so different from that of the British that the young, emerging nation grabbed at it eagerly, as a floundering child taking its first steps might reach for an adult hand.

Commercial enterprises fared somewhat better, and Derek still had three of his original six white managers, including Alan Rushton. Alan had been home on leave and, surprisingly, agreed to return for one more short tour of duty.

"Need that extra bit of cash before I start paying England's prices," he explained to anyone who asked.

CAC, because of its enormity, had people to spare and suffered less than any of its competitors, whereas smaller companies were already cut to the bone. Most commercial ventures were down to one or, at the most, two expatriate managers in each district. It was no secret, though, that they were all slowly winding down or diversifying before the final blow to free enterprise, nationalisation, struck them. Derek expected that sooner or later the position of district manager would be the only one in CAC to be held by a white man. And that would be only temporary.

Derek was eagerly looking forward to the end of his tour, which would mean two months of home leave with his family. If he came back at all, that is. Alan had been deputised to relieve as district manager, on the understanding that should Derek decide not to return, the job would be his for as long as he could hang in. It was quite an ego trip for Alan, who had never in his wildest dreams expected to reach such a high level. It was just unfortunate, he reflected, that promotion had to come under such grim and unsatisfying circumstances.

After two weeks of handing over, desk clearing and generally tying up loose ends, departure day arrived. Derek looked wistfully around his office and wondered if he would ever see it again.

4

It was a tearfully happy reunion at London's Heathrow Airport, with such a lot to talk about. It seemed as though they were anxious to say everything within the first hour of meeting. Debbie was bursting to tell Derek about her new and recent experience as a mother of schoolchildren in England, while Peter and Susan bubbled over with stories of their adventures. The fact that they were a year behind others of their age groups didn't seem to bother them. There was a magic of belonging which they hadn't felt in Africa, where they lived in the adult world of a foreign service lifestyle. There were tales of insect-free picnics, walks through lush green fields and aimless wandering up and down country lanes. These simple pleasures are denied to those who choose to serve their time in West Africa.

Derek knew that he had a lot to tell them about the changes which had taken place over the past few months since independence, but was reluctant to do so. Not yet, at least. It was a depressing topic, and he knew that the subject would only cast a shadow over their long-awaited holiday together; a shadow of what their future may be when the vacation was over.

It seemed to Derek that his children had changed a lot since he had last seen them - more than he expected after such a relatively short time. They had changed not only in stature, but also in character and mental outlook as well. Gone was the indulgent and self-centred precocity which he was accustomed to seeing in all youngsters whose parents took them away to the unnatural life in an African station. They had obviously had no difficulty in adapting to the normality of an English suburb with children of their own kind and culture. He could also sense that they were subconsciously willing him to share it with them.

They all lived every moment of their first few days and nights together, hoping that it wouldn't end. It didn't really have to. After the tender excitement of the reunion, Derek began to feel troubled. All around him was England, where the beer was warm and tasted strange, but the meat was fresh and succulent. England, where the cities were noisy and hectic, but the countryside was peaceful and serene. England, where the weather was foul for much of the year, but amply compensated by the sheer magic of spring and summer. England, where the people were crabby and impatient, but whose underlying warmth and friendliness were sympathetic and sincere once brought to the surface. Derek knew he had to make the choice between his cherished career and the obvious contentment of his family.

Debbie sensed the conflict which was taking place within him, and slowly, patiently drew from him the tendrils of his mental anguish. As a wife, she was devoted to his happiness, but as an equal partner in the marriage she found it hard to suppress the desire to make known her own views. But she was patient. Gradually, almost reluctantly, Derek told her everything. He told her of the unsubtle changes which had occurred since Moresia had become Kumanga. He described the rising frustration and fearful apprehension which had crept over the expatriate population at all levels. He explained how the lifestyle as they knew it, as it had been for decades, had all but disappeared. He explained how it had given way to an insecure and untenable mandate by which those with the required expertise would still be tolerated in Kumanga, but on a very different basis of relationships.

Debbie listened, asked questions, and eventually expressed her own feelings. Although she knew what she really wanted, she did her utmost to be sympathetic and understanding. Had she been the domineering type she could quite easily have influenced Derek's decision, but she knew that the final choice had to be his alone.

By the middle point in his leave, Derek's mind was made up. In a long, descriptive letter to the Director of CAC's overseas personnel he submitted his resignation, citing the state of affairs in Kumanga and his family's well-being as the key points. A blanket of relief fell around him. He would not go back.

Before he mailed the letter, he was surprised and pleased to receive an invitation to a regimental reunion. It had been over sixteen years since he was demobilised, but during this time he had kept in touch, in the beginning at least, with some of his old cronies. He did once receive the curt and formal advice that having left the country without permission from the War Office, his reserve officer status and pay had been forfeited. He learned, with some amusement, that he had been officially posted as a deserter. It was straightened some time to reach him, having been diverted from Kumanga, and the dinner was the out, though, and since then he had kept the War Office, now renamed the Ministry of Defence, fully appraised of his movements. He looked forward to the opportunity of renewing old acquaintances. The invitation had taken very next week. He would take the letter of resignation with him to London and hand it in personally.

The reunion took place in one of London's plush hotels, suitably bedecked with Regimental colours, and attended by several serving officers in formal Number One Dress uniform. To his surprise and disappointment he saw very few of his contemporaries, most of them having become untraceable, like he had been. He found himself at the lower end of the table next to Ferguson. Ferguson, he recalled, was a crashing bore in his younger days, claiming to be related by marriage to the Earl of ..... Derek couldn't remember. Time had not seemed to improve him, despite his moderate success in the stockbroker jungles. They had very little in common in the old days, and even less now. After the usual greetings their conversation became strained, and Ferguson turned away to seek a more appreciative audience on his other side. Derek's other neighbour was a young second lieutenant, who obviously regarded anyone over the age of 30 as a true relic from almost-forgotten wars.

After the third round of the brandy bottle, by which time many a larynx was well lubricated, opinions were made vocal. After decrying the mess of things which the Labour Government had made, the prime lament was the shameful loss of the Empire at the hands of the post-war manipulators. With unconcealed disregard for present company, Ferguson and a few others made it quite clear that those entering the Colonial Service after 1945 did so only because they were unable to "get on" at home, or anywhere else for that matter. They were total incompetents, which explained the woeful state of the Empire, or what was left of it. What do they call it now? Commonwealth, or something equally stupid and unsuitable.

Derek said nothing, although he was aware of several pairs of eyes turned blearily in his direction. After all, he ***was*** the only one present who worked overseas. Obviously, he was expected to reply with some profound comments to the contrary, to defend the actions of his colleagues and the Commonwealth Office. Derek had never been one for arguing with the illogical rambling of drunks, and instead of taking the bait he just shrugged and turned his eyes upwards. Ferguson, convinced in his intoxication that he was on the right track, continued the attack. This time he looked directly at Derek, as though to indicate that the real cause of the Empire's downfall was actually sitting next to him.

"What about India, then?"

"Yes, what about India?" The chorus was taken up by others.

"And the Gold Coast? And that mess in Kenya?"

"What we'll have left at the end of this decade won't be worth having."

The tirade went on and on.

The goading tone began to annoy Derek, but still he said nothing.

"Anyone who lets these foreign chappies dictate to him can't be much of a man, I say."

There was a hush around the table after this last comment. It was as though they were all urging Derek to take up the cudgels and defend his honour, his reputation, his Queen and country etc., in a scenario reminiscent of Gilbert and Sullivan.

Derek looked around the table, then at Ferguson, then back at the faces around the table. Some were tight-lipped and sympathetic, some were smiling with enjoyment and anticipation of a showdown, while others, the vocal few, were waiting to go in for the kill. Derek realised that there was really nothing which he could say to convince Ferguson that he didn't know what he talking about, drunk or not. He carefully and methodically folded his napkin and stood up.

"I'm not going to waste my time and energies trying to explain.

It's obvious you're all too naïve or opinionated to understand, or too drunk to think straight. Permission to leave the mess, sir?"

Without waiting for the Commanding Officer's nod of agreement, Derek pushed back his chair and strode out. He was inwardly seething, but tried to project a controlled calmness. The catcalls of his tormentors and mocking words of Ferguson followed him across the dining room and out of the door.

"That's typical. Run away from it, like you and your lot are doing everywhere. Too cowardly to stand and fight. Just walk out and leave things to sort themselves out. Which they never will...."

The ripple of laughter was lost behind him as he trudged down the corridor towards the mens' room. He changed his mind as he crossed the lobby and headed for the cocktail lounge, where he threw himself down angrily into a corner seat. His mind was in a turmoil. He ordered a double brandy and reflected, as he gulped it down, on the scene he just left and what a complete ass he had made of himself.

If he had kept his head, he could have thought of hundreds, thousands of words he could have chosen to contradict that oaf Ferguson and his cronies, but instead he had hesitated. He had hesitated because those in there just didn't know. Worse than that, he had walked out without even ***attempting*** a vindication. They were all so unaware, that lot, in their secure, insular little cocoons. They were completely oblivious to the circumstances in which colonial and government officers were expected to work and put out their best efforts. Then Ferguson's final remark hit him like a pile-driver. Running away. Wasn't that exactly what he was doing? Wasn't that what his letter to CAC was all about? He took the sealed envelope out of his inside pocket and looked at it, as though expecting it to laugh out loud and say "running away!". He'd had a little too much brandy.

Derek paid for his drink and made his way to his room. His anger subsided as he climbed into bed and switched off the light. Not to sleep, though, since sleep was far away in the carousel of his thoughts.

The following morning, feeling tired, dejected and thoroughly confused, he breakfasted in his room. The last thing he wanted was contact with any of last night's adversaries in the dining room. Running away, again. He ate very little. He showered, shaved and dressed. Then on a sudden impulse he picked up the telephone, dialled CAC's number and asked to be put through to the Director of Personnel.

After the usual series of delays and put-offs by minor officials, according to protocol, he was eventually put through to Peter Smythe-Jenkins. The Director had been a training manager when Derek joined the Company, and over his years of service Derek had come to look upon him as a friend.

"Smitty, I have to see you urgently."

"The feeling is mutual, Derek, I assure you. How's tomorrow at 10 o'clock?"

"No, dammit, I mean urgently. I mean as soon as possible. I'm in town right now, but I might not be tomorrow. I might not be ever, at least as far as the Company is concerned."

"Sounds serious, old man. Tell you what - I have a couple of hours before my next meeting. I was going to spend them going through the mail, but that can wait. Whereabouts are you? Can you be here in half an hour?"

"Be there in twenty minutes."

Derek paid his hotel bill and walked the few blocks to the Underground Station. The ride to Blackfriars was a short one, and he was climbing the steps to CAC's impressive head office within the estimated 20 minutes. The stone structure looked out across the

River Thames like a sentinel of international commerce. A recent sandblast job had brushed away decades of grime, and Derek was surprised to see a gleaming white building in place of the old, grubby, soot-soaked one. London was slowly emerging from two centuries of rampant pollution which had turned the castles of commerce into blackened ramparts. It was even said that fish were once again able to flourish in the cesspool which was the River Thames.

Derek went up to the eighth floor and left his raincoat and suitcase with Janice, who greeted him with the same motherly hug she afforded all returning Coast staff.

"My boys," she would proudly call them.

"He's waiting in his office for you. Seems quite pleased to see you again. Still no sugar with your coffee?"

Quite a memory, when one considers how many coast visitors she sees, and usually only once a year. He was ushered into the sombre, oak-panelled inner sanctum of the overseas personnel department. Smitty was holding the telephone, and smilingly waved Derek to the rear corner of the office where four armchairs surrounded a coffee table. This was something new. Most management interviews were conducted with a formidable-looking desk between the participants, as though to remind the visitor about who was really in charge of the proceedings.

Derek sat down in one of the armchairs and was joined after a couple of minutes by Smitty, who approached with both arms outstretched, as though welcoming a long lost brother. They went through the usual routine of "how-are-you-how-is-the-family?", and so on. Smitty seemed prepared to prolong the social pre-amble, but Derek didn't want this, and withdrew the envelope from his inside pocket.

"This is my letter of resignation."

He paused, waiting for a reaction from Smitty. There was none.

Derek then began to tell Smitty of his dilemma, his family's obvious delight at being in England, his concern about how things were going in Kumanga, and his decision not to go back. Again he paused looking for a reaction, and again there was none.

"Go on," urged Smitty, as though he knew what was coming next.

Derek went to say that he had not mailed the letter, preferring to discuss the matter first. This wasn't exactly true, at least not consciously, but it gave him some leeway to explain his uncertainty. He didn't say anything about the events of the previous night at the reunion, but made it apparent that he was looking for guidance. He knew whose side Smitty was on. Smitty was charged with the responsibility of staffing the overseas positions, not with just anyone to fill the gaps, but with the right people who would do a good job for the Company. Derek knew that Smitty would eventually try to influence him according to the Company's best interests, but he needed to be convinced. He needed to be needed, to have someone advise him, to have someone dissolve his own uncertainty.

Smitty put his fingertips together, cleared his throat, and started to speak.

At this point Janice came in bearing a tray loaded with the paraphernalia of a coffee break. The two men didn't interrupt their conversation while she was in the room. Janice had been the Director's secretary for so long that she knew as much about the operations of the department as the Director himself. Probably more.

Smitty sympathised with Derek's dilemma, as Derek knew he would. Smitty pointed out that the Company could ill afford to lose men of Derek's calibre, as Derek knew he would. Smitty told Derek that this could be a milestone in the Company's history, a turning point which would affect all future operations of the Company, as Derek knew he would. These were all standard responses to the threatened resignation of a valued employee, and Derek expected them. He even used them himself when his African staff suggested that they might look for alternative employment. Smitty said that the Company's strategy was changing, that exciting new venues were being opened, which was a new approach but not entirely unexpected. Smitty also told him that he, Derek, would be in on the ground floor of the changes, which were so far-reaching that they would make all previous operations look pale in comparison. He wasn't, of course, at liberty to discuss them in detail, since he didn't want to tread on the toes of the Marketing Department, but knew for a fact that Derek was an integral part of the plans.

Under this kind of pressure, most of which he anticipated and relished, Derek began to feel a surge of enthusiasm, much like the feelings he had experienced at the start of his career when they explained his very first posting.

An offer was presented. Assuming everything could be resolved satisfactorily on the home front, and subject to acceptance of the detailed proposition which the marketing people would put forward, Derek was being asked to go back for another tour of no longer than twelve months. After this, a "suitably responsible" position would be found in Head Office on his final return to Britain. Or, alternatively, if things worked out for him, he could carry on taking one overseas tour at a time until he'd had enough.

Derek left Smitty's office feeling good about the offer, and went down two floors to Marketing, where the enthusiasm was, if anything, greater than that which Smitty had displayed.

Basically, the plan was to transform CAC from a purely trading organisation to one which was willing to invest in Kumanga's future industrialisation. Over the next two or three years CAC would attempt to shed its image as a purely import/export trader and embark on manufacturing ventures. Negotiations were already well under way with reputable British, European and Asian manufacturers, who at present relied wholly on the import/export trade for representation in West Africa. CAC was in the process of choosing an entirely new name for the fledgling division. Derek couldn't help thinking that whatever the new title may be, it would never command the respect which CAC had enjoyed over the decades. No other trading outfit on the continent could trace its origin back to the pioneering days of Clifford Mores, or could claim to have held a Royal Charter granted by Queen Victoria herself.

Derek's new job would be to oversee this transformation in Ugbeshu Province, which was recognised as a sort of mercantile crossroads, being roughly at the geographic centre of Kumanga. It was described to Derek as a challenging opportunity which would crown his already outstanding overseas career, with the promise of an equally outstanding one at home when it was done. Could Derek afford to pass up such an opportunity for the sake of one more tour?

Derek was now faced with the same dilemma which had haunted him since his return to Britain, except that this time there was something at the end of it, rather than the anxious wondering where it would eventually lead.

Derek conveyed the news of CAC's offer when he returned home that afternoon. Debbie was clearly not pleased. She was disappointed and a bit hurt, but she stuck to her original resolve not to bring any direct influence to bear. She had lived long enough in a Coast family atmosphere to know that anything resembling a challenge to a dedicated Company employee was like tempting a donkey with a carrot. She also knew that Derek was no exception, and would be kicking himself for years, perhaps for ever, if she made him pass up this opportunity. Derek wanted to discuss it with the children, to hold a truly democratic family forum, but Debbie would have none of this.

"I'll pick the right moment; I"ll explain in my own way that this is something you have to do."

Debbie certainly had no intention of going back with Derek and exposing her children to Lord knows what in the new Kumanga. Especially since they had just found contentment in their new life. She told herself that a year would soon pass. It was only about the same length of time she had just spent since she came back, and moreover this time they were already established. She wouldn't have the trauma of finding somewhere to live, and learning to accept the different lifestyle of English suburbia. That was already done. Life can never be perfect, she reflected, or it would be too easy.

Derek thought about it for a couple of days, then called Smitty accepting the offer. He and Debbie both knew that the couple of days weren't necessary - he had already made up his mind when he walked out of Smitty's office. He was asked to call back to the Marketing Department for more detailed information of his new responsibilities.

It was all settled, all decided. There was nothing left of the matter now except to enjoy what remained of Derek's vacation. It was decided that while he was away, Debbie would hunt around for a house of their own, their very first, and direct her energies towards decorating and furnishing it in preparation for the final homecoming.

The day of departure finally came, and it was miserable and painful for all of them. Derek had gained a few extra days by electing to fly back to Kumanga, a mere fourteen or fifteen hours.

Normally he would have taken the Elder Dempster mail boat, which afforded thirteen days of relaxation. He usually enjoyed the ocean voyage, which gave him time to study the masses of paper which Head Office was apt to give its managers when they were returning to an overseas station. On this occasion, though, the extra few days with his family were worth more than a couple of weeks on the high seas. Besides which, on previous occasions he knew that the family would be joining him very soon, whereas this time it was different; he wouldn't see them again for a year.

At last his flight was called, and he settled himself in the first class seat. He felt as though this time it hadn't been as much of a holiday as it usually was. There had been so much on his mind during the past few weeks, so much riding on his decision, that he felt nearer to being weary than being revitalised.

The engines of the Bristol Britannia probed and prodded their way through the cloud cover, and finally pushed the aircraft into the clear, blue spaces above. Ice began to form on the wing edges as Derek's thoughts eased away from the sadness of leaving his family behind. He started wondering, apprehensively, what would be waiting for him when he touched down once again on African soil.

5

The new job promised to be more than just challenging. It was going to take every ounce of Derek's experience in and intimate knowledge of the province's business scene. As already explained to him, the plan was to enter the manufacturing arena in addition, and eventually as an alternative, to the rapidly shrinking import/distribution trade of which CAC had been the undisputed master for decades. Competition from local African and Arab entrepreneurs with little or nothing in the way of overhead was making straight trading less and less of a profitable business in which to be, and CAC's resolve was to move into something with a little better return on capital invested. The days of the Old Colonials were coming to an end in commerce, as well as in government. To diversify seemed to be the only way for CAC to retain its superiority in Kumanga's business world.

CAC would collaborate with several well-known European makers in the local production of high demand commodities such as bicycles, beds, cigarettes, cooking pots and even automobiles. Further and more ambitious projects included a textiles mill, a brewery, a processed meats plant and even its own petroleum refinery. It was simple on paper. The manufacturer would supply parts and technical expertise while CAC, with its superb channels of distribution, would finance and administer the joint ventures, and control the marketing of the products with complete exclusivity. There was much to do, yet, but great strides had already been made.

There was a complication, though. Such had been London's commitment to true and complete self-government for the colony in those bygone days, that no expatriates, whether private or corporate, were allowed to own land. This was in sharp contrast to the conditions in East and Central Africa, where land ownership would prove to be, in the not too distant future, the main cause of racial and social strife. In the West African territories, however, a third party to each enterprise would have to be involved in order to secure some sort of land tenure, and this meant taking a Kumangan national into each venture. This was where Derek came directly into the picture. His immediate task was to select, approach, recommend and finally negotiate with influential African landowners with a view to establishing the various new business undertakings in a proper and legal manner. He was undoubtedly the best qualified person in the province to handle this kind of delicate work, but he soon realised that it would take rather longer than the proposed 12 months they had told him in London.

Smitty was no fool. He knew that Derek would never leave such an important task as this unfinished. Derek wouldn't say anything in his letters home just yet, but privately he estimated that 16 to 18 months would be nearer the mark. This duty wouldn't occupy all of his time, though, and during the periods of waiting for things to happen Derek was still the District Manager.

Alan Rushton was pleased with the turn of events. He was pleased to see Derek return to Ugbeshu, since they had been friends for many years. He was especially pleased to be given the newly-created post of Assistant District Manager, which meant that he would be in charge when Derek was away on this new thing he'd been asked to do. He still had his hardware department to look after, of course, but that didn't take as much effort as it used to. He knew it was only a matter of time before the job became Africanised, so he was glad to have something else to his credit. Like Derek, Alan had left his family at home to try to organise the domestic scene for when he had to return for good. The Rushtons weren't too happy at having to live and work in England again, but like most other expatriates they had to give some consideration to the education of their daughter – there simply wasn't a suitable education system available to them locally.

It was no secret in Ugbeshu that Alan's marriage was past the stage of floundering. He had met Nancy, an 18-year old flirt, at a dance hall during his first four-month vacation, and what followed can only be described as the classic whirlwind romance. He dated her every evening during the following couple of months, ending with a clandestine weekend in a south coast resort during Alan's final few days. After his return to Moresia they had kept up a lively and erotically-flavoured correspondence for a few weeks until he was shocked into numbness by her news that she was pregnant, and "what was he going to do about it?"

His first reaction was to apply for a transfer, perhaps to the far north, and beg CAC not to give out his new address. However, before he had chance to consider his course of action, he received a scathing and blasphemous letter from Nancy's irate father, threatening to lay the matter before CAC's Head Office. With an anxious eye on his future career, and not wishing to involve himself in a damaging scandal, Alan decided to take the easy way out and proposed marriage. It was rather lonely, anyway, being a bachelor in the colonies, and it would be fun to have his own woman around, legally and morally.

Within a short time it was all arranged. The Company agreed to fly Nancy out to join him, and to foot the bill for the wedding. While not quite as sumptuous as Derek's would later turn out to be, the wedding provided them with a good start to their new lives. The couple spent an idyllic week at the General Manager's private bungalow on the beach near Ivebje, and their daughter was born some months later – one of the few native white children in Ugbeshu.

From there, the relationship was all downhill. Nancy became bored with her comparatively dull life in the jungle, with nowhere exciting to go and no-one of her own level in which to confide. No-one of “her class", as Alan unkindly used to say when Nancy complained that the Coast wives were all too "stuck up" to take part in a good, earthy conversation. She became bored with Alan and with his friends. She started to cast around and made a play for what she considered to be "interesting" people, usually week-enders in from the bush with appetites for whatever was available. It was no secret that Alan, on his frequent business trips into the bush, had reverted to taking his pleasures where he could find them, from the man-starved teachers at the girls' schools to whatever black mistress was presented to him by his sub-depot staff.

Neither could afford to go through a divorce, and they grew to tolerate each other's misgivings. They even established a sort of do-your-own-thing relationship within their marriage, a comfortable co-existence which suited both of them. It was no surprise, then, that Alan welcomed the chance of taking on some of Derek's work with its extended touring. With Nancy safely tucked away back in

England he didn't have to pretend any more, knowing that she was probably doing the same thing back home.

Derek had not been shocked, or even surprised at the way things had turned out. He had cynically but correctly prophesied that the Rushton marriage was doomed from the start. He had a soft spot for Nancy, though, which had nothing to do with the undisguised if unacceptable proposition she had once made to him. She was dark, petite and very vivacious, with a zest for life which made her totally unsuited for the role as a "correct" Coast wife. He couldn't do anything to help them, and would probably been told by Nancy to go to hell and mind his own business if he had tried. He had seen the same situation many times during his career, and as long as Alan did his job satisfactorily, his private life was his own concern.

Derek settled into some sort of a work routine, somewhat different from his former one, but very absorbing. He had a new, spacious office in one of the recently completed commercial blocks which were springing up in every major town and city in the country. This was Kumanga's way of heralding a "new era", a "re-birth", to quote but two of the propaganda slogans being bandied about. How these costly building were being financed was open to speculation, but Derek was pretty sure that the taxpayers of some affluent United Nations country were eventually going to foot the bill. Meanwhile, it suited Derek's requirements, since it was near enough to CAC House to make it easy for him to take care of both his responsibilities. Eventually, as the import and distribution business wound down, all the remains of CAC's former trading empire would move into this building along with the new ventures.

It wasn't long before Derek began to feel comfortable with his new job, and he secretly wished that it had been around a few years earlier. It was going to be a busy time, wearing two hats, but it would help the time to pass more quickly. He would pass on to Alan as much of the D.M. work as he could, since once he started to travel he would be away quite a lot. This time mostly by air, thankfully, rather than the dubious, bone-shaking network of what passed for roads. He had heard, though, that an Italian company was about to receive a fat contract to do some major road construction. A useful and much needed way of spending the IMF contributions, much more useful than the luxury image-builders such as television, sports arenas and convention centres which the government had decided the country needed. Derek had often wondered whether they had been waiting for the American Air Force, the originators of much of the road systems during the war, to come back and repair them.

Then the words of John F. Kennedy rang out across the world. The challenge was down, the swords were drawn, as America stood eye to eye with the Soviet Union, unflinching and uncompromising. Premier Kruschev had assured President Kennedy that Cuba would not in any way be involved in the race for arms supremacy, and, ultimately, world dominance. There was nothing in the Soviet plans which called for missile sites on the island of Cuba. Kennedy had not believed him. In fact, he knew the statement to be blatantly untrue, since American reconnaissance planes had spotted and photographed at least fifteen surface-to-air launch sites. It had also been learned that some twenty five Soviet ships, all suspected of carrying deadly SAM missiles, were on their way to a western hemisphere destination. It could only be Cuba.

The evidence was there, the danger very real. Obviously, the next step was up to the United States. This was no petty squabble. This was not one of the seemingly endless Cold War threats which had been part of everyday life in diplomatic circles for the past fifteen years. This was a serious political conflict which could destroy, or at least irreparably damage, not only the two most powerful nations on earth, but also the planet itself.

President Kennedy threw a blockade around the island of Cuba and made his message clear and simple. Turn back, or we'll fight you back. We'll fight with all our strength and all our might to protect our country and our Allies from this flagrant war-like menace.

And the world held its breath.

The Soviets hesitated, pondered and looked well into the consequences of their next move, playing the chessboard of life with real pieces. Slowly, very slowly, they turned their ships around. The time was not yet ripe for the confrontation which someday must surely come. They extracted a promise from the Americans that Cuba would be left to its own devices, in exchange for the complete removal of the missile sites.

The two leaders agreed to these terms, and the world breathed again. World War Three had been averted, for the time being, by the twin elements of courage and wisdom.

On the day of Kennedy's statement, the European and American expatriates in Kumanga were shocked by the brazen effrontery of the Soviets in attempting to threaten America's back door. The Kumangan government, on the other hand, appeared to be taking the opposite view, obviously prompted by their new Soviet benefactors, and loudly decried the "imperialistic threats by the opportunist American meddlers". These and many other standard phrases from the communist propaganda factory were bellowed across the land by the state-controlled Radio Kumanga during the following day. The whites became uneasy with the prevailing mood.

Derek was no exception as he listened to the BBC Overseas Service reports on the happenings. He had sensed Kumanga's shift in loyalties since independence, and wondered what the next move would be. Despite the fact that the matter had been settled, however temporarily, to the satisfaction of the main protagonists, there was no way of measuring any ripple effect.

The town of Ugbeshu fell silent as night closed in, seemingly blacker than ever. There was an uneasy feeling among the remaining expatriates that something was about to happen – something disturbing and unpleasant which would bring about a radical and unprecedented change in their lives.

6

Derek's semi-hypnosis was shattered by a noisy interlude as four more prisoners were brought in, still wearing their night attire and protesting loudly. Derek knew all of them. Frank Smith from the airport; Vasili Kamerakis, manager of Dopoulos Trading; Mike Hailey, Associated Tobacco's sales manager. Last but not least, there was Benny Gold, whom Derek had met on several occasions, mainly in the Club. Benny was the president of a U.S. tractor firm, a hard-drinking, loud-talking man who seemed to spend most of his time travelling the world visiting his overseas markets.

"But have you seen his wife?" commented Alan on one occasion.

"It's no wonder he likes to get away. Refuses to take her, too, I bet. I know I would."

It was just Benny's misfortune that he happened to be in Ugbeshu at this moment, including him in the round up.

Derek's hand waving towards the guard checked the fusillade of questions which the four recent arrivals were firing through the bars as they were pushed into the adjacent cell.

"We don't know," James told them, anticipating the obvious.

"We just don't know."

Alan had been quiet long enough. And anyway, Jean had long since pushed his head away.

"What are we going to do? We can't just sit around."

"We don't have much choice. Be patient."

James put a firm edge on his voice.

"Why don't we," Jeremy spoke for the first time, "why don't we call the guard in, then jump him? We could pretend that, er,...you," indicating Jean, "you could faint, or something. I've seen it work in films. There's enough of us."

"What a stupid idea."

"Use your brain."

"Grow up."

James was a little more kind.

"It won't work, son. We'd get ourselves killed. Don't believe everything you see in films."

Jeremy sank back into obscurity, his face crimson with embarassment. The newcomers were muttering among themselves, the pitch of their voices rising occasionally as they gave vent to their feelings.

Derek glanced around the cell. He had never been in a detention block before, never seen the inside of a jail, a prison, or even a police station beyond the front desk. There were bars on three sides, unbroken apart from the sliding door. The rear wall, originally whitewashed, was grimy and covered with scribbled, crude obscenities and smears of blood, vomit and - he hated to think what else. The furniture in the eight by ten feet space consisted of three rusting iron bunks covered by filthy and torn blankets over equally filthy and foul-smelling mattresses. On these they were reluctantly obliged to sit, if they wanted to sit at all, since the stained concrete floor was even less inviting. A combination metal wash-basin and lidless toilet completed the amenities. Derek hoped that no-one would feel the necessity to make use of these facilities, since it would be extremely embarrassing to everyone. For one thing there was no water in the toilet. Fortunately, the high temperature humidity allowed body liquid to escape by perspiration, and it wasn't as though they had been offered anything to drink.

Derek fell back to meditating. He was totally stunned by the audacity of it all. Escape was impossible at present. They could only hope that someone would realise their predicament and authorise an immediate release, with apologies.

Several more prisoners were brought in, and Derek realised that the same cell block was being shared by the intrinsic core of Ugbeshu's economic controlling body, along with some key technical personnel. But why?

The early sun was well into its ascent when the sound of booted feet along the concrete floor of the passage heralded some long-awaited action. The door of their cell was flung open and a tray-laden constable, accompanied by two armed companions, tried to smile pleasantly as he entered.

"Some chop here. African food. You like it if you hungry enough."

He put down the tray and chuckled as he went on to serve the other cells.

No-one was hungry. No-one had even thought about food until now, and the six dishes of oily, orange soup with chunks of tough-looking meat bobbing around in it did little to stimulate their appetites. There were also six mugs of weak tea which they would not drink, since it was very unlikely that it would have been made with boiled and filtered water. The risk of tummy-palaver was one they had no wish to run.

"Run," muttered Derek with a smile. "How appropriate."

The others had no idea what he was talking about, but they didn't feel like following it up.

After about half an hour the same policeman, still covered by his gun-toting colleagues, returned to pick up the untouched bowls of gari stew.

"Dere be no more chop now till night," he advised them. Then, with a touch of insolence in his voice, "Your majesties go be very hungry it you wait for roast beef to come."

The other two roared with laughter at this gem of wit.

"We go get dishes from odder rooms, den you go back to charge room."

This sudden but welcome news made them leap to their feet, convinced that the ordeal was now about to end. After a short delay the occupants of all the cells were herded back into the charge room. Several policemen were lounging about, rifles cradled, and each with a look of nervous disdain on his face.

"You stay till Chief come," said the constable, then he disappeared into the inner office.

"Stand here, in line", barked a young corporal. His bleary eyes and unsteady manner suggested that the palm wine had been flowing liberally.

"Look de goats waiting for market."

This made the others almost collapse laughing, and provoked further jibes.

"Ya - dem got soft white meat for cook-em and chop-em easy."

"We no fit cook-em. Just put-em for sun an' go red!"

The stream of abuse developed into a cascade as each of the Africans found the courage to put forward his contribution. Then Jean stepped forwards, hands on hips.

"That's ***enough!*** Shut up, all of you! Now go and tell Over-what's-his-name I want to see him. ***Now!"*** The forefinger on her right hand stopped within inches of the corporal's nostrils.

Somewhat surprised by this outburst, yet conditioned from birth to respond to such commands, the Africans stopped their taunting, still not sure about which side had the upper hand. The corporal backed off, then made his way to the office, his eyes wide and fixed on Jean's menacing finger.

Derek realised that he didn't know much at all about Jean, other than the stories which were passed along the top of the bar in the Club. He had learned from experience that stories were not to be trusted. What some men cannot truthfully boast about, they tend to invent, especially where their so-called "image" is at stake. Jean Whatever-her-name was evidently no angel in the moral sense, but even if her reputation outside the hospital were a little on the colourful side, there was no disputing her efficiency in the wards. She was a model of competence, patience and understanding. Derek hadn't really expected her to break down or display any of the usual female emotions when confronted with a difficult situation such as the present one. In fact, he didn't know quite what to expect.

He was not prepared, however, for the outburst of foul-mouthed obscenities which she directed to Ovremwe as he came out of his office frowning. She made it clear in a language which anyone could interpret exactly what she thought about him, his superiors and the country's administration as a whole. Then without waiting for a response she angrily stepped back into line, her face a mask of fury and disgust. The men held their breath, not knowing which way Ovremwe would jump. Derek was certain that if any of the men had delivered such a mouthful, he would have been taken back to the cells and flogged.

"She's attractive," he thought, "in an overpowering sort of way. Not the sort of girl you would take home to mother, and yet...."

Jean, it was later learned, had left school at the age of seventeen, as did most pupils of the grammar school levels. She had a good record of G.C.E. passes, especially in sciences, which meant that she could be eligible for a state scholarship to university. She could either enter the general B.Sc. program or elect a more specialised line of professionalism. She chose the latter and graduated in nursing. This brought her to the age of twentyone when she went out into the world, thinking that she knew everything but realising after a few months that she really knew very little. Her theory was excellent, but experience was a more thorough teacher than all her books.

Jean's career progress from then on was centred around finding the right people to give her the right results. She answered a Crown Agents advertisement five years ago for qualified nursing personnel to go out to the Colonies in a supervisory capacity to help train native staff. What Jean lacked in practical experience she made up for not only in theoretical knowledge, but also sheer, brazen dynamism. She was offered one of the vacant positions. She excelled at her job, and everyone involved with her had to admit that she had a knack of being able to motivate her charges in a professional and successful manner.

Her private life, as she was quick to point out to everyone, including the government auditors, was very much her own affair. She had the ability to convey her feelings and opinions without suffering the retribution which others might have received.

Ovremwe's frown deepened. He was clearly taken aback by

the unexpected verbal onslaught, more unexpected yet having come from a woman. In his culture women just didn't talk to their men like that. But then, these were European whites; they did strange things. In all his years of associating with whites he never had been able to figure them out. He stood for a long time glowering at Jean, who met his gaze with defiance. Then, with a shake of his head as if to convey his sympathies on the white men, he turned to James.

"My instructions are to send you to the Muji Hotel. Why you should be given such luxury is beyond my reasoning, and also my advice. But they don't listen to me. So, into the truck, please."

His voice dropped.

"I'm sure the District Commissioner knows what he's doing. At least, I hope he does."

He couldn't hide the scorn in his voice. Left to him, the prisoners would have been left to rot in the cells, see how they liked being bullied around for a change. But, his orders were that they were to be shipped to the Muji.

The prisoners were loaded in the back of a 1-tonner, all 25 of them, and driven away from the police station. They were glad to get away, but horrified by what they saw as they bumped through the town centre. It had obviously been a night of wildness and unfettered riot. Shop fronts were smashed and looted, with trails of what the raiders dropped leading in all directions. Vehicles were overturned and burning, and the roadsides were littered with bodies in various stages of mutilation. Drunken Africans were roaming the streets, staggering, bleeding, vomiting or just crawling around totally incapable.

Derek noticed that most of the victims were Syrian, Lebanese and Indian traders, whose reputation for ruthlessness made them obvious targets. Most of them were independent operators without either corporate or consular backing. A large percentage had, in fact, become Kumangan citizens so that they could carry on with their business without the discrimination which was being inflicted on expatriates. It made no difference to the Africans what kind of passport they held - they were still foreigners, gouging the African peoples in their own lands.

These ethnic groups tended to turn in on themselves, belonging to neither the African nor the European worlds. They preferred the security of their market caverns and living quarters above to any outside social contact, no matter how successful or prosperous they might be. The Africans resented them for their commercial skills, and the accompanying affluence. The Europeans, and the British in particular, would never accept them as social equals, reluctant to believe in those days that no Arab or Indian trader could ever be successful and completely honest at the same time.

Some of them had tried to defend themselves, their property and their women by producing and using whatever firearms they had been able to acquire and hide, in the event and ever-present possibility of just a situation. This was evident by the number of dead and dying Africans outside and in some cases inside the ruined shop fronts. It was not a pleasant sight, and as the sun rose higher, it would not be a pleasant odour. Pray to God that enough sanity would return for the streets to be cleaned of at least the bodies.

The town of Ugbeshu was typical of provincial centres in West Africa. It was an enormous clearing scythed by a giant's hand out of the jungle, a sprawling ants' nest of activity in which eighty thousand souls battled the familiar effects of hunger and poverty. There were several moderately broad streets entering a vast shanty town of mud and corrugated iron, which seemed to stretch out endlessly in every direction. Running off at distorted angles were smaller streets and passages, muddy in the rains, dusty in the heat where the rooftops of the low shacks appeared to touch and even overlap. Occasionally a stone-built two-storey house advertised itself as the proud domain of a local businessman who had been comparatively successful in his dealings, legitimate or otherwise.

There were no drains, apart from the conventional dirt-encrusted, slime-filled trenches, stagnating and stinking, the ultimate receptacle for everything no longer needed. Electricity had recently been introduced to the town, each outlet a stringy, dangerous spider's web of multiple plugs and hazardous wiring. Radios and hi-fi's blared out the addictive rhythms of highlife, shrieking and wailing at full volume as though telling the world where the action was to be found. There was no sense of urgency in "the town", nothing which couldn't wait until tomorrow or the next tomorrow after that.

In the centre of this nightmare of non-planning the widest and busiest of the main roads was lined with the laterite-splattered concrete buildings of government and commerce. Like an oasis of formality amid the confusion of squalor, the offices and warehouses of foreign-owned business empires conspired with government buildings to bring a degree of efficiency and authority to the ramshackle scene.

The tropical hot-house of African cities encouraged the growth of all kinds of life form, and the diversity of human beings that thronged the streets never failed to intrigue Derek.

There were scraggy Arab women perspiring inside their dowdy black dresses and veils. They contrasted sharply with the Indian ladies in their shimmering saris, with precious jewels in their pierced nostrils and golden sandals on their feet. They exuded class as they snapped orders to the myriad of attendants in their wake.

There were African peasant men, muscled and dignified. They wore loin-cloths or cast-off rags of Western clothing with the same jaunty self-confidence as the successful lawyers in their bespoke tailoring. Their round-faced and curious women, bare-breasted under their cloaks, padded behind, with short leather aprons high on their strong, glossy dark thighs, swinging as they walked. Conical headdresses of ochre and mud and plaited hair made carrying their chattels a near- impossible task, but somehow they managed it. Infants clung like fat little leeches to their breasts, indifferent to the world around.

There were the white women, remote and cool, in dresses home-made from gaudy local material, or brought out from London two years ago and fading under the tropical sun. They were usually followed around by a house boy as they shopped, or they would glide by in the seclusion of a chauffeured limousine. The men wore light linen suits and soft collars, regarded as "proper" for business in the tropics. Unless, of course, they were engineers engaged in "rough" work, in which case khaki shorts and an open neck shirt would suffice. Except at weekend, when casual attire meant faded white shorts and a shirt with the collar rubbed threadbare. Many of the Europeans were beginning to yellow around the edges of their tan, the result of exposure to the sun and rich foods. Derek supposed that he looked like one of them, or soon would do.

And of course there were beggars; beggars of every type and deformity, offering the blessings of Allah for a couple of pennies. Beggars polite and pestering, diseased and brazen. Derek wasn't offended by beggars - he just avoided them.

The street scene was one Derek loved, a scene which he hoped he could enjoy for many more years.

The senior officers and managers charged with the responsibility of keeping commerce and government wheels turning did not live in the town. In an effort to provide as much of a "home-from-home" atmosphere as was possible under such circumstances, the employers of European personnel had built and maintained a housing suburb known as "the reservation" on the fringe of the town. Although they were all described as "suitable" accommodation, the quality and grandeur varied according to status. Each and every one sat in its own compound with its own amenities, its own privacy. Except, perhaps, for the bachelor residences where three or four may be found in the one compound, for maintenance economy as much as for companionship. In all ways it was all a far cry from the conditions of the township dwellers.

The streets of the reservation were all paved and tree-lined. All houses had electricity, piped water, adequate drainage and a gardener to look after the expansive grounds. It was a touch of suburban England affording every white resident, whatever his level of seniority, the chance to live like a gentleman for as long as he chose to remain in West African service. Recently, though, it was being noticed that some successful and newly-promoted Africans were opting to move to the reservation, but this was for purely prestige reasons. In most cases, the families didn't share the enthusiasm to live in white man's territory.

Derek's two-storey house was set like a square white jewel on a bed of perennial colours, surrounded by the lush greenery of a tropical back-drop. The house was really too large for just the four of them, having a complete guest wing in addition to the usual family accommodation. It had at one time been the General Manager's house in the not-too-distant past when the lack of telephones, air travel and even roads had made each district almost autonomous. The house was said to have been in those days second only to the Residency in splendour. However, a recent influx of oil-hungry Americans, with their money and flamboyance, had built residences which made even the noble Seat of Government seem unobtrusive by comparison.

Debbie had done her best in the five years they had lived there to make the place an attractive and comfortable home, rather than merely the house of a senior manager. Evidence of her needlework and furnishing ideas was everywhere. She had even brought back some wallpaper from one of her home leave visits, only to find to her chagrin that she had to paste it up herself. None of the local decorating tradesmen had ever been called on to apply anything but paint, and didn't know where to start. The stewards watched with open-mouthed amazement as Madam worked herself into a sticky frenzy to fasten these long bits of paper to the walls. There was nothing wrong with walls, so why try to cover them? Strange ideas, these oyibos. Hassan's well-meaning but untimely offer of a box of thumb tacks provoked a stream of abuse from Debbie which he privately thought was quite unfair.

As the truck with its human cargo cleared the town and approached the suburbs, the evidence of the riot was less noticeable. Most of the houses had been ransacked, but the occupants were well clear. Most of them had either already gone home or were arrested in the swoop. They couldn't shake, though, the acrid smell of smoke and stench of bodies starting to rot, even as they turned into the driveway of the Muji Hotel.

They left the truck and walked up the steps. As they entered the lobby of this familiar and popular gathering place, formerly known as the Ambassador Hotel, a flood of memories from happier times swept over all of them. Here they had dined, danced, entertained and succeeded, at times, in escaping, however temporarily, from the pressures of living in Africa. The glow of nostalgia faded as they became aware of soldiers in every corner, leering, waving their guns and defiantly wiping their dirty boots on the Wilton carpet and Persian rugs. It was made apparent that the Colonial Office visitor or commercial traveler would no longer find comfortable, familiar refuge in this former oasis of luxury, this once blissful retreat.

They were again split into their original groups. Derek and his friends were shown to a suite on the third floor by an effusive Indian desk clerk, who could not break the habit as he ushered them in like valued paying guests. The suite consisted of three bedrooms, a sitting room, a kitchenette and the usual bathroom facilities. To their surprise but great relief they found a selection of their own clothes, taken randomly from the wardrobes of each and every one of them.

This brought a smile, the first for several hours.

Alan Rushton spoke what was in their minds.

"Well, I'll be damned! At least it looks as though they plan to keep us alive for a while longer."

His optimism, if not his cynicism, was shared by all of the perplexed members of the group as they bathed, shaved and generally cleaned themselves up. They were further surprised at having an appetising breakfast sent up to them. White man food, this time. They learned later in the day that Vincente, the Italian chef, had refused to leave his post while there was still a chance that there would still be people around to appreciate his culinary talents. Vincente's reputation was legend throughout Kumanga, especially with visitors from Ivebje who remembered his day as a sous-chef at the Royal Empress Hotel in the capital.

Vincente's artistry was, by cordon-bleu standards, only slightly better than average, but after two dusty days of bland rest-house food the menu at the Ambassador Hotel in Ugbeshu was almost a gourmet's delight. Vincente had been able to send home enough money to his brothers in Turin to open their own family restaurant.

"Some-a day, some-a day," Vincente would say when asked how long he planned to bury himself in Africa. "When I am-a too old for-a the heat, then I go back to Italia." Thank goodness he hadn't yet gone!

Events seemed to be taking a turn for the better. After breakfast the detainees began to mellow and talk in a more optimistic tone. No-one was tired. There was a chance that something might be missed while sleeping; there was much speculating to do. Especially after an Army captain called in during the morning to say that "someone important" would be coming to explain why they had been detained.

They waited with immeasurable curiosity for about two hours and a half until, with great flourish and ceremony, the captain returned to announce the arrival of the Important Person.

It was His Excellency Chief Anthony Bartholomew Agamoru, now the Governor of the Province of Ugbeshu.

7

Tony Agamoru needed no introduction to any of them. His family owned almost half of the land in what was now called Ugbeshu Province, and had done so for generations. It was said that their wealth and power were the spoils from the incessant tribal wars fought in bygone days on behalf of the Oba, when the kingdom of Ugbeshu stretched for hundreds of miles in all directions. Tony's father claimed to be related to the Oba himself. No-one had ever dared to dispute it, since the family had a reputation for making their claims stick.

Tony's power lay not only in his wealth and position, but also in his physical and mental superiority. He exuded charm and cordiality and bore all the traits of an African leader whose upbringing has been greatly influenced by western standards. His whole character was one of forceful dynamism, gentle but ruthless, diplomatic but compelling, and he commanded the respect of everyone he met.

Tony had been educated in Ivebje at an expensive private

school to which only the sons of European diplomats and influential chiefs were admitted. There had been no difficulty in securing an under-graduate place at Oxford, where by applying himself diligently to his studies, both academic and social, Tony attained an honours degree in law. His rise in government circles had been swift and smooth. Long before independence, Tony Agamoru was a respected member of the Moresian Trade Delegation in London, with a shining future ahead of him. When the Trade Delegation became a fully-fledged High Commission, Tony was an automatic choice for a Vice-Consular appointment while still in his twenties. He was accepted by London's diplomatic elite and became one of the most popular party guests.

A personal scandal involving Consular funds and young, blossoming female socialites brought Tony a severe rebuke and cast a shadow on his diplomatic future. Nothing was ever proven, and such was the family's political pull that his penalty was nothing more than a demotion in rank, and he had settled for the District Commissioner's job back in Kumanga when the last British incumbent retired. During his short time in office he had already been able to restore much of his esteem, and was steadily re-forging his political ambitions. An arranged marriage to the daughter of Prince Efik, heir to the throne of neighbouring Abakoka, had not only smothered the growing inter-tribal bickering but also brought Tony recognition as a peacemaker.

Tony was an avid sportsman, having a golf handicap in the single figures, an expert tennis player and had been a keen member of the Club since it was forced to open its doors to non-whites. One of Tony's regrets at having been recalled to his native country was that Kumanga did not have an active cricket team.

"Some day, perhaps, we may put something together. We did with soccer, so why not cricket?" He had to admit, though, that both the rules and the enthusiasm for the noble and rural game of cricket would be hard to instil into his countrymen.

Tony's politics were confusing and contradictory. His upbringing and training led him privately to favour the situation as it had been before independence.

"British aid used to be like a water tap. Where there is a need, you simply turn it on and help yourself. When the need is temporarily satisfied you turn it off until next time. That doesn't happen any more. Pity."

In the interests of his career, his country and, not incidentally, his own well-being, he had found it expedient to throw his considerable energies behind the drive for nationalism, which was almost a religion or even a disease with those in power who could do him the most good.

"Give us our freedom and we will come together as one family. We will work twice as hard because we are free. This is not India, you know - there are no petty quarrels here to divide and weaken us."

He didn't believe a word of it, and knew that his European friends didn't either, but it was what his fellow Kumangans wanted to hear. It was this sort of rhetoric which kept him popular with leaders and followers alike.

Tony had, in fact, been instrumental in the expulsion of several expatriates who were less than enthusiastic about Kumanga's approach to self-government. The difference between them and the white people still around was that they had been foolish enough to vent their feelings in public. Like the frustrated and slightly drunk British diplomat who had been heard to declare that Kumanga's was "the only constitution in the world to have been put together on the bloody telephone." Even Tony couldn't let that one pass, even if he did privately believe it.

"The trouble with you British," Tony had once said while sitting around the Club's bar, "is that you have no imagination, no colour, no sense of pageantry. Oh, sure - you follow the historic and required traditions such as your coronations and such. But otherwise your lives are dull, monotonous, anaemic and grey when compared with the African. When the British Empire crumbles, as it surely will, it will be because you bored it to death."

When Tony entered the hotel suite with his usual taciturn charm, they all assumed that it would be with apologies, that their current predicament would immediately be resolved. This was their friend Tony, their golfing partner, their bar-stool colleague. They were not prepared for what was to follow, for the change in Tony's attitude towards them as he began to explain why they and several hundred like them had been detained all across the country.

"My friends," he began, as he lit a Benson & Hedges, "and I still think of you as my friends, despite this - this inconvenience over which I had no control. I'll come straight to the point."

"Please do," rebuked James, refusing the offered cigarette. "Someone has a lot of explaining to do, so it might as well be someone we know."

Tony smiled in a pained way, like a small boy caught with his hand in the cookie jar, but wanting to assure everyone that it was both necessary and justified. He offered the cigarettes around but only Alan took one.

"As you are aware, your friends and greatest creditors have more-or-less declared war on Soviet Russia."

"Now look here," spluttered Alan, who had never really liked Tony all that much since the day he was made to look foolish on the tennis court. "That's not true." He coughed as the smoke hit his throat while he was still talking.

"Russia threatened America with those damn missiles, so the

Yanks told them to..." He didn't use the phrase which had first come mind. "....to clear off out of Cuba. So would you, or anyone else, under the circumstances."

Tony ignored him and carried on as though nothing had been said. In his opinion Rushton was a semi-literate idiot, and didn't deserve an answer.

"Although you all know that I am certainly no communist, we can't ignore that fact that my government has found warm friendship with the Soviet factions, who appear to have a deep appreciation of our problems. They've given us a great deal of help since independence - help which has played a big part in our development so far."

"Oh, come on, Tony. You don't..."

James's comments were choked off by the army captain, who stepped forwards with his hands up.

"You will address the Governor as 'Your Excellency'. As you used to address those appointed by your own people in London. You are no longer on a level...."

He, in turn, was interrupted by Tony.

"That's all right, Captain. I know these people well. To them I will still be 'Tony'. For the time being, at least."

The captain stepped back, and James continued.

"You, above all Kumangans, surely don't buy that. The Russians are just out for what they can get. Which is control. And they'll control you in a far more ruthless way than the British ever did. They're playing with you."

Tony shook his head.

"Their view of us is vastly different from the colonial one which has subjected African peoples everywhere to a state of virtual slavery in our own countries over the past century."

This sounded like something from a Soviet propaganda

speech, and Derek couldn't help a little snort. Tony noticed it, but carried on, a little less enthusiastically.

"Our president, -er- with the full backing of his cabinet, considers the attitude of the United States and her allies to be one of extreme aggression, and has declared his support for our new friends. He has acted by ordering the expulsion of all nationals who support America's grave and warlike threat."

"Rubbish", exploded Alan, still coughing, but unable to contain his frustration any longer.

"You've lived in the U. K. long enough to know that this is a typical Soviet move to get a foot in the door, like she did in Asia, in India, in Cuba and God knows where else. Surely you don't believe this propaganda bullshit?"

Tony smiled, then addressed the captain who was lounging by the door. He spoke rapidly in Jibi, a language which Derek had long ago given up as impossible for a European to master. The captain left the room.

Tony re-arranged his gleaming white agbada, and lowered his voice.

"What I believe or don't believe is academic right now. I'm looking after my country's interests, which at the moment happen to be the same as my own. My instructions are simply to obey orders. I am what the Americans refer to as 'on a roll'. I didn't wangle the D.C. job by expressing my true beliefs. My predecessor did that, and he is no longer D.C. In fact, he is no longer."

He paused at the dubious humour of what he had just said. They all remembered Alhaji Yusuf. As a northerner who had made good in the south, it was only a matter of time before Yusuf's strong pro-British views would spell his demise.

Tony continued.

"If it makes you feel any better, I personally believe that the

Soviets will have a short reign in Kumanga. Or anywhere in Africa, come to that. Pure communism does not mix with traditional African tribalism. But, in the meanwhile, we have to live with it, and all I have to do, as your Whitehall men are always saying, is keep my nose clean."

"Thanks a lot!", was Alan's reply. "Where does that leave us?"

"Just coming to that - ***old boy***." He leaned heavily on the last two words, as if to convey his opinion of Alan.

"I wondered when you'd get to it," commented James. "Why us, specifically?"

Tony leaned back in his chair and put his fingertips together.

"It's not just you specifically. You, along with many others, have certain skills and resources which are essential to the smooth running of our country. Such has been Britain's tight control over our affairs in the past century that it's been made impossible for us to govern ourselves effectively. Yet. Oh, I know all about the Great Plan, the Supreme Proposal to lead under-developed countries to independence. The - what is it called? - 'introduction of controlled self-government'. Now there's a contradiction in terms if ever I heard one."

Derek had to agree. It was typical Whitehall jargon. But he would never admit it to an African.

This statement and Tony's waving hand silenced the expected protests which were jumping to the lips of his audience.

"Let's not kid ourselves. You British had no real intentions of giving up. It was lip service, a show for the rest of the world, a conscience gesture after the fiasco in India. Don't think we were fooled by that, not for an instance. I lived in London long enough to realise what you ***really*** think. We knew what would happen, and it did. We have been left high and dry, and we're supposed to come crawling back to Britain with tail between legs saying, 'we can't manage on our own - please come back and rule us.' But that isn't going to happen. We ***will*** make it on our own. Or, at least, with a little bit of help from Soviet Russia."

"With...a little bit of help....." He broke into the lyric from a recent London theatre hit.

The prisoners glanced at each other apprehensively. There was obviously some substance to their detention. They weren't going to be released unconditionally.

Tony resumed his explanation.

"This is where you come into the plan".

There was a shuffling of feet as the others changed position, as if to make sure that not a syllable was missed.

"We are not so ignorant as to think that we can run everything ourselves just yet, or rely totally on the Russians, who are, after all, strangers to our system. So we are forced to enlist your co-operation. We still need your help. Yes, even the cleverest of my colleagues have to admit it However, there's always a chance you may not give it willingly, so we have to take some measures to be sure of your co-operation."

"What the hell are you talking about?"

"Let me spell it out for you."

"Please do!"

Tony's gaze swept around the room, then came to rest on Jeremy Wilson.

"Jeremy Wilson. You are the clever boy who keeps the power going in our city, and much of the province, too. Without your guidance and expertise we would probably blow up the generators in less than a week. Like they did in Lagos last year. Even the Russians don't have anyone who understands those machines as well as you do. You will keep the power flowing for us."

Jeremy paled, but sat still and silent.

"And don't even think about making anything go wrong. If it does, we'll immediately think you are deliberately sabotaging things. You can just imagine how upset certain people would become with that. So I'm sure we can count on your co-operation."

There was no friendliness in his voice now. Jeremy looked at James as if for guidance, but the older man just shrugged.

Tony then turned to Jean.

"Forgive me, matron, I'm forgetting my manners. I should have talked to you first. Your function is obvious. Everyone's aware of your great value at our hospital. Everyone likes and respects you. What's more, they all obey you, since there's no doubt that you know best what the hospital needs. You are, to be quite honest, not replaceable. Not yet, anyway."

"So", was Jean's only comment.

"So, my dear lady, you will continue with your duties as though nothing has happened."

He waved his hand to silence Jean's next retort, which he expected would be one of defiance. He then looked at Henri Gaudet.

"Mon chèr ami. Ton rôle est très important." Derek's French wasn't good enough to follow the conversation, but he picked out some words which indicated that Henri was being told to keep his trucks moving. Derek knew that Tony spoke three or four European languages, and this was a typical gesture. This was one of those classy touches which had made him such a hit in the diplomatic world.

After Henri's spluttering and gesticulating had subsided, Tony reverted to English.

"If any of you didn't follow that, I was merely explaining to your French friend what his part will be. I'm sure he will share the news with you later. Now, you three."

He looked at James, Derek and Alan in turn.

"James, you still have great financial power in this area. You have the means of financing whatever projects we may wish to put into effect, basically through your bank's influence with overseas creditors. That's one area where the Soviets fall down - they're not too free with the ready cash. Roubles troubles, if you like."

He stopped and smiled at this witticism, looking for support. There was none.

"It's not just the keys to the vault we are after. Your main function will be to persuade governments and financial institutions of Europe, Asia and America to maintain a good credit rating for Kumanga."

James half rose from his chair, but sat down again when Tony raised his hand.

"You're out of your mind. No-one will take any notice of me, even if I agreed to do it."

"Oh, they will when they hear our terms. Especially coming from you, a prestigious and respected pillar of our major bank."

"Now - our good friends from C.A.C."

He smiled pleasantly at Derek, and paused as though expecting the favour to be returned. It wasn't.

"You have at your disposal a great deal of merchandise on import license. You will continue to bring it into the country until the world recognises Kumanga as a serious and creditable nation in its own right. You will, of course, continue to do your business with the markets as normal, but government requirements will have priority. That includes discounts on pricing."

He knew as well as Derek that 'discounts on pricing' meant that the company would be lucky if it saw any payment at all.

"We're already doing that. Can't cut it down much more or we'll not make any money at all."

"My friend, you've been making money, big money, out of Africa for decades. It's time to put a little back. But this isn't the time to discuss the finer points."

It was all very obvious now. Tony had been delegated by his masters to bring the outline of the plan to the six detainees, and probably to all the others, to explain in an informal way what was happening. Gone was the camaraderie, gone were the golf partnerships, the tennis, the hours of friendly discussion, the innumerable drinks bartered back and forth across the bar in the Club. In their place was a cold, practical official explaining to his former friends why they were now his prisoners, his servants. He was, as he had said, keeping his nose clean.

This time James did stand up and pointed a finger.

"It's madness - sheer lunacy. You'll never get away with it. As soon as the world realises what's going on they'll close the door on you with a bang. You don't really expect a crazy idea like that to work, do you? You expect bankers and suppliers to keep sending out what you demand, under these conditions? They'll cut off everything as soon as the word gets out."

Tony sighed, and lowered his voice.

"Don't point your finger at me, James. I'm not a dogon yaro. As I explained to you, what I personally expect or think is of no consequence. I'm just doing what I'm told by our government There are wiser men than I who feel that as long as we have you here, plus all the others like you throughout the country, your companies and governments will be happy to co-operate in exchange for your continued well-being."

This made them all look up sharply. It was the first time Tony had alluded to their personal safety.

"Hostages."

Jean's face was a mask of cold fury.

"You mean we're to be bloody hostages. You're all mad."

Derek was privately hoping that she would come out with another mouthful like she gave Ovremwe. It would be interesting to see Tony's reaction, with his sophisticated upbringing. Probably write it down for his own use. But it didn't happen.

"And just how long is this expected to go on?", Derek asked.

"That's not for me to speculate," answered Tony. "Or should that be 'not for ***I*** to speculate'? I never could get that construction sorted out. Used to drive my English prof. crazy."

"To hell with the construction."

Alan had been quiet for too long.

"How long do you plan to keep us, you scum-bag?"

Tony's tone changed as he stood up, and Derek groaned. Alan and his big mouth again.

"Mr Rushton," Tony snarled, "You would do well to mind your manners. I don't like you, as you are well aware. You're not totally indispensable to this scheme, and certainly in no position to carry on treating Africans like vermin, as you have for most of your career. That's all over now. So keep your mouth shut and you'll live. Understand?" He softened slightly. "And that goes for all of you, too."

He calmed down and continued in his original voice, but without the mellow look which his face had held so far.

"I didn't come here to give you guarantees or answer your questions. I came to tell you why this is happening because I thought you would take it better from me than from some jumped-up civil servant. I don't make the rules, I just interpret them. All I know is what I told you. Co-operate and I will personally see to it that you are treated well. Have I not persuaded them to let you stay here instead of holding you in that abominable police station? Have I not secured some of your own clothes and found you some decent food? Believe me when I say I'll make life as pleasant as I can for you. But if you fail to co-operate, and it will be out of my hands. And I can promise you that it will be very ***unpleasant***."

He glowered at Alan and called out in Jibi. The captain was there instantly. Probably been listening in to everything anyway, thought Derek.

Tony glanced at the Rolex on his wrist.

"Now you must excuse me. The pressures of office, you know."

The smile returned to his face as he strode towards the door which was opened by the captain. He turned as he stepped through the doorway.

"Please continue to look upon me as a friend. It never hurts to have someone you know on the inside".

He waved, and left.

The old charm is still there, thought Derek, even if he did come near to losing it. Must speak to Alan. His mouth could get him into a lot of trouble right now. And all of them, come to that.

Although Derek had had very little sleep before his rude awakening, he was not tired. Shocked, dazed and bewildered, but not tired. He sank back into one of the armchairs and pondered what he had just heard. There was a buzz of conversation all around him as the others discussed and questioned. Because of Britain's close ties with the U.S.A. and America's ultimatum to the Soviets, he and his companions were to be detained and forced to take whatever action their captors demanded. An ironic twist - they were the slaves now and the Africans were the slave-masters.

There was no doubt that the Russians would be pleased with this move. They would encourage Kumanga to extort whatever they could from capitalist sources before the world closed its eyes to the fate of the hostages. It was a classic idea, if a bit far-fetched, but it might just work for a while. Sooner or later, though, the flow of money, goods and services would be choked off as the foreign powers grew tired of the blackmail. But this could take weeks, months. Then what?

This was what Ovremwe had meant when he referred to persons of "political or commercial value". He had meant that everyone on whom Kumanga still relied to prevent the country from grinding to a halt would be held to ransom. And then the Soviets would move in and increase its fawning influence to a degree where Kumanga would become hopelessly dependent. Like Cuba. The striving and scheming for a piece of Africa had finally paid off. So-called experts had said that Africa would never lend itself to communism. Perhaps they were correct, but that doesn't stop a struggling country accepting help when the timing is right. There would be many, many other Kumangas unless the western nations removed their heads from the sand.

Derek's lifted up his head, eyes wide, as another thought occurred to him. Of course! It was probably Russia's plan in the first place, conceived long before President Kennedy's anticipated reaction. No Kumangan would have the cunning or the audacity to hatch out, let alone execute, such well-timed, well-planned strategem. All the Soviets had to do was make the proposal then turn the screws on Kumanga, using the missile crisis to draw gullible African minds further into the spider's web.

Derek couldn't help feeling a twinge of admiration for the Soviet intellects responsible for this plan. He also realised with increasing alarm that the next few weeks, months, or even years could, at best, be very uncomfortable for him and his companions. At the worst - he didn't want to speculate on the possibilities. The master-servant relationship was now turned around, and the Africans had centuries of grudges to avenge. It was clever and dirty, typical of the tactics and intrigue which the Soviet Union would use in an effort to further its strategy.

Derek glanced around the room. The others had fallen silent, each trying to untangle their own confused thoughts. He wondered if they were drawing the same conclusions.

"It looks as though we are well and truly trapped", commented James to break the silence. "Locked up for being too efficient. Ironical, isn't it? One really can't win".

Henri Gaudet swore in French, long, loud and leaving no question as to his feelings.

"I agree", said Jean. "Don't understand what you said, but I bet it matches what I'm thinking".

They began to talk, analysing the situation and projecting the consequences of various forms of action. They talked round and round in circles, but were unable to come up with anything which might offer some hope of escape from their predicament. In due course an excellent lunch was served to them, after which they dozed, trying to catch up on some of the sleep they had lost the night before. The rest of the afternoon was spent in agitated anticipation.

Tony Agamoru, to give him credit, had tried to make conditions bearable for them. He sent in extra beds, magazines, playing cards and even a radio. The latter wasn't much comfort, though, since all external stations had been jammed. All they could find was high-life and propaganda declaring the glory of the republic and the lengths to which it was prepared to go to ensure "democracy, free from colonial oppression, for all loyal Kumangan citizens". The telephone was still there, but was as dead as the corpses they had seen at the roadside. Jeremy Wilson tried to revive it, but without success.

"I'm an electrician, not a telephone engineer. I would be

surprised, though, if it ever worked at all, judging from the wiring," he commented, with an obvious hint of personal experience in his tone.

By late evening they were feeling bored and tired - tired through physical inactivity and mental strain. Derek thought how Debbie would react when news of this situation leaked out. She would probably go into a panic with a touch of "why am I not surprised?" thrown in. And she was right – the threat had always been there, however remote it had seemed. But it was too late to do anything about it now, except try to figure out a way round it.

No-one was able to add anything new to the speculation about what the future would be like. They sorted out their sleeping arrangements. Derek and James would take one bedroom, Alan and Jeremy the second, leaving the smallest one for Jean. This was after Alan had more than just jokingly suggested that Jean share with him.

"You never give up, do you?"

Jean was plainly neither pleased not flattered by the offer.

This left Henri Gaudet, who was quite content to stretch out on the large sofa.

Despite the lack of sleep over the past 24 hours, Derek had trouble in relaxing his active mind sufficiently to drop into slumber. The situation was not helped by the relentless plodding of the sentry outside, and the monotony of his tread even penetrated the air-conditioned seal of the bedroom. It contrasted sharply with the bored and silent vigil of the night-watchman who patrolled Derek's own house.

Musa, whose job description record referred to him as a "mai-gardi", was undoubtedly the happiest and most affluent person on Derek's staff. Musa didn't know how old he was. The staff files gave his age as 45, but he looked nearer to 80. He was from the desert Buzu tribe, and as the senior mai-gardi on CAC's payroll in

Ugbeshu it was to him that the privilege and honour of guarding the D.M.'s house fell. He had few possessions; a kettle, teapot, chop-dish, tin mug and prayer mat were all Derek had ever seen, apart from the clothes he wore which he never seemed to change.

Musa's needs were scant. He slept for most of the day in the shade of a flame-of-the-forest tree near the boys' quarters, and Derek knew that he was fed by Pious on whatever escaped from the kitchen. He slept for most of the night, too, sometimes all night, awakening only in time for his morning Sallah, the religious ritual with which every devout Moslem starts his day. It didn't really matter if he slept or not, since as long as he paid his protection dues to what the whites referred to as "the thieves union", he knew that the premises he was guarding would be exempt from burglary.

Musa would introduce a substitute watchman every May just before the rains came, then he would disappear back up north for six months. He would resume his duties in November, releasing his "brother" to stand in for some other mai-gardi who wanted a holiday. Derek could think of no-one else who could afford to work for only half a year, saving a very large percentage of his meagre wages so that he could take a vacation for the other half. Nice idea, he thought. Six months working, then six months holiday; he could do with only a six-month tour right now.

With this pleasant if impractical idea tugging at his semi-conscious, Derek finally drifted into a troubled sleep, punctuated by Jim's snores and the thoughts of what Jean was wearing to bed, if anything.

8

The next morning they breakfasted well and leisurely, a rare treat which was usually enjoyed only on Sundays and holidays. There was absolutely nothing to do afterwards except browse through the magazines and talk among themselves. Jeremy thought about seeing if the swimming pool was still operative, but couldn't get further than the door of the suite, which was locked from the outside. The radio was still offering propaganda and nationalistic drivel, in which they had no interest whatsoever. It was obvious that the immediate problem was going to be acute boredom unless something happened soon.

They talked, they speculated, they predicted, they even hatched an improbable escape plan, but nothing led anywhere. There were long periods of silence when no-one could offer anything new, and each became wrapped up in private thought. Derek's reflections were about his family, and his bitter regret at having accepted this assignment when he didn't need to. It was just to satisfy his ego, regardless of what it was doing to his family. Or was it that the thoughts of living in bleary old England just didn't appeal to him after Africa?

Later that afternoon their boredom was broken by the arrival of Axel Svenson. Svenson was known to all of them. In fact, Svenson was known to everyone in the province. Svenson's reckless exploits as a bush pilot were almost legend, and had earned him the title of "Axel the Mad". They were not pleased to see him in their midst; he was a known rebel and brought trouble everywhere he went.

Axel Svenson was from Sweden, the son of a rough, hard-drinking dock worker whose wife had run away when Axel was only five years old. Borg Svenson had tried to bring up his son the best way he could between extended bouts of drunkenness and frequent work lay-offs. This did little to groom the young Axel for a life of genteel respectability.

During most of his father's periods of neglect, Axel had found himself in the care of foster homes and state institutions, where an effort was made to educate him in the basic academic needs. That was between escapades of running away, being thrown out as unmanageable or living by his wits. These episodes were sporadic, however, since Svenson senior always returned, employed and sober, to claim his son with a promise of reform and parental responsibility. The promise usually lasted only until the next lay-off. It was no surprise, then, that Axel grew up tough, uncouth, and well able to take care of himself in a man's world at the age of fourteen. He had a knack of being able to remain one step ahead of the police, unlike many of his colleagues.

"Sometime they make stupid mistake; not smart people. Have to think smart an' you no get caught," was his philosophy on law breaking.

After lying about his age he was taken on as a deck-hand by the captain of a Liberian-registered freighter, and developed a keen interest in marine engines. Without any formal training he became skilful at repairing, servicing and even replacing the powerful engines, which made him a popular source of cheap labour for money-oriented ships' masters. It was to his advantage, though, and after five years of roaming the oceans he returned to Sweden with a sizeable bankroll. His interest switched from marine to aeronautical engines, and by sheer determination and conscientious study he obtained a commercial pilot's licence while still in his twenties.

The world was now at his feet. He drifted from country to country, flying a variety of missions about which he showed no curiosity, picking up experience along the way. He saved his money, learned as much as his limited reading capacities would allow, and kept well away from liquor. The same restraint couldn't be applied to his sexual practices, though, and in the interests of personal safety he was forced to make many a hasty take-off before it was scheduled.

During the early fifties he found himself in northern Moresia with a small share in a one-machine air freight company which asked no questions and obeyed no laws except gravity and self-preservation. The reason for or purpose of his missions did not concern him. His job was to fly, land, then take off again whenever he was bid, for which he was handsomely paid. On one such mission his two partners were gunned down while loading, prompting Axel to take off hurriedly and save his own skin. He had no way of knowing if his colleagues had been killed, arrested, jailed or had escaped. All that was important to him was that they never came back, leaving him the sole owner of an air freight business with one dilapidated plane.

As British control in Moresia began to loosen, Axel moved his business to the more populated and lucrative southern regions. He increased his fleet by the purchase of a used but serviceable Piper Cherokee, and built a service hangar in a corner of Ugbeshu airport. The legal side of his enterprise was maintained by a Royal Mail air service contract to remote corners of the country. It was a known if unproven fact that most of his profits were derived from operations on the fringe of the laws governing contraband. He was an expert in the art of bribery, and found very few gates closed to him.

Axel's many years of successful work almost came to disaster when it was announced that the new Republic's policy was to allow only Kumangan citizens to handle official documents, including mail. Mr. Svenson could expect to lose his contract unless suitable arrangements could be made. Without his legitimate reasons for travelling, Axel's other activities would fall under greater scrutiny and would mean, at the very least, a considerable drop in his income. Through his many contacts and expertise in lining the right pockets, the "suitable arrangements" were made, and Axel overcame the other hurdle by simply becoming a naturalised Kumangan citizen. Even this, though, had not exempted him from being classed as a "foreigner with useful potential", hence his appearance at the Muji Hotel under guard.

With his comic-book English, coloured by pidgin, he proclaimed with great energy what he planned to do to his abductors once the situation reverted to normal. He had refused to submit to a physical search, and his six feet four inches of towering rage and muscle did nothing to persuade his captors to enforce this requirement. In fact, he had been subdued only by the certainty of a bullet or two had he continued with his defiance. The four soldiers escorting him thankfully retreated after they had pushed him into the suite and thrown in a mattress behind him. He whirled on them with a growl as they left, a stream of what sounded like very uncomplimentary Swedish following them.

Derek and James exchanged glances. Whereas the Swede would be an invaluable asset to their group if ever things got rough, the reputation of Axel the Mad would be of little use to them in a situation requiring tact and diplomacy.

The Swede glowered at them. These were not his kind of people. They were snobbish, socially correct, dull, self-opinionated and too clever by half. "Poncy", was the word the English used. He realised, though, that they were there for the same reasons as he was, and resolved to be tolerant of them to a degree. Especially the nurse-woman; he could be very, very tolerant of her.

"They want me to fly my planes wherever they tell. Maybe they pay, maybe they don't. I Kumangan now, but I don't like they tell me what I haf to do. You the same?"

Realising that Axel was struggling to be friendly and communicative, which he never had in the past, Derek was quick to answer him. Between them, the captives told him what they had learned, and Axel started to realise that perhaps he had misjudged them in the past. Perhaps they were "ordinary" people, after all. Perhaps he could get along with them.

"Then we all in the same boat. Or the same hotel."

He laughed at this humorous gem, and was pleased to see that they laughed with him. They thought it would be expedient to do so, until they had gained the confidence and respect of this uncouth giant.

Jean kept her distance from Axel. She was as aware as everyone else of his reputation as a womaniser. Not that he didn't try. At one stage he sat on the sofa next to her and put a big, hairy arm around her shoulder. Jean reacted by pulling a safety pin out of her pocket and pressing the open point into Axel's flesh.

"Now move it. And don't try it again."

Axel yelped, frowned at her, then laughed as he removed his arm, a red spot appearing at the point of puncture.

"A fighter. I like that. But", as Jean started to protest, "Am sorry. Maybe later."

"And maybe not," replied Jean as she moved to a different seat.

Axel didn't try it again, much to Derek's relief.

After the third night their patience was wearing thin, despite the luxury which the hotel afforded them, and tempers became short. Alan Rushton quarrelled with Henri Gaudet over priority use of the bathroom, bringing up the Battles of Waterloo and Trafalgar and France's historic animosity towards the English. Jean argued with James for asserting the authority which he didn't have, except by seniority, and was joined by Jeremy in depicting the world to be designed for the younger generation, not the older. And just about everyone was on at Axel because of his manners.

"Or lack of," as Jeremy put it. "The man behaves like a pig. Worse, in fact." A good job Axel didn't hear that, thought Derek, or there might well have been a homicide.

After breakfast on the fourth day, the captain came to tell them that they should gather up what personal belongings they had, since they were being returned to police headquarters for further briefing.

"Not that ghastly place again," said Jeremy. "I feel ill just thinking about it."

He really is a sort of spoiled brat, thought Derek. Jeremy had hinted in the past that his father was quite rich, so what he was doing in a place like Kumanga was a mystery to everyone. He was even suspected of being queer, but then everyone without a wife in West Africa was suspected of being queer at one time or other.

Unless they took a black mistress, that is, and then they were thought to be just depraved.

As they re-assembled outside they wondered what possible further briefing there could be, over and above what they had already been told. Perhaps this was the re-assignment of duties, the doling out of responsibilities, or whatever they wanted to call it. They were loaded into the back of a one-ton lorry. Perhaps the same one which had brought them here? There was only one guard, a docile-looking constable, desiring to be courteous to them but not daring to disobey the instructions he had been given to keep good watch over the prisoners until they arrived at HQ.

Derek noticed with a faint twinge of alarm that Axel Svenson had purposely positioned himself on the guard's right near the tailboard of the truck. He felt a queasiness in the pit of his stomach, and it had nothing to do with breakfast.

The truck was of a typical commercial design, but fitted to military standards, with a canvas cover supported by steel bars. There was no glass in the large window cavity which separated the driver from the load area, and the top of the cab had a large turret hole through which a machine gunner would protrude when on patrol or combat duty. There was no gunner today, though, and the driver was alone in the cab.

They bumped and swayed along the rutted road surface, and their solitary escort, having satisfied himself that there were no apparent immediate problems, turned his gaze to the black strip receding behind the vehicle.

They had only covered a mile or so when Derek and Alan saw Axel slowly and silently remove a short, stubby screwdriver from the ample waistline of his crumpled and baggy trousers. Derek started to reach forwards but was held back by Alan. Rushton's eyes silently pleaded with Derek not to interfere, and Derek slowly sank back on to his hard seat. As if by telepathy, James turned his gaze to the rear of the truck, and they all witnessed Axel's arm rise to its fullest extent, then describe a swift downward arc as it plunged the two-inch blade up to the hilt in the base of the black throat. Axel's left hand covered the African's mouth to stifle the croaking gurgle, and blood spurted furiously from the severed carotid artery. It sprayed Axel's front, the floor of the truck, the canvas sides, and even reached Derek's face across the other side of the vehicle. Henri vomited over the side where the canvas flapped loosely.

Jean sat quietly, a sombre smile escaping from the corners of her mouth. Despite the training which had schooled her to rush instinctively to the aid of the injured or sick, she made no movement. She even seemed to delight in watching the blood pulsate from the severed artery, as though viewing a laboratory experiment where there was no real suffering. Derek, Alan and James between them pulled the bleeding and gurgling figure from the tailgate where it had slumped, and silently laid it down on the floor of the truck. The blood spread out in all directions, surging and receding as the vehicle acknowledged the twisting, pot-holed surface of the road. Derek didn't realise that a human body could expel so much blood. Jeremy didn't move, except to flinch as the trickle of sticky, red liquid reached his open-toed sandals.

Axel wiped the blood from his hands on to his trousers and grabbed the rifle as it slowly fell from the grasp of the dying constable. He pushed the muzzle through the window opening and into the driver's left ear.

"Keep driving," he barked. "You partner him dead, and you go be too if no do what I say. Savvy?"

"Yessah, savvy." The driver was suddenly aware that he was alone in a dangerous situation.

"You do what I tell, and you go live. You no do it, and this first bullet go make you head look like mashed yam. You savvy me?"

"Yessah, savvy you well well. Please, sah, make you no go shoot me. I go do what is it you want. I have piccins, sah, - no shoot me."

The driver sat very still, his concentration riveted on the laterite borders of the road in front of him.

"Make you turn for right next road. That mean this way."

Svenson gestured with his right hand, just in case there was any confusion as to which was the right.

"To airport, fast, but no tricks."

"No, sah, no tricks. I promise. But no shoot me, sah."

"Axel, where are we going?"

"You hear me tell driver. To airport. Is where my plane is, is it?"

He mumbled something in Swedish, which Derek didn't understand, but he couldn't mistake the scorn in the Swede's tone of voice. He knew that Svenson had little time for social graces, and even less tolerance of so-called gentlefolk who were afraid to get their hands dirty. Or in this case, bloodied.

"Yes, but what then?"

"Wait and see. You haf to trust me."

Axel particularly didn't care for Alan Rushton. Alan had once had him suspended from The Club for a whole month for "disorderly conduct, unbecoming a member of the European Club". All he had done was get drunk and throw Nancy Rushton in the pool fully clothed. Little bitch was asking for it anyway. And more. And she got it. He smiled to himself. It was a secret only the two of them shared. And she had promised not to tell.

They sped through the suburbs, avoiding the town centre. Derek had a curious feeling of excitement percolating inside him. It was a feeling of horror and nausea at the stabbing and elation at being once again in some sort of control of the situation, mixed with apprehension and uncertainty of what lay ahead. What if they were caught? Would it mean death? More impressively, what if they got away? What if he and Jean found themselves........? His imagination was running wild, and it had to be checked right now. It did seem, though, that she had been giving him warm and friendly looks since they were thrown together.

Derek pulled his mind back to the immediate predicament as they emerged from a narrow side street, and turned on to the road to the airport. Their luck was holding, at least so far. The remaining two miles passed in silence, save for the steady whine of the engine and blare of the horn, warning cyclists, children and goats to make way for a vehicle on official government business. The pool of blood gushed against the tailgate and began to drip through the crack, leaving a spotty, red trail.

Axel, peering through the windshield of the vehicle, noticed with some concern that the entrance to the airport, some two hundred yards before the main terminal, was blocked by a barricade manned by armed police.

"Don't stop. Drive through it."

"No, no sah - I hit de barricade and maybe de glass break right in my face."

"Is worse than a bullet in you chicken brain?", snarled Axel. "Maybe de glass miss you; but for sure I no go miss you head wid dis gun. Pass building and take right to my shed. Savvy?"

"Savvy, sah, yessah."

Scarcely had he finished speaking than they were at the barrier and through it, the yellow and black striped wood splintering around them with a crunch. The guards, startled out of their early morning complacency after an uneventful night, slowly recovered their wits in time to fire half a dozen badly-aimed shots at the back of the speeding truck.

The vehicle rounded the corner of the terminal and raced across the apron towards Svenson's hangar, leaving a tell-tale wake of red spots as it bumped and bounced over the uneven surface. They screeched to a stop by the plane.

"Surely you're not proposing to put seven of us in that?", asked Alan, eying the Cherokee with suspicion.

"You stay if you want. Then only six. Is made for six. Easy. Goodbye, you stupid English."

"No, wait. If you think it's O.K., of course I'll come."

An alarm bell sounded somewhere in the terminal, and shots began to ring out. James had been under fire many times during the war, but for the others it was a new experience. They didn't waste any time scrambling aboard the aircraft.

"Take me, sah, please, I beg you", pleaded the terrified driver. "Take me, or they kill me for let you get away. Please...I'm begging you as a Christian...."

The gibbering wretch was on his knees trying to grab Axel's bloodstained legs. Then he rolled over still and silent as the edge of the Swede's hand came down on the base of his neck.

"Axel, I don't think...."

"Shut up and get on the plane."

Derek did as he was told and squeezed himself into the freight compartment of the plane. It was really all freight compartment, since the Swede had removed all of the seats except for the two front ones. James had already commandeered what would have otherwise been the co-pilot's chair.

Svenson jumped aboard, secured the door and strapped himself into the pilot's seat. There was no time for the customary instrument check, nor the run-up once the engine had splutter into life. It seemed like no time at all before they were speeding across the barren earth in search of the runway.

Several vehicles could be seen heading out from the direction of the terminal, some with guns blazing. The comic cross-country race ended as Axel wheeled the plane on to the end of the runway and boosted the power as high as he dared.

"Everyone should now be praying", he boomed over his shoulder, and he unexpectedly crossed himself in the manner which Derek normally associated with Catholics. There's a surprise.

"Tanks full and one extra person. And no time to take full runway. Everyone hold on. And pray."

A Land Rover filled with police and weapons cut out from the pack and headed down the runway on a direct collision course. To Derek it spelled the end. Then the driver of the vehicle changed his mind as the certainty of death occurred to him. The Land Rover passed by the starboard wing with inches to spare.

"Here we go," yelled Axel, as he eased back the stick.

At first the response was negative. Sweat oozed out of every pore, mixing with the blood on his clothing to form a pinkish hue which reminded Derek of childrens' wallpaper. Axel tugged more firmly on the stick and the small plane lifted its nose, wobbled on the cushion of air beneath its wings, and began to gain height. Cars, trucks, trees and buildings gradually slid downwards, and the end of the runway passed beneath them as their upward glide continued.

There was a howl of jubilation from Alan, quickly taken up by Jeremy, Derek, Henri and even James, as the realisation of escape hit home. Axel was not so jubilant. He busied himself with his instruments, as he had done countless times before, and set a north-westerly course. This wasn't the first time he'd been obliged to make a hurried get-away, but never before with six passengers. The Kumangan Air Force had jets which could make his little plane look as though it was going backwards, and blast them out of the sky with one shot. He could only hope that they were otherwise occupied, grounded for lack of spare parts, or didn't think that a little Piper Cherokee filled with suicidal Europeans was important enough to bother about. He wouldn't say anything to the others - they were all so happy, and at the moment looked on him, Axel the Mad, as a sort of saviour. He relished the thought with a ironic smirk on his face as he turned to address them.

"We fly over border one hour. Then we fly three hundred miles in Bujavi, land in Qedar where I have friends. Get more fuel to go French Territory."

Almost as an after thought he added, "Sorry, no food here. Small bit of water for drink, but not too much. Go careful."

His passengers settled themselves as best they could to an anxious but inactive few hours. There was nothing to do, and very little space in which to do it even if they thought of something. What about bathrooms? Derek instinctively glanced at Jean. As though reading his mind, she smiled and shrugged her shoulders. He should have sat closer to her. Perhaps.... Forget it, he told himself. Suffice it that they had all got away unhurt. From now on they were totally dependent on the skill of this strange but fascinating, unpredictable but confident Scandinavian pilot-saviour.

9

The heat in the plane began to rise, as though the sun were retaliating for this invasion of his celestial territory. The runaways chatted, they dozed, they pondered and they perspired, their sweat making muddy puddles in the dust on the floor as they shifted positions. This was decidedly less comfortable than the hotel-prison, but they were aware of a far greater mental ease knowing that they had, for the moment, regained their freedom. It was only after Svenson had mentioned the word "food" that they realised they would have to go without lunch. It didn't seem to matter, though; there was too much tension, too much excitement to think about food. What did start to trouble them a little was the pitiful lack of drinking water. It was probably sufficient to satisfy the pilot and perhaps one passenger, but hardly enough to quench the thirst of seven of them. No-one talked about it. An unspoken bond told them that anything, even temporary thirst, was better than being a captive in an African country gone crazy.

The mesmerising drone of the engine gave Derek a feeling of timeless seclusion, like a passive dream from which he would soon awaken and find everything normal again. And yet, what was "normal"? Was it normal for a European, brought up in the tradition of order and sanity based on centuries of culture and history, to be thrust into the perplexities and frustrations of West Africa? Was it normal to endure heat, humidity, insects and the aggravations of an alien culture? To try to instil into emerging peoples a sense of balance, propriety and honesty amid such an atmosphere of confusion and graft? Was it normal to yearn for life like it used to be in the old colonial days, knowing that every age yearns for the one they have just left?

After a couple of hours the tone of the plane's engine dropped and they began to lose height.

"We land now at Qedar", boomed the Swede over his shoulder. "Haf friends here. We refuel, buy food, then fly French Territory - maybe nodder two, three hours."

The aircraft circled once and lined up with the uneven concrete strip which served as a runway to those daring enough to risk a landing. Svenson had done it dozens of times.

Qedar, as they all knew, was a semi-important town in the insignificant and impoverished nation of Bujavi. The next country along from Kumanga, Bujavi's northern border fringed the Sahara desert, and the vegetation was as sparse as the population. Throughout all of Bujavi a very strong Arabian influence had mingled with the Negro strain to produce a third group - a remarkably handsome blend of both.

Bujavi had escaped the land grabbing of the Berlin Conference and its empire-building boundaries, and had never been colonised or even occupied. History relates that the territory had originally been offered, by international agreement, to newly-liberated slaves during the 18th and 19th centuries, and was thereby inviolate. The unofficial version was that none of the European colonists wanted it because it wasn't worth having. Whatever the reasons, Bujavi had been allowed to drift into the twentieth century at its own clumsy pace, like an orphan attaining the age of majority without parental guidance.

The outcome of this slow self-development was pitifully evident to visitors from other parts of the busy West African coastline. Even the neighbouring native populations, and in fact everyone and anyone who had ever benefited consciously or otherwise from direct colonial rule, tended to look down on the Bujavis as being primitive in the extreme. Derek was not alone in classifying them as a sort of African hill-billy sect, trying to keep pace with the rest of the world but not knowing how.

This impression of stark primaevalism greeted the seven fugitives as the plane touched down and bumped and rolled along the rutted concrete. Svenson had been here before, and showed no surprise at the cluster of dilapidated buildings which served as the terminal. Although he had radioed his intention to land, there had been no response. Either because they weren't listening, or, more likely, couldn't be bothered going out into the sun to greet the aircraft.

Svenson taxied to a stop, and they all jumped out, thankful for the opportunity to stretch their cramped muscles. After Svenson had taken a large and lusty gulp from the water can, his first since they became airborne, Derek noted, he led them to the shack marked "Customs and Immigration" in English, French, Arabic and an unfamiliar script which Derek took to be a Bujavi dialect. A sleepy-looking official in a dirty khaki uniform slid from his chair to greet them.

"Sannu, Abdul", barked the Swede, his right fist held high in the traditional Arab greeting of the sub-Sahara. "How youself, you wives, piccins? Lafiya lau?"

"Dey good, sah. All good. How your own wives, and other peoples?"

He giggled delightedly as Svenson, roaring with laughter, slapped him heartily on the back. This was obviously some routine, thought Derek, which the two of them were accustomed to enacting.

"Na dade rabona da ganinka, Abdul. Ina chief?"

"Next room, sah. I get 'am. You bring some good ciniki today?"

The official eyed the other travellers with interest, and in particular the dried blood splattered on their clothing. This must be an important trip. Perhaps profitable, too.

"I always bring good business", boomed Svenson. "You savvy that. Always plenty ciniki - plenty dash for my friends." He winked slyly at the African, whose grin spread even wider as he disappeared through the rear door.

"You obviously know your way around here, Axel."

"In my business we haf to haf friends everywhere."

No comment to that, thought Derek.

There was a delay of several minutes, after which the man re-appeared, closely followed by an equally dishevelled officer who was distinguishable from the first only by the dull metal bars on his collar, American style.

The senior official shook hands with Svenson, then frowned.

"Marhaban, Mistah Svenson. I fitty see you papers, please."

With a grunt Svenson produced a bundle of documents wrapped in plastic from inside his shirt.

"Here is pilot license, registration for plane, commercial

permit, and....You savvy them; you see them plenty times before. And here", he continued, producing a roll of American dollars which Derek had seen him take from under the seat of the plane, "is money to buy food, fuel, and what we will call co-operation." His eyes twinkled.

The lieutenant gazed at the documents and at the money which Svenson was waving about. He knew from past dealings that the Swede was very generous, and his first impulse was to take what was offered and comply with the wishes of this big, strange-sounding man. He would be able to take home more than three months' salary, even after paying off Abdul. But this time Svenson had brought along six other people. Why? This was most unusual.

"What of papers for other people? I know you, but I no know dem. Who dey, and why dey here?"

"These all my friends. We leave Kumanga quick-quick, an' no time to find papers. You savvy, I think?" Svenson winked at the lieutenant. Again he waved the bundle of notes and again his eyes twinkled.

The lieutenant turned to Abdul and they both sank into Bujavi. Eventually Abdul shrugged and picked up the telephone. The lieutenant turned back to Svenson.

"Mistah Svenson you know de rules. You and me we do business plenty time, an' no problem. You good and honest man." Derek winced as he heard this doubtful opinion. The lieutenant glanced at him with the air of one who has just been accused of an error in judgement, and carried on speaking. "Dese other get no passport and no visa and this na different. Unless dey want buy temporary visitor permit, maybe?" He rubbed his thumb and forefinger together in an unmistakable manner.

"Sorry, but we have no....."

"How much?", barked the Swede, his air of joviality

evaporating as it slowly dawned on him that something was different.

"Nawa kudin?"

The lieutenant mentioned a figure, and Svenson leaned over the counter and grabbed him by the lapels of his dirty shirt.

"Careful, my friend - don't get too greedy. Remember all the good things I done for you."

"Just a minute, Axel." James prised Svenson's hand away and stood between him and the official.

"My dear chap." It was almost laughable, thought Derek. James was going to try to reason with the man - try to use reason over corruption. Always an optimist. A very polite optimist.

James continued.

"You see, my friends and I are in a bit of a pickle. We had to leave Kumanga in a hurry - a damn big hurry. We don't have any papers, and certainly don't want to buy a visitor's permit. We just want the chance to buy food and fuel, them we'll be out of your way. No problems, no fuss, and no-one will ever know we were here."

He smiled benevolently. The lieutenant frowned at him and glanced at all the others, who were nodding in agreement. What was that about a pickle? They have strange ways, these whites.

The lieutenant shook his head and said, "You are really illegal immigrants. Your plane is out of fuel, so you can go nowhere. So you are in the country illegally. However, for a small consideration, Mistah Svenson, I will...."

There was a yelp from Abdul, who lowered the telephone and began to jabber excitedly in Bujavi. The lieutenant's eyes opened wide, and he grabbed the receiver. He spoke rapidly for several minutes, while the fugitives looked at each other, a feeling of apprehension sweeping over them. Finally the lieutenant snapped an order to Abdul, who went into the back office and returned almost immediately, handing his superior a pistol.

"So you are not only illegal immigrants. You are murderers, too. Now we know why you left Kumanga in such a hurry. And it explains the blood. You are under arrest. No, Mistah Svenson it is too late for your money now. For the moment, anyway. This time I get something more valuable".

And probably a promotion, thanks to the kindness of fate which has brought you to this airstrip....

He yelled out in pain as Svenson's big, hairy fist slammed down on the hand holding the gun, sending it slithering across the floor to land at Alan's feet. Alan picked it up and pointed it at both Africans in turn.

"Thanks, mate - just what I could do with right now. Both of you together, and no funny business".

"Funny business"?, thought Derek. He thought people only said that on B-class films.

"And we want to see the British Consul. Unless, of course you are just going to let us fuel up and get the hell out of here."

"No British Consul here, no Consul any kind unless at Zekwi, and that four hundred miles away." Svenson knew where to find the officials. It was his business to know these things. Derek remembered reading something recently about the British Consul in Bujavi having been recalled to London for some trivial diplomatic reason. Not much help there, even if they needed it.

"You ungrateful pig," snarled Svenson. "All the good ciniki I bring you, all the dashy you get, and you no fit help. Give me gun - I go kill this cockroach now-now."

He swung on Alan to grab the pistol, but Alan moved away.

"You no get away." The lieutenant's voice was cracked as he spoke. He knew that the Swede would kill him as soon as look at him under these circumstances. "Guards already on way - plenty guns. You no fit get away. Listen!"

The sound of powerful vehicles could now be heard, increasing in volume as they approached. Jean, who was nearest the door, looked outside. She saw three GM trucks, bristling with rifles, about 100 yards away. In no time they were at the door, weapons pointing at the Europeans.

"Shoot! Shoot! Give me gun, I kill some!"

"Don't be stupid, Axel. We shoot at them and we're all dead. There must be about 30 of them."

Slowly they retreated into the far corner of the room, and the pistol was knocked from Alan's hand by the barrel of a rifle. Trembling noticeably, the lieutenant drew himself up to his full height and mustered what dignity he had retained.

"You are under arrest. There is a charge of assault and, and....and pointing a weapon at a government official. In addition to your original crimes."

Derek noticed that he spoke intelligently and precisely. Gone was the pidgin with which he had conversed with Svenson. Just an act, that, Derek supposed, to encourage the "dash".

Further protest was pointless, and for the second time that day, although the last occasion seemed like an age ago, they were loaded on to the back of the truck. This time there were no fewer than ten guards on the truck with them, and a further truckload following closely behind. What happened to the third truck was not made apparent. Probably gone to pillage the plane for what they could make use of.

This could be tricky. Apart from the alleged assault, thanks again to the reckless Swede, there was nothing else on Bujavi soil for which they could be taken to task, assuming the suggested bribes could be effected. They might just be able to talk their way out of it, fill up the plane and be on their way fairly soon. Then again they might not.

The journey was a short one, the terrain sandy and uninteresting. Derek couldn't help wondering how much more mental strain they could take before someone began to crack up. The Frenchman looked tired and flushed, and was sweating profusely. Jean, on the other hand, was cool and composed, leaving the course of events for the men to decide, and following their lead with calm detachment. Not much of the "weaker sex" about her, thought Derek, with a strange feeling of arousal. Alan was mumbling to himself, no doubt cursing the Swede, the Africans, the country and everything else which had contributed to his present circumstances. Perhaps even me, mused Derek. Svenson was probably saying the same sort of things as Alan, but in Swedish and in a voice which carried well above the whine of the vehicles' engines. James sat ponderously, as usual not showing his emotions. Jeremy was just plain scared - it showed in his eyes, his actions, his demeanour; he's obviously led a sheltered life, and might well be the first to cave in.

Qedar was a small, dusty town whose only claim to fame was that it was once a major defence stronghold against the invading Arab hordes in the many Jihads of bygone centuries. Although the defence of this arid and undesirable bit of land was now neither practical nor necessary, the garrison had remained. In fact it was the main training depot for the large but ill-equipped army which the nation's pride insisted on maintaining. Of the seven visitors, only Axel had ever been there before. Only Axel had ever had occasion or desire to be in the country at all. Derek hoped that he wasn't trying to figure out another valiant but ill-conceived attempt to resolve their dilemma by forceful means. Let's hope he can patch up his quarrels and help to get us out of here peacefully.

They should really try to contact the American Consul, who was probably their only ally. A lot would depend on how soon this worthy gentleman would be able to act on their behalf as a fellow white man. Derek smiled as the thought occurred to him that the American Consul might not even be a white man.....

These thoughts and many like them were racing around in his mind as they drove through the township and came to a halt on its outskirts. This was not, as expected, at a military or police depot, but outside a large, two-storey house set back from the others on the row, and surrounded by a thick lining of neam trees. The guards jumped down and motioned their captives to do likewise. They did so without hesitation, and climbed the steps leading to the front door.

They were met in the doorway by, surprisingly, an African clad in the familiar faded white uniform of a steward.

"Good afternoon, madam, good afternoon, sahs", he beamed as he ushered them in. "Boss phone an he tell me say look after you. I give you chop an you stay here till he come talk to you."

"What is this place?", asked James, resuming his self-imposed leadership role.

Whatever it was, it was certainly no jail. Their hopes rose.

10

The hall-way was spacious but gloomy, due to the dark coloured panelling around the walls, an unusual feature in such a colonial style house.

"This government rest house. Qedar have no good hotel, no fit for European, so sometime people stay here. I Peter. I cook-steward. Make you maybe sit for lounge, den I pass chop, small time"

The mention of food brought their hunger, temporarily forgotten, back into mental focus. They hadn't eaten since early morning, and the suggestion was welcomed by the travellers. The lounge was well furnished with armchairs and couches, all locally made with the typical wooden frames supporting brightly coloured repp over foam cushions. There was a large, cumbersome coffee table in the centre of the room and several drinks stools scattered between the chairs. A faded Persian carpet adorned the centre of the floor, surrounded by dulled terrazzo, where decades of feet had worn away the once-glossy finish. The curtains hung limp and faded, and a shower of dust fell from the blades of the giant ceiling fan as Peter switched it on.

The room was clean and neat, slightly musty and showing its obvious age and lack of frequent use. It reminded Derek of the visits he used to make to the doctor's waiting room as a boy, a room where people came and went, but never stayed long enough to be concerned about its upkeep. The only thing missing was the occasional whiff of antiseptic when the doctor's surgery door opened.

The visitors sat down and allowed the faint breeze created by the ancient and creaking fan to dry their sweat and soothe their minds, as Peter bustled in bearing a tray of assorted drinks. Jean wandered off to find a bathroom, but noticed that an armed guard was never very far behind her wherever she turned.

"I'll be damned if I'll let you follow me in here," she exclaimed as she found what she was looking for and slammed the door in the soldier's face.

The men didn't speak for a while, busying themselves with the drinks. Henri Gaudet was still sweating, and had a noticeable tremble. Perhaps a couple of brandies will settle him, thought Derek, although he didn't seem to be very well co-ordinated. James broke the silence.

"Well - what do you make of this? Are we prisoners or are we guests?"

Alan answered him.

"Who knows?. But then I never could think too well on an empty stomach."

"Then your stomach must be empty most of the time M'sieur Alan."

This remark was uncharacteristic of Henri, but it produced a perceptive smile among the others, and prompted Alan to throw a newspaper at him.

The men took turns with the bathroom as Jean returned and poured herself a liberal quantity of Scotch.

"I see you're a chotapeg person," Alan commented, with a smug expression on his face.

"I might agree with you if I knew what the hell it meant," replied Jean, icily. "If you're trying to impress me with your knowledge, don't bother. You probably learned it from the back of a Chanduri corn flakes box, anyway."

"Now look here - I was just….."

"All right, you two; let's all relax and try to get along. We're going to have to, somehow, for goodness knows how long."

Before anything further could develop, Peter called them to the dining room. Although they were puzzled by this unexpected turn of events, their hunger prevailed and they sat down eagerly to enjoy whatever was being served.

Peter's little-used culinary talents surprised them all. The meal was plain but well presented, in the usual simple but wholesome style of a rest-house cook. Between each mouthful of food they learned that Peter had picked up his talents while working as a houseboy several years ago during an American seismic company's search for oil. In fact, this very house was one of several which the Americans had leased to accommodate their technical staff, and it had been maintained thereafter by the Bujavi government as a suitable resting place for visiting dignitaries or commercial agents.

Over coffee and a cheap but palatable brandy their tensions began to ebb. It was evident, as James pointed out, that they were not being treated as criminals. Their surroundings and treatment were comparable in a small way with what they had experienced at the Muji Hotel in Kumanga, and although they were still prisoners, they were at least being afforded some measure of respect and regard.

"They could quite easily have thrown us in some smelly jail for the night. We really should try the telephone. If Peter is to be believed, it was working this afternoon. You never know."

Where Svenson had proved his leadership in situations requiring action and force, James had obviously taken it on himself, by virtue of his seniority, to direct their tactical course. Alan would have liked to, but wasn't given the chance. Derek reckoned he could make as good a job of being the leader as James, but didn't feel it was worth rocking the boat. No, if James wanted to be in command, he was welcome to it.

After several attempts via the operator to reach the office of the American Consul in Zekwi, James decided to try a different tactic. His plan was foiled, however, and he was startled by the ring of the bell, denoting an unexpected incoming call.

"Now who on earth could that be?", asked Alan, with a frown on his face.

James shot him a glance which needed no words to say that his guess was as good as anyone else's. He picked up the receiver with an apprehensive "Hello ....".

The voice at the other end was loud, and could be heard by all the occupants of the room, although they couldn't make out the words. The caller identified himself as the Deputy Secretary of State, though James missed the name, and asked to whom he was speaking. James identified himself.

"Good, good; just the person I want."

The Voice dropped in volume, as though to indicate that at this stage what he had to say was for James' ears only. The gist of the conversation was relayed to the others after James had hung up the receiver. The caller had indicated, in an apologetic tone, that a line could not be made available for several hours, due to technical difficulties.

"You know how things are in these places, the problems we come across. Nothing ever goes smoothly. But don't worry - we're working on it."

The Voice went on to say that he would personally, using his executive powers, undertake to make the connection at the first opportunity. Meanwhile, they should avail themselves of whatever meagre facilities were at their disposal, and should anything be needed to aid their comfort, the guard commander was under orders to attempt to obtain it.

"Within reason, of course."

The atmosphere of euphoria which had begun to build up at the first taste of food burst like an oversized bubble as they realised that they were still very much in trouble.

"Last meal of condemned man," commented Svenson morosely.

"Rubbish," replied Derek. "They probably don't know quite what to do with us. I'll bet they aren't altogether used to situations like this, so they need time to figure out the options. We're all aware of the speed with which the African mind works when it's faced with the unfamiliar."

Alan took up the commentary.

"And we've had enough experience with telephones on this continent to know what the word "delay" means."

Derek and Alan punctuated their optimism with a nod to each other, and smiled weakly around the group. "The best thing we can do is find a bed to sleep on and wait for something to happen. It's a pound to a penny there's nothing we can do right now to **make** it happen."

But the Swede would not be compromised. He turned his

back on them and stared through the window into the descending twilight. The garden was faintly illuminated by speckled leaf shapes, thrown down by the distant streetlights.

"You don't know African like I know African. Nobody here is being in Africa as long as me, work with them, live with them, shoulders together with them like I haf in twenty year. You can not make reasoning."

He turned slowly to face them.

"I say we escape."

"And I suppose we catch a bus at the corner," sneered Alan, "and ask to be put off at the airport. Oh, of course, we must make sure they have a plane ready for us, all fuelled up and ready to go."

Axel clenched his fists.

"You laugh at me. You English gentlemen", (it came out like "shentlemen"), "you all too coward to fight. 'Less you haf an army and a Union John behind you."

Axel took a step towards Alan, fists still clenched. Derek stepped between them, still smiling at the "Union John" reference.

"Calm down."

The order came from James, who addressed his next remarks to Axel. "There are at least half a dozen guards out there, all armed, all trigger-happy, and God knows how many more at the garrison. We wouldn't get past the end of the street, and there's no point in risking it. Not yet, at least, until we find out what the score is. What we should do now is work out some sort of bluff. We have to convince the deputy something-or-other that we really are what we say we are - fugitives from a country gone mad, running for our very lives. The Bujavis have been telling the world for ages how independent they are, how they are masters of their own affairs, how they answer to no-one. Let's see if they really mean it."

He turned abruptly before Svenson could reply.

"Guard!"

Peter came scurrying in.

"Some dese guard not know English, sah. I go get chief. I talk for you."

"Talk for me, yes. I suppose that means interpret. And bring more brandy."

Peter turned and nodded while still retreating.

James walked over to Jeremy, who was hugging his knees.

"Jeremy, lad; you've been awfully quiet. Are you all right? Is there anything you'd like to share with us?"

Jeremy got up and walked towards the window. He started to speak, then closed his mouth. It was obvious to the others that he was very choked up, and not talking was his way of hiding it. He shook his head and gazed through the window, the same one through which Axel had stared a few minutes earlier. Then he turned around and a rush of emotion poured out of his mouth.

"If you must know, I've never been so miserable in my whole life. I never wanted to come here in the first place. 'Go abroad, see the world', my father said. 'It'll make a man of you'. More likely make a bloody corpse of me."

James walked over to him and put a fatherly arm around his shoulders.

"I know how you feel, and...."

"No, you don't bloody well know how I feel." Jeremy threw off the arm. "You couldn't possibly. I, er - I, I'm sorry. I know you're only trying to help, but it doesn't. Nothing can, except to get out of this bloody mess and go home."

"We will, lad, we will."

Jean went to the window and took Jeremy's hand.

"It does help to talk, you know. Believe me - I know. Seen it hundreds of times."

She led him back to the sofa and urged him to sit down next to her, still holding on to his hand. Derek felt a pang of jealousy, then reproached himself severely.

Jeremy sat silently for a while, then cleared his throat. The others moved closer to him and sat around, like a kindergarten class about to hear the teacher tell them a story. With a stern look Jean reproached them. They moved back and adopted a casual disinterest, but straining to hear every word.

"My father is Frank Wilson, chairman of Midland Electric."

Derek had heard of them. They were a small but hugely successful enterprise, a thorn in the side of such greats as General Electric, Black and Decker, Philips, and the like. Jeremy continued.

"It wasn't always that way. He started with nothing and built the firm to what it is today by sheer guts, hard work, and determination. Now he's worth a million or two. All I wanted to do was join the firm and be an electrical engineer. Perhaps work my way up through the shop like others do. But he has other ideas. He wants me to be groomed for a top job, to be shaped in his image, to be a real manager, a boss. And some day take over from him. But not until I've been "properly trained". And part of his training was to wangle me this job with the Kumanga government. 'You're an electrical wizard,' he said. 'You'll have no trouble in that job - you'll be supervising it, not doing it.' He doesn't know much about African workers. 'Then we'll see what you've learned about life after a few years abroad.' I hate his plan. I hate it here. I hate the thoughts of being an executive. All I want to do is be an electrician, fix things, make things work, do what I like doing best. Not spend my time fixing up other peoples' incompetence".

The pathetic flow stopped and Jeremy turned his head to hide the tears. It was as embarrassing for the listeners as it obviously was for Jeremy, but at least now they knew what made him tick. Or, more appropriately, what stopped him from ticking in a normal fashion.

Jean dropped the hand.

"I can see your point to a degree, but can't help thinking that you are being a little selfish. And ungrateful. I really think you should start thinking about others for a change, instead of just yourself. I can see why your daddy wanted you to go out and fend for yourself for a while - oh, yes, I can understand his reason."

She returned to her own chair, leaving Jeremy with his mouth open, all signs of self pity brushed away by the unexpected rebuke.

"Time to grow up."

Well, that ought to jerk him into life, thought Derek, as Jeremy's anger began to mount. Strange that they are both about the same age, and yet Jean is so much more mature. A vicious little cat.

"But you were the one who said that...."

"It's O.K., lad; I think Jean was just trying to get you out of your melancholy. And it looks as though it succeeded."

Jeremy stood up, as though contemplating this revelation from on high. He sat down again with a puzzled expression of his face.

"Well, I think we've pursued that topic far enough. Where the hell's that guard?"

Axel against Alan. Jean against Alan. Jean against Jeremy. Who would be next? There was no limit to the possible number of permutations.

They settled themselves back into their armchairs.

"God, I need a bath." Jean spoke the sentiments they all had. They had been in the same clothes for several hours, since early morning, in fact. Fourteen hours of heat, humidity, sweat, dust and laterite. They all felt unpleasantly dirty and offensive.

Peter came hurrying back into the room bearing a tray laden

with glasses, a bottle of brandy and an assortment of locally-bottled soft drinks.

"Sorry, sahs, no more ice yet. Maybe one hour, or two. Fridge very old. This Corporal Odima, guard chief."

Behind Peter was the tallest African Derek had ever seen. He reminded Derek of the pictures he had seen of that East African tribe - what were they called, the Whatus, Watusi, Whatsit, or something - who were all alleged to be about seven feet tall. And he was quite broad, too, and not one ounce of it was fat. It was easy to see, in this survival of the fittest arena, why he was the chief. No one would dare oppose him.

Odima spoke to the Europeans in a strange, as though expecting them to understand. Peter translated.

"He say you make list of things you need, and guards go get am in market. You pay first."

"No!", snarled Svenson, pulling himself up to his full height but still falling well short of the corporal. "You bring first, then we pay."

Peter conveyed the message to Odima, who shrugged, turned on his heel, and began to leave.

"Wait!", shouted Derek. "Come back, we talk."

Derek was now on familiar turf. His whole career had been spent in bartering, trading, bargaining and even wheedling with such people. Odima came back.

"Pay forst," he said in English.

"How can we pay when we don't know what cost?", asked Derek with a dazzling smile.

Odima looked at Peter, who translated, then frowned, hand on chin, as though taken aback by this completely unexpected revelation. People rarely opposed his word. Derek took advantage of the corporal's dilemma to push home his proposal.

"Why don't we make list, find out price, then we give you half. Then we pay balance when have things for hand. Peter - a pencil and paper, please."

"Yessah, right now."

Peter paused to pass the information on the Odima, then raced away to find the writing materials. Odima continued to frown, as though finding it hard to comprehend such a complicated way of doing business.

The visitors held a hurried discussion and made up a list of the things they needed, noting down the prices as quoted by Peter. It was mainly toilet requirements and clothing they wanted. Derek knew that both Peter and Odima, and possibly the captain himself, would profit to some degree. When the list was completed, Derek reduced its total to two thirds, and instructed Svenson to hand over half of that amount from his bundle of cellophane-wrapped notes.

"Now," began Derek, with the charm he had developed over the years. "These prices are too high. I know this - my job is trading, so I savvy market. Here is half of what I think should be the price. Tell the corporal to go get am, then we pay balance. And we never tell Deputy Secretary that people try to cheat us."

He winked slyly and Peter giggled.

"Yessah, I tell him," as though he had no complicity in the matter whatsoever.

Odima listened to the exchange, and at the words "Deputy Secretary", for which there was no Bujavi equivalent, his eyes narrowed. Perhaps finding a flaw in his scheme, thought Derek with amusement. Peter conveyed the message, and Odima shook his head. Peter jabbered on some more, repeated the bit about Deputy Secretary, and Odima slowly and reluctantly took the money and list and departed. Derek reckoned that he would make about twenty-five percent profit on the deal by buying, begging or stealing the required items from his brothers in the market. There really would be no sense in his running unnecessary risks. Especially since the oyibos seemed to be connected with the Deputy Secretary somehow. The D.S. was, in effect, his master. Right at the top, where it could do the most harm if he became upset.

The evening gave way to the early but total blackness of the African night. The rest-house guests talked and they drank; they tried to read the outdated magazines, but concentration was lacking. All that was on their minds was what tomorrow would bring, what the so-called Deputy Secretary would be able to do to hasten their release. They were not really prisoners, yet they were. There was no real reason to hold them, yet something was not quite right. It was so confusing, so wearying, so "if only". If only they had not been in Kumanga on that night; if only the plane had been a little larger and could have taken them a bit further. If only the lieutenant had accepted Svenson's bribe; if only.....if only.....if only they had never heard of Kumanga, or Moresia as it was then, in the first place!

The corporal returned with a passable selection of garments and toiletries, and Svenson reluctantly parted with the rest of the promised money. Jean was offered first call on the ancient, stained bathtub, but declined, reasoning that if the men used it first, she could go last and take as long as she liked.

After bathing and changing clothes, they all resumed their seats in the lounge to talk some more and drink the cheap brandy. Tiredness began to creep up on them.

They started to think about sleep, since it was obvious that nothing else would be happening that night.

Derek realised that Alan was no longer with them. He had ambled off a while ago, mumbling something about needing the bathroom, not feeling too bright. He still hadn't returned. With mild curiosity Derek went searching, followed as always by a gun-toting soldier. There was no sign of Alan in the bathroom or any of the bedrooms. Mystified, he went towards the kitchen. He followed the sound of a shrill, female laugh to the back porch where he found Alan, rather drunk, trying to make himself understood to a young, full-bosomed African girl. She was obviously enjoying the attention she was being given by this white man, whose intentions were plain in any language. The guard looked on, approvingly.

Derek's voice took on a hard tone as he stepped out.

"Alan - for God's sake! This is neither the time nor the place. We're in enough trouble as it is. Don't make it worse."

"Whoops! We cot gort. I mean, got caught. Got caught by th' boss. My boss, not your boss." Alan's speech was slurred. He continued to ogle the girl, making her giggle.

This made Alan giggle also.

"Alan!" Derek's tone was harsh and firm.

Alan turned his bleary eyes towards him, then back to the girl.

"Got t'go. Boss says got t'go. No fun t'night. Cheersies."

Alan took another swig from his glass, then it slipped through his fingers and shattered on the stone floor. Peter came running in and began to sweep up the shards of glass, clucking his disapproval.

"Sorry, Peter, my old Peter pal. Peter pal - thass funny. Don't you think thass funny, Derek?"

"No, I don't. I don't think it's funny at all," rebuked Derek as he led Alan away from the kitchen and towards the staircase in the hall. "You're drunk; go to bed."

Now it was Derek against Alan.

Peters swept up the remains of the glass, thoroughly enjoying this exciting deviation from the dull routine of looking after an empty house. With tireless energy he gathered up the discarded garments and set about washing them in the bath-tub. He was reliving his former days of glory as chief house boy for sophisticated people such as his present guests. Quite nostalgic for him, really.

Peter was one of those energetic individuals whose intelligence far outweighed their station in life. If he had been given the benefit of a proper education, if his father had been wealthy enough to send him to college, if he had not been expected to provide for the rest of the family, he would surely by now have been a high government official. He often thought of himself as being more suited to command men, instead of being commanded by others as he now was. He was lucky, though, to be employed at all, when seven out of ten of his fellow tribesmen had no work, no money, no hope. Lucky, that is, if one discounts the fact that most of his earnings went to support those others without work. He was at a loss to understand the attitude of many of the neighbouring countries who were striving hard to be rid of the White Man. It was only during the brief stay of the White Man in his country that he remembered there ever being any sort of prosperity around.

Peter hung the clothes outside in the warm, dry air, and returned to the lounge. He addressed himself to James Barrett, who appeared to be the chief of these white people.

"S'cuse me, sah. If no more, I close now. Go sleep."

James raised his head, which had sunk down on to his chest.

"Eh? Oh, yes, of course, Peter. That will be all."

"T'ank you, sah. If need me, tell guard chief to come get me. Goodnight, madam; goodnight, sahs."

A chorus of "goodnights" followed him to the kitchen. He picked up the cup of brandy which he had previously set aside. A well-earned, if not quite legitimate, reward for his evening's labours.

There was silence in the lounge, apart from the interminable night noises filtering through from the outside. Crickets, frogs, cicadas and an infinite variety of other insignificant but collectively vocal insects maintained an unending symphony of life in the trees, the grasses, the weeds and the bushes outside the open windows. Moths, flying ants and even dung flies, attracted by the lights inside the room, crashed carelessly into the mosquito screens, fell to the ground, then rose to try again, until they died of exhaustion. Translucent geckos traversed the ceiling in search of unsuspecting intruders, their rapier-like tongues collecting flies, mosquitoes, ants and anything else which were not quick or alert enough to get out of the way.

James stretched his arms high above his head.

"Well, I, for one, am going to get some sleep."

"You mean for two," corrected Derek. "Alan was asleep before he hit the bed. The brandy helped, though."

James and Jeremy moved away, and their measured footsteps could be heard on the wooden staircase. The others sprawled lazily in the lounging chairs. Derek had already tried to coax the ancient, battered radio set standing in the corner into life, but without success.

"Even the Voice of America has deserted us," he observed with a wry smile.

There were four bedrooms in the rest-house. The two smaller ones each contained a standard single bed. There was one spacious one with two single beds, and the fourth held a double bed, a rarity for West Africa. Svenson thumped the chair in which he was sitting, and declared that he would be all right there. Since his exciting and unconventional lifestyle had seen him spending more nights out of bed than in one, no-one objected to this proposal. Henri Gaudet declared that he, too, would stay put, making use of one of the relatively soft and comfortable sofas. Obviously, Jean would have to have her own room. James and Jeremy had taken the twin room, and Alan was already tucked away in the other single. This left Derek with the double bed, an unexpected but not unwelcome pleasure.

Axel fell asleep instantly in his chair, his snores gradually increasing in volume until the others could stand it no more.

"I suppose we should try to get some sleep," said Derek as he stood up and walked towards the stairs. "Henri, are you sure you'll be O.K.? You don't look too well to me. How are you feeling? I'd be happy to stay here if you are going to be better off in the bed."

"Ah, merci, mon ami, but I will be fine. Even that noise," he waved towards Axel's inert figure, "will not damage my sleep. Bonsoir. Et bonsoir, mam'selle Jean."

Derek and Jean went upstairs, noting that two of the soldiers assigned to guard them followed at a discreet distance.

Derek heard one of the guards sit down with a grunt outside his door. He'll probably be asleep before me, Derek thought.

Apart from the sentries patrolling the grounds outside, the house fell into an uneasy sleep.

11

Derek came to life instantly as he realised that his bedroom door was slowly being opened, then closed just as silently. He became aware of someone else's presence in the room, and in the gloom he could pick out a figure slowly advancing towards his bed. He didn't know if he was going to be robbed or murdered, but his and other friends' experiences with night prowlers had taught him that the best policy was to lie still and feign complete ignorance of what was going on. Most burglars were only after valuables, but usually came armed, any sudden movement might provoke a knife in the heart if the intruder felt that he was cornered.

As the shadowy figure crept closer, he realised that this was not a prowler, not a burglar, no-one intent on causing him bodily harm. Bodily contact maybe, but not harm. The figure became recognisable as Jean. Jean Whatever-her-name was. Jean let fall the sheet which had been draping her and stood poised and naked by the side of the bed. Her long, blond hair glinted dully in the moonlight which forced its way through the partly open wooden louvres of the window.

Still Derek didn't move. Silently, Jean lifted up the mosquito net and slid between the sheets next to him. Derek's first impulse was to roll out the other side and tell her to leave at once, but the words wouldn't come. All he could bring himself to utter in the sheer exciting mystery of what was happening was a futile "hello". He knew that it was wrong, that it shouldn't be happening, but he was still a man under stress, and here was a woman willing to help him forget that stress for a while. No-one else would know. It would be their secret. It was what his subconscious had been willing since they were first thrown together; he didn't realise, though, that it had been so obvious to her – there had been no subtle signs. His body yielded to her demanding, caressing gestures and they lost themselves with scarcely a word in sublime closeness. There were no feelings of guilt at that time; they were in a desperate situation from which they may never escape alive, so who could blame him for being human?

As the first feeble rays of dawn forced their way through the slatted shutters, Derek vaguely and sleepily became aware that Jean was disengaging herself from him. She wrapped herself in the sheet and cautiously stepped out into the corridor. After making sure that captives and captors were still sleeping, she went back into her own room. Derek smiled to himself as he thought of Alan. Alan the Lecher, whose pride would have been furiously hurt had he known that Derek was the one who had been chosen. Pity he will never know. No-one would know, Derek told himself as he lay back on the pillow with a gratified look on his face. The look hardened as guilt began to take over. Debbie would be devastated if she ever found out. But then chances were she never would.

Derek had never been one for vivid dreams in his younger days. His life had been orderly and uncomplicated, and it was only in recent years, as his steadily increasing workload threw a greater demand on his mental capacities, that his subconscious refused to switch off during the night. The events of the past few days played havoc with his imagination as he slept during what remained of that first night in Bujavi, to give him the worst nightmare he could remember.

He found himself running as fast as he could towards a building which he could see far away on the skyline. Despite its distance from him, he knew that it was CAC's London office, but the faster he ran, the further away it seemed. Behind him were hordes of black dogs, snarling and snapping, with a strange red light shining from their eyes. Derek was carrying a heavy briefcase marked "fragile - do not drop". He had no idea what was in it, only that he didn't dare put it down. His legs were aching, his lungs were bursting, but he knew he couldn't stop.

The office building vanished. It its place was a colossal tower, its top hidden in the dark grey clouds which obscured the sun. Standing in the doorway of this improbable, enormous light-house shaped structure was Smitty, waving his arms beckoningly. The tower was no more than a few yards away now, but just as Derek came near to the open door, Smitty ran inside and slammed it shut. The dogs were close behind him now. A tribal chanting began all around, the rhythmic chanting he had heard work crews use to co-ordinate their efforts. Derek could see Svenson fighting with the dogs, picking them up and breaking their necks. But the dogs wouldn't die; in fact, they began to multiply and surround him.

Then the tower was no longer there. In its place was a fast-flowing stream of green slime, the kind of slime he had seen on top of stagnant drainage ditches at the side of the roads. And he could

see Jean, her arms held high in the air, as though willing herself to be pulled down and lost forever in the hideous mess. He wanted to run and save her; she was his conscience, and had to be saved. But it was too late. He couldn't move, couldn't do anything to save her. What
was done, was done. He began to despair. Then the dogs were on him. He went down fighting and kicking.

Suddenly a white hand grabbed him by the shoulder and pulled him up. The dogs vanished, and in front of him was James Barrett, shaking him violently and calling him in a very distant voice.

"Come on, old chap - snap out of it. I don't know where you've been, but it must have been one hell of a journey."

Derek forced open his eyes to see his colleague, James, peering anxiously at him, the mosquito net draped around his shoulders. At the foot of the bed was Peter, tea tray in hand, looking most concernedly at the distraught white man. Derek's terror subsided, and he sank back against the wet pillow. He was drenched with sweat and still trembling.

"That's better. What on earth were you dreaming about?" James released his grip on Derek's shoulder. "You gave Peter here quite a fright. He though you were having a fit, or had been possessed by ju-ju, or something. That's why he came for me."

Derek grunted a reply as the realisation of where he was and what had happened took full possession of his thoughts.

Peter resumed his customary cheerful smile.

"Morning, sah. I bring tea."

He put the tea tray down on the bedside table and pulled back the mosquito net. Then he opened the shutters, allowing the brilliance of the early sun to flood the room, and causing Derek to close his eyes again for a while. Peter placed a neat pile of clothing at the foot of Derek's bed, and shuffled off to attend to his other guests.

Derek sat up and accepted the tea which James had poured for him into the china cup.

"You can put your own milk in. Had us worried for a bit, you did. Must have been quite a dream."

Derek nodded, and sipped his tea.

"It was. Nightmare, in fact. And we were all in it."

James shot him a curious glance.

"Been dreaming about future plans, have you. No wonder you were so excited".

He stared intently at Derek, a whimsical smile playing on the corners of his mouth.

He knows, thought Derek. And yet he couldn't possibly. Further speculation was cut short by James's next remark.

"Better get going as soon as you can. The long-awaited Deputy Secretary fellow has just arrived." His gaze dropped. "With, - I don't know if you are ready for this - our good friend Tony Agamoru."

Derek nearly splurted out a mouthful of tea.

"What the hell is he doing here. What has this got to do with him?"

"I gather we'll find out when they have everyone together downstairs." James left the room.

Derek felt a cold chill hit his spine. Tony Agamoru. Tony had no business in Bujavi. But it certainly was no coincidence that he was here, at this rest-house, right where they were, right at this time. As he shaved and dressed, Derek felt as though his nightmare was catching up with him. The tea was left unfinished. He and Debbie had always maintained that no-one outside the English race could make a decent cup of tea, anyway.

He washed his face, threw on his clothing and went downstairs to confront the newcomers. Axel Svenson, looking much the worse for wear after his night in the armchair, was glowering across the room at Tony, who was accompanied by an immaculate, dapper African who were seated by the window.

Tony jumped up as Derek entered, his hand outstretched in greeting. Derek took it, only to be hospitable, but not in any gesture of welcome or friendship.

"Derek - what an unexpected pleasure! Oh, this is Mr. Nsenji, the Deputy Secretary of State for this fine country. I gather you spoke with him last night. Or, at least, James did." He nodded in James's direction. "Now we just have to wait for the rest of your companions before we can get down to business."

The smaller man bowed then shook hands with each of them.

"I trust that you had a comfortable night and that Peter looked after you well."

He spoke concisely, with a faint trace of American drawl. Derek couldn't be sure, but thought he could detect a slight American drawl.

"Please be seated until the rest of your companions arrive. I have no wish to repeat myself, as I told your rather unpleasant friend here." He inclined his head towards Axel, who snorted.

Nsenji returned to his seat next to Tony, who had also become seated. Derek and Jim glanced at each other, then sat down without a word. Derek had a bad feeling. This was not going to be plain sailing, not even a pleasant meeting.

Mr. Nsenji was impeccably dressed, from his shiny black shoes to the neatly knotted tie. Windsor, thought Derek. He didn't learn that from an American. Gold cufflinks adorned a spotless white shirt, a whiteness and brightness rarely seen under the tropical sun. All that was missing was the black jacket to complete the picture of the well-dressed businessman usually seen around the stockbroker belt. It was an obvious indication of his rank, and he made the others in the room look drab and shabby by comparison. Except Tony, of course, who was clad in a multi-coloured agbada denoting "One Kumanga" in many places.

It was customary for the clerical grades in Derek's experience to dress for the long, hot hours in the office in casual and comfortable clothes, whereas Sunday would find them resplendent in their best, and probably only, formal suit. Including, occasionally, a snap-brim hat made fashionable by gangster movies in the 1940's, or even a bowler hat. For the expatriate management staff the opposite applied. Senior executives were able to sit in the comfort of an air-conditioned office, and would dress in the same manner as Nsenji now was. Those whose rank didn't merit an air-conditioner would more than likely wear shorts, dark blue for middle management and white of khaki for the juniors, but always with a clean, well-pressed shirt and sometimes a tie. Their Sunday ritual, though, regardless of status, was to throw off the trappings of business formality completely, and spend their day of leisure in a T-shirt and faded, sometimes threadbare, shorts.

Derek wondered what Nsenji did on Sundays. Perhaps he just added the jacket to complete the formality of his appearance. Or perhaps he was westernised enough to go for the shorts.

They had to wait another fifteen minutes before the rest of their party put in an appearance, during which time Peter bustled around serving coffee or tea. Again there was a warmth of welcome from both Nsenji and Tony as they greeted each of the newcomers by name.

Jean was unmoved by all the politeness. She refused the seat and stood in the centre of the room in a belligerent manner, feet apart and hands on hips. What a difference in attitude from just a few hours ago, Derek thought. He was hoping to catch her eye, but she avoided looking at him.

"Why don't we cut out the smooth talk and get straight down to business. Are we getting out of here or not. And what's he doing here. I'm sure it's no coincidence."

Tony seemed to squirm a bit at this attack, but Nsenji was not at all unsettled by her manner of defiance. He met her stare with an equally aggressive one.

Henry Umoh Nsenji, unlike his Kumanga counterpart, had not had the benefit of a wealthy and influential family on which to base his rise to power. From a background rife with poverty he had attained his present position by sheer determination and devotion to work, plus more than a little deceit and corruption. He had trodden down everyone who had threatened his progress, and was neither obligated nor indebted to anyone. Except, perhaps, his three brothers whose muscle had been called into use on more than one occasion, and whose services had been rewarded by secure if ineffectual government positions where their comparative illiteracy would not be a hindrance.

He stood before his guests now, 36 years old, only 5'3" in height, but emanating authority in a manner which Derek had rarely seen in an African outside of chieftaincy. He would go far, this man, and would not let anyone or anything stand in his way. He waited until Jean had backed down and taken a seat, then he did likewise.

"Well," said Jim. "Now what?"

Nsenji looked around the room, embracing all the questioning stares with one swift glance.

"Chief Agamoru, if you please."

Tony cleared his throat, clearly uneasy at being out of his own jurisdiction.

"Since we - er - that is, since our independence, which all of you will remember, being - er - in Kumanga at the time - that is, when it was still Moresia, of course, and...."

"Stop stammering and get on with it."

This was Alan, who had been silent so far. He was looking very rough. Tony took a deep breath.

"Since independence, it has become clear to my government that our new benefactors from the Soviet Union do not altogether have Kumanga's best interests in mind when it comes to....

"I told you that yesterday. We've all been telling told you that, for ages. We said you'd regret it, but still you..."

Jim stepped in.

"All right, Alan. They're realising now how wrong they were. But that doesn't help us much right now. Do go on, Tony. I have a feeling that this is going to be fascinating."

And probably unpleasant, for us at least, Derek thought.

"Anyway, we have realised that we have to get out of it somehow. Going back to Britain, with cap in hand, is out of the question; we would be the laughing stock of the entire world. What we need is someone in similar circumstances, but who have been independent for quite some time. For all time, in fact. Someone who can advise us, can guide us, who can steer us away from apparent pitfalls. We have now found such a country. We have......

"Don't tell me....you don't mean....". Alan nodded his head towards Nsenji. "You mean you're expecting this cowboy outfit to...."

He forced a laugh, which was more like a shriek.

Nsenji appeared to ignore this affront. He withdrew from his briefcase a slim, gold cigarette case and offered the contents around. They all refused except Henri, who really would have preferred what Jean referred to as his "stinking Gauloise", and Alan, who realised that he had just destroyed another resolve to give up. But then he gave up every few months, and was coaxed back into it by far less stressful situations than this one. Derek had been a smoker, but was persuaded by Debbie to give it up when it was suggested a couple of years ago that smoking may be linked with cancer. Jim was an infrequent cigar smoker, and Jean had never started. Nsenji selected a cigarette for himself and lit it slowly and deliberately while Tony attempted to regain some dignity.

"As I was saying, we need help from someone who isn't interested in controlling us, like the so-called super-powers are. We need a hand from people who know how to govern themselves, preferably with available resources, how to assist without exploiting."

"And you think that this backward bunch of neolithic retards can do that. What do they get out of it?"

"That will do, Mr. Rushton. Remember you are a guest in my country. Your superior colonial smugness doesn't wash here in Bujavi. I could have you jailed for talking like that."

Derek felt that it was time to step in before Alan got them all jailed.

"All right, all right; that's not going to get us anywhere. Give it up." It came across as a command from a district manager to a junior, and sent Alan back into a glowering sulk.

"Thank you, Mr. Scott. I will continue with what Chief Agamoru is attempting to put across".

And not very well, Derek thought. I've never seen him so stuck for words.

Nsenji took up the narrative.

"For many years, since the Americans abandoned their attempts at finding oil in our country, we have been searching for an opportunity to improve the living conditions of our people. As you know, we are a poor country with very few known resources, little or no technology and very few trained experts of our own. With that sort of situation our chances of raising our living standards are pretty remote, as you will appreciate. I was fortunate enough to complete my education in the United States, where my eyes were opened wide to the inequalities of the world."

So that's where the slight drawl comes from. Must impress the hell out of his fellow countrymen.

"Damned if I can see what that has to do with us right now. What's your point?"

"I'm coming to that, Mr. Barrett."

There was a trace of impatience in Nsenji's voice. He inhaled deeply on his cigarette. Not a man to be trusted, thought Derek. The temperature was rising as the sun once again took control, throwing spiky shadows through the window as it cleared the tree tops. Henri was already sweating copiously, but Nsenji remained arrogantly cool.

"I must insist that you hear me out, then you will better understand the position in which my government finds itself. It has a lot to do with you, as you will learn if you let me explain."

Derek detected a slight hint of apology in the last comment.

"You people have become important pawns in our negotiations."

He paused, as though expecting an argument, then carried on.

"We were never colonised. Whether that is a good thing or not is open to much debate, since we appear to have sacrificed the expert guidance which neighbouring countries have received at the hands of the so-called "great" powers of Europe. We have had some limited aid from the U.S. and from the U.N., and, more recently, from the Soviets. These were no more than hand-outs, and not by any means enough to pay for any improvement plans we might wish to make."

Probably found its way into numbered accounts in Zurich, was the first thought Derek had. He often wondered how people got hold of a numbered account in the first place.

"In consequence, we have been looking for a way to improve our lot and pull Bujavi away from the bottom of the "most impoverished nations" list."

He leaned forward slightly. This was obviously one of his favourite topics, one of his crusades.

"The pace of the world is too fast for us to cope with on our own. We need help, real, material help, not just hand-outs and promises. We need someone to take an interest, to help us to develop and share their prosperity with us on an equal basis. We need someone to share their advances in technology, in education, to teach our people better ways to live. In short, we want to join up with a more progressive nation on a partnership basis. But we will never," he emphasised the "never" as he sat up straight, "go begging to the West or the East. We will not be exploited in a colonial fashion."

"I get it," said James. "You team up with Kumanga, who have the money and expertise, and who have had their fill of Russians, and you benefit from their prosperity. Current prosperity, I should say, since who knows how long it can last without proper help.?" He addressed his next comments to Agamoru. "But what do you get out of it, giving your goodies to...what did you call it...a "most impoverished nation?"

Tony eagerly took the floor again.

"Oil, my friend. They have oil, and lots of it."

He nodded his head in emphasis. A glance from Nsenji made him sit back again.

"When the Americans left," Nsenji continued, "they did so not because they failed to find oil. It was because the reserves we have were more costly to extract than those available to them. At the time. Now that the Middle East has become so unsettled and their own oil sands projects seem to be more expensive than they originally thought, they will soon be looking elsewhere. The same applies to the Soviets, too. We will be ready, and our prices will be attractive. Don't get me wrong - we're not going to give it away, but working as a team we'll do well."

Tony nodded his head and waved a hand in Nsenji's direction.

"We have the money and the knowledge, they have the raw materials and the labour. And they are not under anyone else's thumb." He nodded again.

"OK, OK; very cosy for you. Why are you telling us this? Where do we fit into this pantomime?"

It was Alan's turn to speak out.

Nsenji smiled. His cigarette had burned itself out on the ashtray, and he methodically withdrew and lit a fresh one. This time he didn't offer them around. Derek noticed that it was a State Express 555, advertised as the "Passport to International Success". Some irony.

"Understand that we do not intend to give away our inheritance. That is most important. What we have in mind is more of a pooling of resources, an amalgamation where our two countries can develop harmoniously as one national entity. There will be no conquerors and no conquered. There will be no masters and no servants. There will be only one common unity working towards one common goal."

This is getting ludicrous, thought Derek. It'll never work. You can't even get different tribes in the same country to live in harmony, let alone peoples of different nations. They tried it in Rhodesia and Nyasaland, and look what happened there. They tried to link Egypt with Syria, and that was a disaster.

Nsenji's eyes gleamed fanatically as he prepared to continue. He pulled deeply on his cigarette, sending a cloud of blue smoke into the powerful cloak of sunshine. The shadows shortened perceptibly on the floor and walls.

"We have now found such a country which is willing to align with us and help to pull our oil reserves out of the ground and eventually join forces in all political and economic circumstances."

Derek felt as though he should be hearing fanfares and violins, such was the drama in Nsenji's oratorio. As if reading Derek's mind, Jean stood up and turned to look through the window.

"Makes you feel like vomiting, doesn't it?", she muttered in James's ear, but in a voice which they could all hear.

Nsenji continued, oblivious to the disdain.

"The final details haven't yet been ironed out, which is why there hasn't yet been a formal announcement. This is where you come in".

The visitors all lifted their heads, intent on catching every word from now on.

"The country from which you have escaped, unlawfully, is soon to be part of our common nationhood. It was just bad luck on your part that you happened to pick Bujavi to make your landing, since...."

"No, no; - we have to stop for fuel. No fit go any more."

"Yes, thank you, Axel, we all appreciate that. It wasn't your fault". James's tone was mildly reproachful, despite the words.

Nsenji continued, as if to reinforce James's comments.

"Obviously, you didn't know what has been going on behind the scenes, so to speak. You haven't really escaped - you just gave yourselves up again. When I heard that a light plane containing seven white people had landed at one of our airfields, I knew it had to be you. Most unfortunate".

"So," snapped Jean, whirling around. "Why bring us here? Why the big pretence, the comfort, the service, the luxury? Luxury for this place, at least."

"Why? Why didn't I just have you thrown in jail? Because, my dear friends, Bujavi is still a neutral country, technically speaking, and we have no wish to run foul of the U.N. when you have committed no crimes against us. Unofficially, though, for the moment, we are under an obligation to do our future political partners the service of holding you and handing you over to them. It will be, shall we say, our first act of partnership and co-operation. It will be well publicised and timed to coincide with the announcement declaring the federation of our two nations. That way we shall be doing our patriotic duty while not upsetting the U.N.. I understand that the charges against you are quite substantial?"

It was a question partly directed to Tony Agamoru, who was eager to jump into the conversation, but was not given the opportunity.

"Against Mr. Svenson, amongst other things, - murder. I wouldn't be surprised that as a Kumanga national," Nsenji turned back to Tony, "you might be sentencing him to hang. Publicly. The rest of you, possibly accessories to murder, but certainly complicity to treason and escaping lawful custody."

Tony nodded his head vigorously. He really is being subservient today, thought Derek. Not like him at all.

James spoke in Tony's direction.

"Already telling you how to run things, it seems. You're making a big mistake".

Tony shrugged as Nsenji turned to Jean.

"For you, madam, a reprieve."

"What do you mean, a reprieve?"

"In Bujavi we do not normally negotiate with women; they are still regarded as inferiors and do what they are told. You, however, in deference to your western emancipation, will have a choice. Chief Agamoru here has generously agreed to look after you personally, take you back in his private plane, make sure no harm comes to you and repatriate you, and so on. He will no doubt explain the details himself...."

The tone and content of Jean's reply came as no surprise to Derek. She told Agamoru in language Derek hadn't heard since his army days what she thought of his idea, his parentage, his attributes, and ended by suggesting a totally impossible physical action which Tony should try. Tony began to expostulate while Nsenji smiled, amused by the totally unaccustomed refusal. Most women in his country would be flattered at being invited to join such a prestigious harem.

"The alternative, madam, is to remain with your friends here, and take your chances. I cannot be held responsible for the actions of my men."

Jean turned and told Nsenji in no uncertain terms what actions she would like to see performed on him, and he raised his hands in the air as if to indicate that his efforts to help had been rejected.

"What about our right to contact the American Consul?", demanded Alan, who had been quietly enjoying Jean's descriptive outburst, with total approval.

"Unfortunately our telephone system is quite antiquated and unreliable. We are trying to make contact, but..."

"Liar!", shouted the Swede. "You on purpose stop us from talking. You make sure we don't talk to anyone. And after all the help I do for your people, all the favour!"

"Ah, yes. I was going to overlook the matter, but since you bring it up I may as well include it. I have been informed that you attempted to bribe one or more of our border officials. And not, apparently, for the first time. That will also have to be taken into consideration."

"Now." He stood up, indicating an end to the visit. "I'm sure the admirable Peter has prepared an excellent breakfast for you. I advise you to make the most of what you can while you can."

He turned to speak to the guard near the door.

Axel had silently worked himself up into a near-frenzy. While Nsenji was still turning he lunged at the two black figures while they were pre-occupied and sent them sprawling backwards. He wrenched the rifle from the startled guard's grasp, silencing him with a vicious swipe across the jaw with the butt of the gun. James saw his opportunity and mustered his well-used and well-remembered combat training to drop Tony Agamoru to the floor in a carotid choke hold. Derek and Alan jumped to his assistance, but James needed none. Tony was out cold. By the time the sound of the commotion had attracted the attention of the other guards, Axel had the rifle pointing squarely at Nsenji's nose.

"Tell soldiers put down gun, come in here hands up, or I shoot you. Already haf trouble for killing, one more no make no matter."

Nsenji's characteristic calmness had left him. He croaked out the orders in Bujavi as he squinted into the solitary eye of the rifle. The bewildered Africans stood still, wild eyed, mouths ajar, not heeding.

Nsenji screamed at them and they slowly dropped their rifles, advancing into the confusion of the lounge at their master's order. They all lay face down on the faded carpet.

"Peter!" James picked up a rifle as he called for the steward. The trembling houseboy crept into the room as James's voice rang out again.

"How many guards? Not all here, I think".

Peter glanced at the inert figures and raised three fingers.

"T'ree more - outside, I t'ink".

"Bring tie-tie, quick. Someone go with him, keep an eye on him". Gaudet picked up a gun and shambled off after Peter as he ran from the room. James went towards the front door.

"Wait". Jeremy and Jean both picked up a fallen rifle and followed James as he went in search of the other three guards. Peter came back with the rope which had held their clothes the previous evening. At the same time the scuffle of booted feet told that James had located the sentries. There was a sound of rapid footsteps on the gravel, followed by a single shot. Then silence.

After what seemed like an age the scuffling resumed, and two of the sentries entered the lounge, their hands high in the air, followed by James, his rifle raised.

"James - you didn't...?"

"No. He did. Had to, or else the blighter would have got away and raised the alarm."

Jeremy appeared in the doorway, a glazed look in his eyes, a faint curl of smoke at the muzzle of the gun which was now pointing towards the floor.

"I had to. I didn't want to, but I had to, didn't I?"

"Of course you did," said Jean soothingly. "It was him or us. You saved us. You saved me. He tried to run away, but you stopped him. I'm proud of you."

The dull glaze in Jeremy's eye was replaced by a defiant, fiery stare.

"Too damned right, I had to. I've never killed anybody before, but, you know, I don't feel half bad. Not as bad as I would have felt if I'd known beforehand I was going to kill someone. I'd do it again."

He's pathetic, thought Derek. But thank God he had the

gumption to do it. At least all the guards were accounted for.

With a groan, Tony started to come round.

"Tie him up," commanded Axel. "Tie all up."

"Haven't got enough rope. Any more?"

Peter shook his head.

"Wait - I've thought of something." Alan swallowed hard. "When I was downstairs last night trying to find somewhere quiet and private to, er, to...you know what I mean..."

"No, we don't. What ***do*** you mean?"

"I know," cut in Derek. "Go on, Alan."

"Well I saw a door cut into the wall and asked what it was for. She said it...."

"Who said? Who's 'she'?"

"Never mind about that, now." Derek showed his impatience. "What did she say Alan?"

"She said that it was a sort of cold storage room, you know, a root cellar, and if the door closed accidentally we couldn't get out."

"Excellent! Just what we need! Alan, I congratulate you. And her, whoever she is. Show us. You too, Peter. And you, Tony. Not the slimy one - he's our ticket out of this place."

They hauled the guards to their feet as Alan led the strange procession out into the hall and down the slippery staircase to the cellar. Axel and Gaudet stayed behind with rifles trained on Nsenji.

The official had by now recovered some of his composure.

"If you think you can get away with this, you're very much mistaken. In a few minutes my people will realise...."

"Shut you mouth," snarled Axel. He rammed the muzzle of the rifle into Nsenji's open mouth, causing a trickle of blood to form at the corner. "I don't like you. You make me think of snake. I look for chance to kill you when I finished with you."

They sat in silence until the others came back, minus the

Africans.

Jeremy spoke.

"There are two vehicles outside, a Jeep and a flashy American limousine. Can carry six easily - eight at a pinch."

"Good. We'll take 'em both." James was back in command. "No point in squeezing up all together if we don't have to. Anyway, we don't want to leave vehicles lying around, just in case there's another guard we haven't dealt with. Axel, why don't you and Jeremy take our smooth friend here," he indicated Nsenji, "in the Jeep, and lead the way to the airport. The rest of us will follow in the limo. While we have a live duck we have a powerful bargaining hand."

They went outside, cautiously at first, and crept around the building. They spotted the Jeep first, and Axel jumped in behind the wheel. Jeremy sat next to him, pointing at Nsenji in the back seat with a pistol taken from one of the sentries. The Jeep eased its way to the end of the driveway. The others found the Desoto Diplomat, with banner unfurled, in the shade of a huge flame tree. There was a uniformed figure fast asleep behind the wheel, oblivious to all the conflict which had recently taken place. Alan gently poked his rifle into the man's ear.

"One bad move, my friend, and I blow your head off."

The driver opened his eyes wide and started a surprised gurgle, but thought better of it as he saw another gun pointing at him from the other side.

"Out!", snapped Alan. "Lie down in de dirty."

The man didn't need telling twice.

"We can't risk another gunshot. We got away with it the first time. No-one heard, or at least no-one took any notice. Next time might be different. We will have to be a bit quieter in future. Don't shoot him."

Alan looked at James in astonishment.

"I wasn't planning on doing. You didn't expect me to... in cold blood?"

"What were you going to do? Tell him a bedtime story and hope he goes to sleep? Let him run off and get help? Go on – go and get in the car."

They climbed into the limousine feeling distinctly queasy. After a few silent seconds James joined them, pausing only to wipe the blade of a kitchen knife on the grass before sliding it into a makeshift sheath in his belt.

"Well, what are you all looking at? Do you want to be caught again? Let's go."

He sat in the front seat, which had been left vacant for him. It was automatically assumed that he would be taking charge again.

With Gaudet at the wheel, the big car slid through the gates to follow the Jeep.

12

Gaudet chased the Jeep along the sparsely-treed boulevard as Svenson drove madly towards the haze which they took to be the centre of the town. The smoke from cooking fires mingled with the dying reaches of the harmattan. The Swede obviously knew his way around, and all Henri had to do was to follow him. Or, at least, that was the theory of it. Svenson could go as fast and as madly as he wished in the rugged, versatile Jeep, threading his way through narrow streets and scattering all forms of life in front of him. A limousine bearing a government standard, though, has to show some degree of decorum, and it was all Henri could do to keep the Jeep in sight while maintaining a more sedate, more respectable pace. There were a few moments of tension as the two vehicles approached a major intersection where a khaki-clad policeman, perched high on a platform in the middle of the crossing, was making a magnificent show of directing the meagre flow of traffic. He had everything well under control until such times as two vehicles came from different angles at the same time. His only recourse seemed to be to stop one until the other had passed by, regardless of direction. He spotted the limousine and the escort Jeep when they were half a block away, and dutifully stopped all other traffic approaching the intersection. Henri tried to cover his face with his hand, knowing that a white driver of a government vehicle would immediately be suspect. His fears were averted, however, when the officer jumped to attention and saluted smartly as they passed, almost dislodging his gleaming white sun helmet.

Strange, thought Derek, how the topi had all but disappeared after such a long tenure. For decades, no white visitor had been brave enough to venture into the tropical sun without headgear for fear of severe sunstroke, or even death. That seemed to change during the Second World War, when military personnel abandoned not only their helmets, but shirts also. They were none the worse for their daring disregard for tradition and safety, and the use of the topi began to decline. Perhaps heads are better made now than they were in those past decades? Well, perhaps not physically, but with a much greater understanding of foreign climates. It was a pity, in a way, though. The topi was a fitting garment for the colonising British - formal, inflexible, indispensable and without comparison in its genre. Now that it had almost disappeared, was it not an indication that the British Empire was not far off doing likewise?

As they approached the town centre Derek became cynically aware of how typical this city was of every other large African metropolis. The road first ran through suburbs, which had been thrown without any apparent plan around the city's core. It bulldozed its way through a mess of shanties where the real truth of a town's poor quarter has to be seen to be believed. Narrow streets, hardly wider than the size of a large car, branched off the main roads. These side streets were ill-paved and dotted with deep, bone-rattling craters. The buildings on either side were of corrugated iron, timber or just mud, or a combination of two or all three.

When iron begins to rust, as it must in humid climates, it has the effect of totally destroying whatever artistic values the building may once have had. In fact, it evokes a feeling of despair in the beholder, a sinking of the stomach, a shuddering revulsion, a sensation of "there but for the Grace of God....."

The drains ran typically open and in gullies along the sides of the streets. Thanks to the actions of the sanitation department and thousands of gallons of disinfectant, they were not quite as smelly as would be imagined - until they were disturbed. The violence of the sun didn't seem to deter the flies, though, which would thrive in such a haven of excrement. Definitely not, thought Derek, the sort of abyss to fall into, as Debbie once had. Derek couldn't remember the exact details, except that Debbie, in her usual obliging fashion, had agreed either to deliver or pick up something for someone at a roadside shop in the township. Derek had stopped the car close to the shop, but had been unable to park by the concrete paving block which served as a bridge over the drain. Debbie, thinking that the cruddy appearance indicated a solid surface, energetically stepped on to the crusty, dusty mess and began to sink slowly and gracefully into it. At first Derek didn't realise what was happening, being higher up on the road and on the opposite side of the car. He became aware of a commotion and saw some African tradespeople rushing to pull Debbie out of the waist-deep mire, and sluicing down her legs and clothes with their precious water. Debbie was taken straight home and dumped unceremoniously into the shower, still fully dressed. Her clothes had to be destroyed, and the familiar stench of African township drains seemed to hang around the car for ever.

The city of Qedar was already into its daytime hustle and bustle. The main roads and side streets alike were crammed with people, from beautiful, naked children to extravagant, influential tradesmen to arrogant, aloof government officials. Styles of dress varied from nothing to scant loin cloths to expensive traditional robes to very expensive and totally inappropriate business suits from London, Paris and New York. Dress style and quality was very much an indicator of status, almost as much as the automobile, for those affluent enough to possess one.

As the two vehicles entered the heart of the city their progress was severely slowed, despite the recognition and courtesy afforded the insignia of a government car. The peculiar, acrid smells of Africa pervaded the car's air-conditioned seal. The aroma was mainly that of palm oil, the universal cooking base. At first the smell is repellent, but after a while it comes to represent the whole life of Africa. It evokes a sensation so completely tied together with visual memories, that distant scenes of Africa dance across the subconscious whenever the smell of palm oil reaches the nostrils.

Here and there amid the squalid shacks were the more substantial, more appealing edifices of the affluent few. These had high walls with straw thatch on the rooftops, sometimes thickly splattered with mud baked hard by the fierce sun. The walls were heavily inscribed with geometric designs and Hamitic messages of goodwill, and surmounted by blunt spikes which looked like donkeys' ears. Typical Arabic influence, thought Derek. And yet, still African. It makes sense, really, when one considers that the origins of this part of the continent lay deep in both ethnologies. It was once a fringe portion of the mighty Sokoto Caliphate, way back in what Europeans like to call the Middle Ages. As a result of the perpetual conquests by Muslims and infidels alike, there had evolved a nondescript architectural muddle denoting no real, definable characteristic.

At first glance the town seemed like a conglomeration of old and very old, with a sprinkling of concrete which spoiled the pseudo-Arabian Nights scene. Along the sandy ditches which ran along both sides of the streets, naked and grinning piccins amused themselves in the filth. They waved and shouted excitedly as the two vehicles threaded their way towards the outskirts of the township. Apart from the children and the toothless old crone who took time off from her pestle to stare, the presence of motor vehicles went unnoticed. Donkeys, bullock carts, cyclists or, more predominantly, just pedestrians, paid little heed to whatever urgency the Europeans might display. There is no urgency in Africa; tomorrow will still come, regardless of today's pace.

Derek was reminded of his earlier days with CAC when he had served a whole tour as relief manager. "Nomads", they were referred to in the Company, filling in for a couple of months here and there in all parts of the country where leave schedules or sudden emergencies would leave a gap. A temporary transfer to just about anywhere could be expected for someone on the nomad list. Derek had spent a total of six months in Maikuma province, CAC's most northern trading area in Moresia, which was more like being in Arabia than in Africa. The terrain was sandy, the climate very dry and the populace thin-faced and light brown in colour. What he remembered most was the atmosphere being so dry that his skin would crack, and papers would curl up. And then in contrast to the baking heat of day, the nights were cool enough to add another blanket or two to the bed covers.

It was in the North where he had picked up his working knowledge of Hausa, the universal language of the Sahara fringe. It was very much akin to Arabic. Not that Derek could make any claims to knowing Arabic, but he was always able to make himself understood by Arab traders when he addressed them in Hausa. With writing, though, it was a different story - the version most foreigners learned was transposed into a phonetic English-style alphabet, which obviously made it easier for expatriates to learn. This was something of a breakthrough for the British. In most cases they had been content to get by with pidgin, considering it to be the duty of the natives to learn the White Man's language instead of vice versa.

Derek had become quite proficient in Hausa during the short time he had spent in the north, and kept up his knowledge through Hassan and the itinerant traders who travelled the southern regions peddling their wares from door to door. Hausa didn't help much with the traders in the south, but at least gained him some credibility as a genuine, trustworthy dealer who had at least made the effort. It also earned him a cash bonus from the Company.

Derek hadn't cared very much for the north, and was glad to find that his next posting was back in the rain forests of the south. One very valuable asset he did treasure from the north was Hassan. It was rare for a domestic to move from the north to the south, being virtually a different country apart from the artificial geographic boundaries, but Hassan had taken such a fancy to Derek that he not only agreed to but requested the move.

Qedar was situated at the southern end of one of the great Sahara caravan routes where strings of camels could still be seen bringing groundnuts from the French territories, blankets from Timbuktu and leather from Morocco. Or rather, back from Morocco - most of the leathers attributed to Morocco's fine workmanship began as West African hides. The town of Qedar owed some of its reputation to having once been a major trading centre for two other important commodities - salt and slaves. Not all that long ago it was a notorious slave market where thousands of human beings were bartered and sold with no more consideration than that given to animals. Male or female, young or old, beautiful or ugly, they were all disposed of without discrimination. Some of the cruellest deeds that unthinking Mankind has ever perpetrated were done in and around Qedar. The unfortunate slaves, victims of inter-tribal feuds, were forced to march under the lash across the hot, waterless desert down to the slave markets such as the one still standing (albeit unused) in Qedar, day after day, week after week.

It was estimated that not more than twenty five percent made it to the slave ports of West Africa or the Mediterranean, and their tracks were marked by human bones in both directions. Everywhere the traveller passed in those bygone days he could see the signs of oppression and suppression. Even after international pressures put an official end to slavery, there was very little a concerned outsider could do to enforce the multi-lateral decision without the full co-operation of all factions. Slavery is still being practised under differing legal names.

Svenson directed the Jeep towards the enormous cavity which had once been the main gate of this ancient walled city. It had always struck Derek as ironic that the invention of the firearm had almost overnight made the intricate fortifications of these old cities quite obsolete. It was a bit like the North American West, where the forts of the soldiers were adequately protected until the Indians also acquired heavy guns. In a philosophical mood, he mused that nothing could now protect Mankind against himself, not even the possession of armament equal to that of his attackers.

As they approached the gate Derek looked at the mosque in all its splendour, standing like a sentinel of defiance to all infidels who dared to criticise its dominance. In contrast to the general air of decay and regression which prevailed in the town, the mosque was bright, vibrant and breath-taking in its glory. Its blue, marble-like dome glinted in the sunlight, and high on a tall minaret could be seen the muezzin calling the Sallah. His mournful voice was picked up by a powerful amplifier and flung across the town, beckoning the faithful to prayer. Already a hundred or so devotees were gathered, waiting to pay homage to Allah, their white and pastel robes forming a mosaic of soothing colours against the khaki background of the sandy laterite.

When Derek was in the North he had been invited into a mosque by one of his important traders He referred to it as the "Masjid". On certain festive occasions the members of the Masjid extended greetings and hospitality to certain infidel acquaintances, not in an attempt to entice or convert, but simply to demonstrate that Allah is merciful and welcomes all those who pose no threat to Islam. It was an interesting, sincere and entertaining occasion, the likes of which he had never experienced in a Christian church.

Assallam alaikum.

The two vehicles crept through the thirty-foot thickness of the gateway, dodging arrogant-looking camels and load-heavy donkeys whose drivers were expertly if noisily guiding them to the market place. They turned on to a black-topped road which Derek remembered from the previous day as being the route to the airport, and Svenson put his foot down hard, sending the Jeep shooting away. Gaudet tried at first to keep up with him, but, knowing that the spectacle of a government car driving at high speed would surely attract attention, relaxed his progress and allowed the limousine to fall behind. There was no chance of getting lost now - the prestige-fired road led only to the airport.

As they travelled the sparse, rock-strewn countryside they could not escape the fact that they were in groundnut territory. Huge pyramids of this important cash crop had been built on both sides of the highway, waiting for transport which would take them on the long haul to coastal ports. Derek was again reminded of his brief stay in northern Moresia when one of his many duties was to take inventory of such groundnut stock piles. On a concrete base, each pyramid was assembled by gangs of sweating labourers who would pile bags of the commodity in an ever-decreasing ascendancy, until the very last bag was carried ant-like, amid cheers of encouragement and achievement, to the pinnacle of the hill. The final bag of yet another groundnut pyramid was always an excuse for a few hours off and a noisy celebration, where the palm wine flowed freely. To take stock of a groundnut pyramid seemed to Derek an impossible task, until he was given the formula. He remembered it well. Provided that the base layer was correct, there were eight hundred and fifty tons at thirteen bags to the ton - that made eleven thousand and fifty bags of groundnuts per pyramid, if all had gone well. Derek dismissed the thought, thankful that this onerous task was one which he had left behind many years ago.

The surrounding countryside was still under a thin blanket of harmattan mist which the sun was valiantly trying to penetrate. This was another reason why Derek wasn't too keen on the northern part of West Africa. The harmattan was a steady wind from the north east which picked up minute particles of sandy dust on its travels across the desert, then deposited them on everything in its path. It spread a choking mist all around, thinner than fog but thick enough to blur and distort shapes and colours. Early in the morning during harmattan the sky was saffron, then ochre, changing to anaemic light brown, and eventually a hazy dull yellow as the strengthening sun managed to penetrate the murk. The greatest annoyance was the silting up of the nose, mouth and eyes. Car engines, and carburettors in particular, had to be cleaned out every few hours to prevent the vehicle from seizing up. Harmattan was a bane to house-boys whose efforts at dusting and polishing furniture and floors were pointless. Qedar, being relatively further south, wasn't as bad as most places Derek had visited, but the pallid yellow of harmattan enveloped the earth in a choking cloud.

As Gaudet began to reduce the distance between the two vehicles Derek's wandering mind was jerked back into full alertness. Down the road ahead of them he saw a small, dark figure throw itself over the side of the Jeep, bounce on the laterite, then come to a halt at the side of the road. Gaudet applied the brakes with a screech.

"Qu'est-que..."

The words were choked off as a thunderous explosion lifted the Jeep into the air, disintegrating as it rose. It came crashing down in a mass of flames and smoke as Gaudet brought the car to a stop just yards from the wreckage. Derek and his companions scrambled out, and were knocked flat by a second explosion. They remained on the ground, faces buried, until the only sound they could hear was the crackling inferno which had once been the Jeep - and their friends.

Derek raised his head and felt sick. He saw the dismembered remains of Svenson and Jeremy being rapidly consumed by the flames. Mercifully they would have felt nothing after the first blast. It was little consolation to note that Nsenji was also quite dead, his head crushed by a large rock at the side of the road where he had dived out of the speeding vehicle. He would no doubt be regarded as a martyr, a true patriot, when the facts became known.

Alan absent-mindedly picked up the gold cigarette case and put it in his shirt pocket. Derek picked up another object which he saw gleaming in the sunlight. It was a grenade fragment. Nsenji must have known that all military vehicles carried hand grenades, and had taken the only course he could think of to try to stop the escape. Unfortunate that he had chosen to leap out right where a semi-submerged boulder, obscured by the soft, drifting sand, lay waiting to smash his skull.

They were all stunned. They were more stunned by this than

anything else which had happened to them during their exciting few days of flight so far. Even Jim, Jim the logical, Jim the stabling influence, couldn't bring himself to think of what to do next.

Jean, with professional calmness, tried to stem the flow of blood from Jim's head, which had been hit by a piece of flying debris from the second explosion. She did look rather shaken up, though, Derek conceded. It was understandable, given the circumstances.

Derek was anxious to run as far from the scene as possible before the locals, attracted by the explosions, came to investigate. He knew well enough that a deserted stretch of road could, as if by magic, suddenly be teeming with population when something happened. He had himself had experience of that when his car went out of control once during a violent storm. The tires could not grip the slick road surface, sending his vehicle over a culvert and into a river. Before he could get out of the car, there were dozens of faces peering down at him, even though the road had been empty seconds before.

"What now?", asked Alan, who couldn't think of anything else to say which wouldn't bring the nauseous feeling in his stomach up through his throat.

"Let's get the hell out of here, before all the local yokels for miles around are on us."

They climbed back into the car. Henri muttered a prayer and crossed himself. The others guiltily murmured an "amen", ashamed that they had not thought of it first.

"No use of going to the airport now, mes amis. I suggest we head west, to the border."

No-one had any better plan, so Henri turned the big car around in the direction from which they had come, in search of the main highway west. James had again positioned himself next to

Henri, as though it were expected of him. He glanced upwards through the windshield.

"If my orientation is correct," he said with an effort "we should turn right as soon as possible. That should take us in the general direction of the border sooner or later."

Derek nodded. If they could, by some stroke of luck or Divine assistance, reach the border with Séjumé they would be safe. If....

They fell to their own thoughts as the minutes and the miles ticked away. Their situation was now more desperate than it had ever been. They were total strangers in a country which would soon be searching for them behind every rock, every tree, every bush. They had no food, no water, no money. Eventually the big car would run out of fuel and there was no-one they could turn to for help. If they ever came out of this alive it would surely rank as one of the world's untold miracles.

13

The world's news agencies had scant information at first about what came to be known as "the Kumanga Affair". This was hardly surprising, since the government of Kumanga had gone to great lengths to drop a news black-out over their activities. Many foreign journalists had already been expelled from the country on the pretext of "biased and unfair reporting" about the gradual but noticeable swing towards the Soviet Union. Those who remained, along with some of their Kumangan colleagues, were either detained or severely censored under the guise of security. Besides which, the Kennedy/Cuba incident commanded so much of the world's attention that little heed was being paid to other news, especially where it concerned a little-known and even less cared about dot on the map called Kumanga.

Such is the ingenuity of the experienced newsman with a story to tell, however, that despite the Kumangan government's efforts, snippets of information managed to find their way over the borders and into many of the world's newspapers. Not headlines, by any means, but more like page eight or nine fillers. The stories were described as "unconfirmed", and as such were suspect and of little interest. It was only when the returning deportees and those fortunate enough to make a clean escape began straggling through Europe's capitals did the real extent of the purge become realised.

In due course a sensation-hungry world, tiring of the American/Soviet stand-off, pounced on the reports of injustice, indignity and ingratitude which the refugees brought with them. The initial flush of excitement, though, became unworthy of closer attention when it became apparent that there had been no genocide, no massacre, few atrocities and little sustained violence. Or, at least, nothing which could be proven or substantiated. To most people it was just another incident of an emerging African nation abusing its new-found freedom to put its house in order. Quite commonplace, these days.

"An internal matter," said the United Nations, after receiving several feebly-worded protests from Western countries on behalf of their displaced nationals. The subject very quickly lost momentum, and was placed low down on the priority list. The Red Cross was refused permission to send in an investigation team, and the Vatican referred to the reports as "an unfortunate situation".

To a handful of individuals in London, though, it was far from just "an unfortunate situation". To the wives and families of those still out there it was a matter of deep concern, a personal trauma, almost a tragedy. Debbie Scott was among a group of people who wandered about the corridors of London in search of news. From CAC to the Commonwealth Office, to the Foreign Office and back they went, then to the Kumangan High Commission and the offices of the West African Trading Commission, and back again to CAC, who could tell them nothing. Senior management knew no more than what the newspapers had already told, despite their corporate influence in diplomatic circles. Contact with branch offices in Kumanga had been cut off, and even nearby Ghana, Nigeria and Cameroon couldn't or wouldn't help them. Although Debbie had been subconsciously preparing for some sort of trouble since Derek's departure, the impact of its reality sent her reeling with a psychological sickness she had never before experienced, never before even imagined. Much worse was the not knowing; not knowing where Derek was, what he was doing or what was being done to him. Was he dead? Was he in some foul-smelling prison? Or perhaps he was being tortured and abused beyond imagination by a people whose veneer of civilisation was precariously thin, people who were avenging themselves for generations of colonial suppression. Some of those who had returned told stories of imprisonment, of beatings, of shootings, of torture. Were they true? Was Derek one of these, or was he one of those fortunate enough to have escaped? In some ways having no news at all was worse than knowing for sure what had become of him, while in other ways it held out a hope.

Gordon Blake had left Ivebje, having come to the end of his ten month executive tour, and was already on holiday. He had stepped off the plane quite recently without any inkling of the upheaval which was about to occur in Kumanga, and the extent to which his son-in-law would be involved. It was fortunate for him that his leave came up when it did, or he would surely have been implicated also.

It was often debated but never agreed upon by those involved whether the shortening of a "tour" from twenty months to ten was a sign of respect for seniority and experience, or merely a diplomatic way of acknowledging that a person of advancing years tends to tire more quickly in the tropics. Whatever the reason, Gordon and his senior management colleagues were always glad of the privilege, and were more than eager to replace West Africa's heat, humidity, insects and frustrations with Europe's cool, temperate and pleasant surroundings at regular but short intervals. There was, of course, always a fight to see who could arrange his holiday when England was at its best - that is, between May and August. Obviously, not everyone could go home in the summer, and Gordon was one of those people who really didn't mind being there during the sharp snap of late autumn and early winter.

Gordon and Marjorie had, by carefully preserving their finances over the years, been able to purchase and furnish the average Englishman's dream home - a country cottage in the Home Counties within easy reach of London, but far enough away from the hustle and bustle of commercial life to be able to enjoy a few weeks of carefree, unadulterated relaxation. Gordon was, at the time of the Kumanga crisis, a well-liked, well-respected member of the community, where his knowledge and personal interpretation of the African scene were constantly in demand. The cottage was rented out for ten months of each year, but when the time for retirement eventually came, this would be where he would spend the rest of his years. It was getting close to that right now, with two or maybe three tours ahead of him.

It had already been suggested that when he settled down he should consider accepting a position on the Magistrates' Bench, or perhaps allowing his name to stand in some future aldermanic election. While he felt that he still had quite a few years of active life left in him, he hadn't given any serious thought to either proposal. He had already been asked by the local newspaper to give his personal views of the Kumanga crisis, but had firmly but politely refused to do so while still on the staff of CAC.

Gordon's background was rather different from that of his

CAC colleagues. He had been born in Capetown in 1907, the son of an English-born immigrant to the fledgling Union of South Africa who had risen to prominence in government service. As his father's career expanded, Gordon had spent his early days living in the Cape and Natal provinces, and the family eventually settled in Durban on the early retirement of his father due to medical problems. He knew as much about Africa as anyone, black or white, but grew concerned at the resurgence to power of the Boer element, whom the English thought they had conquered and supressed. He was sent to Wellington School, one of Britain's finest, then on to Oxford, where he was still classified as an "African native". During his passage through university he became more and more disillusioned with South Africa's attitude towards the black population and, like many others in a similar position, began to feel uncomfortable about returning. The opportunity to join CAC came as a blessed solution to his dichotomy. He was given the chance to live and work in his beloved Africa, albeit a different part, while at the same time being permitted to condemn the growing movement which led eventually to total racial segregation under the name of "Apartheid".

Eventually, Gordon began to ignore the South African half of his dual nationality and assumed a countenance as English as any of his colleagues. He met a thoroughbred English lady, complete with horses, tea on the lawn and church every Sunday in a flowered hat and white gloves. He grew to love and respect the "typical" English traditions which Marjorie represented. Whether on tour in Moresia or vacationing in the United Kingdom, this was part of what resolved him to spend his retirement, when it came, in the English countryside. Anyway, there weren't many parts of Africa still available to a white resident, native born or not. He had approved of, and even encouraged, his elder daughter's marriage to Derek Scott, a sensible, level-headed young manager of great promise. The two men became good friends over and above the boss-and-subordinate level, and Gordon's anxieties about his son-in-law's present whereabouts matched those of his daughter..

At the end of a week, and under much pressure from European embassies in neighbouring countries, the President of Kumanga issued a statement. He defended what London called "questionable activities designed to prejudice the well-being of British subjects and other expatriates" in a well prepared speech, stiff with Soviet overtones and phraseology. President Akparu explained.

> ***"The actions of our Government have been precipitated by certain subversive elements which, no longer having the selfish privileges which the previous administration continued to afford them, were attempting to undermine this Nation's political and economic progress. In consequence, they have been removed from positions of authority where their decadent colonial influence could, and probably would, be detrimental to Kumanga's growth as a free nation."***

There was much, much more, most of it outlining in unsubtle terms the alleged "dissatisfied", "bourgeois" and "corrupt" attitude of the expatriate management upper class, and how their "obvious discontent and unco-operative behaviour" was undermining Kumanga's efforts to progress as a potential world power. Some of them, in fact, had resorted to outright spying, and it had become apparent that a "cleansing" of the social strata was overdue.

Gordon Blake smiled as he heard these opening remarks. He knew Adebo Akparu well; he had known him as a well-connected law student, the son of a wealthy CAC trader who had begged

Gordon, amongst others, for a letter of reference to expedite the young, lazy, unmotivated Adebo's entrance to Ivebje University. Gordon had given it, but only as a public relations gesture. Gordon had, in fact, been instrumental in securing a coveted position at the U of I's law college for Adebo. Surprisingly, young Adebo had scraped through with enough credits to be accepted into one of Kumanga's most prestigious law firms, whose English senior partner retired shortly thereafter. Gordon had helped give Adebo a boost by retaining him to conduct some of the Company's legal matters, although it soon became obvious that the young Akparu's interests were more political than legal. In fact he had bungled so many cases entrusted to his care that CAC had reluctantly struck him off its list. This action did nothing to improve relationships, and thus it was with no recriminatory feelings that Akparu had stood back as the ranks of CAC were decimated by the alleged cleansing.

Adebo Akparu had come to realise and accept his inefficiency as a lawyer, and had turned what few talents he possessed to politics. He owed his present position to the enthusiastic support he had given to the "right" people in the early days of Moresia's quest for self-government. He had, over the years during British rule, been prosecuted, outlawed, exiled and even jailed for his Marxist-inspired activities, and the influence of highly-placed friends, some of them fellow ex-students, had eventually secured for him a favoured place in the political arena. Long before the British left, Adebo Akparu had developed a martyr-like following, and it was no surprise to the likes of Gordon Blake to see him elevated to the Presidency when the Kumanga Progressive Socialist Party swept the election. In a country where "election" means tribal dominance, there is little doubt as to who will command the majority of the votes. Adebo Akparu was born to the largest tribal faction in the country, and the KPSP made sure that it could count on the votes of many lesser tribal groups by means which it would never dare to make public.

Gordon knew that Akparu could never have composed sentences as lengthy and as verbose as those which he was now reading out, even if he had studied with a dictionary for a month. It was obvious to him that the text of the message had come from a much higher source of intelligence. The title of "Dr." was a self-imposed honorary one, designed to allow Akparu some level of credibility in the political area.

The President's speech continued.

"To the best of my knowledge, and contrary to the biased rumours being spread by former white residents, no persons, be they white, black or Asian, have been unlawfully arrested, and there certainly have been no executions, as some reactionary elements are claiming. Most of the dissidents have been expelled for the reasons already stated, and those whose whereabouts are unaccounted for are presumed to be in hiding, or to have perished during their imprudent attempts to evade deportation. Henceforth only those expatriates invited by the Government of Kumanga to remain in this country will be permitted to do so. They will be expected to work very closely with our Administration.

"Every effort is, of course, being made to locate those who seem to have disappeared during the exercise. The search may well prove to be fruitless, since those in question appear to be reluctant to give themselves up into the safe custody of the authorities".

Gordon snorted at this blatant and obvious untruth, and choked on the smoke from his cigar. Giving way to a fit of coughing in an attempt to clear his lungs he missed the first few words of President Akparu's next comments. It was a long, rambling dissertation which did no more than elaborate on the foregoing theme. It was vague, inconclusive, and gave unsupported reasons why Kumanga had to rid itself of all reactionaries in order to be able to offer equal opportunities for all men in a free and democratic society. He probably didn't realise it, but he actually quoted passages which Gordon recognised as being pure Karl Marx as to how this was to be achieved.

Gordon's anger mounted with his dismay. It became apparent that the years of service, frustrations and damned hard work given by him and thousands of others who had devoted their working years to bringing this under-developed expanse of terrain into the twentieth century were going to be thrown back into their faces. He recalled an old saying which an African chief had once translated for him from the original Setikiri tongue -

"treat a wild dog too kindly and it will bite the hand".

How true this is, he reflected. Kumanga was certainly biting England's hand right now.

As a foot-note to his speech, President Akparu made a special point of saying that contrary to the opinions of some observers, Kennedy's warning to the Soviets regarding Cuba did not, repeat ***not***, precipitate the Kumangan Government's long-planned actions. It was no more than mere coincidence that the two events had taken place simultaneously.

This was the final insult to Gordon's intelligence. He switched off his radio before being subjected to the Kumangan national anthem, and placed a personal call to the Commonwealth Secretary.

With the exception of the minority of people whose lives had been touched by the Kumanga Crisis, Akparu's statement was looked upon with disinterest. It was no longer news. It had, furthermore, been overshadowed by yet another coup d'etat in South America, where the bloodshed and bodies were real and visible, and the threat of a dock strike at home, which carried far more local impact. The speech from Kumanga was looked upon as just another African domestic affair, and not by any means a deliberate and provoked strike in the long-standing East-West squabble.

The Commonwealth Office appeared to accept the Kumangan President's statement on face value, and restricted its diplomatic activities to a half-hearted attempt at trying to determine the whereabouts of the missing Britons. This was despite a strong protest from CAC and several other large mercantile companies that not enough was being done to locate their personnel and recover their property investments. Questions raised in The House met with the blunt official rebuff that this was not a political or diplomatic matter.

To Debbie and many like her, though, the days of anxiety and speculation seemed to be endless. Slowly and painfully the realisation that Derek might never come back dawned on her. She reproached herself bitterly for having given in to him and letting him go back to Kumanga for this supposed "final tour", especially since he had already put forward his resignation, however reluctantly. Her life collapsed around her. Her children, old enough to know that something was very wrong but too young to appreciate exactly what, seemed to reflect in their faces the distress which she felt. It was cruel to think that they may never again see their father, a father destroyed by the very people he was trying to help. She kept hoping against hope that the stragglers who were still trickling back from West Africa, the lucky ones who had made it back with their tales of horror, could at least bring her some word of what had happened to her husband. There was nothing to tell. Her grief was total.

The English sky was cloudless but sharp with the magnificence of autumn's change into winter. The last flowers of summer suburbia had long since given in to the chilling air, and frost was not far away. There were few leaves on the trees; their brown remnants were choking lawns and clogging roadside drains. Autumn's fresh and tantalising atmosphere had all but disappeared, telling England to prepare for the winter. Although never expected, it would inevitably arrive as it had done for countless centuries and take everyone by surprise.

Debbie Scott was awakened from an uneasy sleep by the insistent double ring of the telephone. Tired, depressed and haggard to a point far beyond her years, she plodded reluctantly down the stairs and lifted the receiver, fully expecting to hear another well-meaning but insufferable message of condolence. Her life had been hell for the past couple of weeks. Despite the sympathy and well-intentioned patronisation of her family and friends, she was in no state to face the future as a widow. Not yet, anyway. Everyone she had spoken to had insisted that "no news is good news", that there was still a chance. Well, so there was, she kept telling herself. But as each day passed she came that little bit closer to accepting that Derek was out of her life for good. She had steadfastly refused to go and stay with the kind people who had offered to "look after her". It was only when those close to her convinced her that in her present state she was hardly capable of taking proper care of her children that she agreed to let her mother come and visit for a while. After all, there was no-one more suited to the occasion than the wife of a long-service Coast employee, as Marjorie Blake pointed out with great concern.

She was in no mood to engage in small talk this morning. She answered the telephone rather tersely, and was surprised to hear a cultured voice give her the news that Derek Scott was among a small group of people known to have escaped from Kumanga after being detained for a few days. It was formal, matter-of-fact and impersonal, as though the process of telling someone about their loved one's escape was an everyday chore.

"You mean Derek is O.K.? He's safe, and coming home?" She was scarcely able to believe it.

"That's not what I said, Mrs. Scott." The Voice fell short of saying "are you deaf, or something?", but conveyed the impression. Debbie formed a picture that the owner of the Voice would be frowning with impatience, eager to get on to the next number on his list.

To CAC's London Office it was simply another case of two more of their hundred-or-so displaced employees having freed themselves from the clutches of a deranged government. The information was unconfirmed but reasonably reliable, having come from loyal forest workers whose bush telegraph instincts were uncanny. But that's all they knew - Derek and his group had fled the country in a plane, but Lord knows where they are now. It was getting to be a routine affair for CAC, a checking of names off a list as people either straggled home or were reported to be on the move. Many of those returning had hair-raising experiences to relate - hiding, fighting, running, stealing and even killing in their efforts to escape. It was the sort of stuff adventure movies were made of. Sadly, though, a great many were still unaccounted for.

But the world went about its business.

14

Totally oblivious to affairs on the international scene, and in fact to anything but their own survival, the fugitives watched the miles slip beneath the wheels as they sped south west in the stolen car. Occasionally they would make a comment about recent events, which they could not change, or on their future destiny, at which they could only guess. For the most part, though, they sat in silence, wrapped in their own private thoughts.

They passed through dry scrub and savannah which had been burned. The burning is supposed to fertilise the soil. The slash-and-burn procedure was never a great success, but it was, and still is, a tradition among many of the world's less sophisticated farming communities. The scientific fact is that the nitrogen released by burning organic leaves is more likely to be liberated into the wind than back to the soil. Besides which, burning kills a lot of plant life and probably hundreds of animals, driving others before it in a frenzied panic. But such has been the custom for so long that it's now hard to stop.

Driving through the burnt countryside was a depressing experience. The whole world seemed desiccated, dry and dead. Derek began to long with a bitter nostalgia for the fresh, green beauty of his native England. Or even the hot humidity of the jungles with which he had been associated for so many years.

The grasslands increased in intensity as they journeyed further south, leaving the sandy fringes of the Sahara behind them. The comical baobab tree seemed to be mocking them, just as it had in turn been mocked by countless generations of humans because of its incredible upside-down appearance. It was as though it had been planted by a giant Divine hand in a giant Divine fit of anger with its roots where its branches should be.

The road was not good. There were stretches of sometimes five miles or more where the surface adopted that corrugated wash-board effect which made steady progress impossible. There were two ways of attacking corrugated roads - either very slowly, taking each trench as it came, or very quickly in the hope of riding the crest of the bumps and virtually flying over the depressions. When confronted with such a situation, Derek usually opted for the first alternative, partly out of deference to the car's suspension, but mainly from fear of personal injury should he mistime the leapfrogging. Henri obviously knew a trick or two, and was able to direct the car along the bumps with scarcely a ripple being felt.

They had been travelling for three or four hours – Derek couldn't remember - when Henri's foot eased off the accelerator, and they approached what appeared to be a traffic jam ahead of them. As they drew closer Derek realised with dismay the cause of the hold-up. It was one of those infernal and infuriating road/railway bridges where trains and vehicles shared the same single track across a river. For most of the time the single-lane span was open to road traffic, which would lumber up the ramp at one end of the bridge on the green light, drive slowly across, trying heroically to avoid the tracks, then down the ramp at the other end to continue the journey. On the few occasions when a train was due in either direction the gates would be dutifully swung across until such time as the train had chugged its way along the track, leaving the bridge free once again for road traffic. It was not uncommon for the gates to close up to an hour before the train was due, and it was pointless to plead and protest. No amount of arguing would influence the officials to let anything through once the gates were closed, not even a car flying Government colours, and the drivers resigned themselves to an unscheduled nap in whatever shade was available. This only happened three or four times a week, and it was by pure misfortune that the fugitives found themselves at the end of a line of a dozen or so vehicles, whose drivers, with the nonchalance of Africa, were happily snoozing or playing chequers by the roadside.

To call West Africa's rail system a network was to exaggerate. Built early in the century as an alternative means of moving materials to and from the ports, the rail lines spread across the countryside like tentacles, single track for the most part. Although timetables were regularly printed and distributed, they were quite meaningless. A train reached its destination only when it got there, and no-one seemed to care if it were a few hours late or a few days. To the custodians of the gates, whether they be in charge of an important crossing like this one or a simple level crossing out in the country, the very rumour that a train was in drumming distance was reason enough to close off the roads and leave traffic to pile up on either side for as long as it took the train to pass. Besides which, a considerable percentage of their income was derived from the refreshments they were able to offer to hungry and waiting drivers.

Derek had waited on some occasions for as long as four hours.

But, as with ferry loading delays, there was nothing which he or anyone else could do but sit and quietly fume, calling down all the curses which he or anyone else could muster on yet another of Africa's frustrations. This time, though, it was different. Derek knew that for every minute they were delayed the greater would be the chances of their escape being discovered, and the greater would be the chances of recapture. Trying to make themselves as inconspicuous as possible, they waited in line for over two hours before nature began to make its inevitable and undeniable call. For the men it was easy, but Jean had to wander deep into the bush to escape the inquisitive eyes of patient but bored occupants of all the vehicles waiting to cross the bridge.

Eventually a mournful wail heralded the approach of the train and two engines, new diesel ones this time, replacing the old-fashioned steam, dragged scores of boxcars, livestock pens and passenger coaches across the bridge at a snail's pace.

"ZEKWE-QEDAR EXPRESS", proclaimed the signs on the sides of the passenger coaches.

"Express my ar--, er, foot," muttered Jim, voicing the opinion they all held, but toning it down for Jean's benefit.

There didn't seem to be any outward signs of difference between the coaches marked "1st Class" and those marked "3rd Class". The open windows of both were crammed with smiling and waving half-torso figures, bantering cheerfully with the people from the vehicle line-up who clustered dangerously close to the railway tracks. It seemed to Derek that there must have been as many people on the roof and hanging on the outside as there were within, presumably catching a free ride across the bridge. Slowly and painfully the last of the train cleared the bridge and the waiting drivers started up their engines. Two grunting and sweating officials, clad in dirty grey uniforms with "Bujavi Railways" woven in above the left breast, manhandled the gates open then scrambled aboard the final carriage, presumably to do the same at the other end. Or perhaps to head for home, knowing that their services wouldn't be required until tomorrow or the day after. Trucks, buses, cars and bicycles trundled up the ramp and jogged along the bridge, catching up with the train and blaring their horns at the pedestrians, all of whom were making better time. They were on the move again, thank goodness.

When he had cleared the opposite gates, Henri picked up speed, overtaking the vehicles in front of him whose drivers willingly and happily gave way to an important Government car. Derek sent up a silent prayer that no similar obstacles would be encountered. Next time they might not get away so easily.

At first their progress had been sandy, especially when they had to drop the three inches or so off the side of the thin tarmac strip as a vehicle approached in the opposite direction doing likewise. They breathed and swallowed the fine, choking sandy dust which penetrated the limousine's door and window seals, making a mockery of the air-conditioned comfort on which the car's reputation rested. Gradually the sandy wastes had given way to fine soil, then sparse grass, ever thickening as the travellers chased the sun southwards. The khaki-beige of the road-side safety shoulder slowly turned to a brick red as the sand changed to laterite. Almost imperceptibly the vegetation began to encroach on the fields which flew passed them as they entered the fringe of the enormous rain forests bordering West Africa's humid coastline.

They passed a busy roadside market, acknowledging the waves and smiles of the villagers, who had neither knowledge of nor interest in the reason for the car's passing. They were quite accustomed to seeing Government vehicles, whose occupants could be white, or black, or Asian - they really didn't care. This was only a small market, nothing to compare in size or variety with those which Derek had visited in places like Onitsha or Ibadan on his many trips to Nigeria. Derek was at home in the market, as was Alan, since that was where most of their trading was done, directly or indirectly. The traders, mainly women in big, colourful head-ties, were packed together as tightly as hens in a battery, offering anything and everything. They displayed pots, pans, textiles, food, hardware and many other daily requirements. They displayed ju-ju artifacts such as monkey skulls, bat wings, deer antlers, dog paws and a multitude of mysterious and forbidding concoctions with traditional but doubtful medicinal properties. And most other requirements between - it was a boast that "if you don't see it, just ask - we either have it or can get it quick, quick". And they could!

These women, referred to as market mammies, were exceptionally strong, gaily dressed and with an endless capacity for chattering, arguing and bargaining from 6 o'clock in the morning until long past dusk. Their God was their inspiration; their second God was money. Each woman probably had a husband somewhere, who may also be trading or be perhaps a civil servant, a company clerk, a carpenter, a driver. The market, though, belonged to the women, without whom it would be lifeless, insipid, dull and undeniably less profitable. Their life was to gossip, nurse their babies, barter, feed their cluster of child helpers, then pack up the unsold goods ready for the long trek home. This procedure would be repeated the next day, and the next, and the next, until they became too old and feeble to do anything but hand the business over to their daughters. The amount of money these women made was staggering. Despite their illiteracy, they knew to the nearest penny how much profit had been made each day, and this was reflected in the amount of credit which the major trading companies allowed. Yes, Derek was very much at home in the market.

A panoply of blazing colours sprang at them from the passing trees. Reds, golds, blues, maroons and a dazzling variety of hybrids filled the gaps between the inevitable greenery as the travellers penetrated deeper into the sombre tunnel of interwoven branches. Derek couldn't help feeling a welcome sense of security as the jungle tightened around him. It reminded him of his childhood when he would pull the bed covers up to his face as a protection against whatever lurked in the deep, dark corner shadows of his bedroom.

With the car's fuel gauge dangerously close to empty, the rain forest eventually engulfed the voyagers totally, its ageless trees forming a giant's cathedral which the tropical sunlight could scarcely penetrate. They had travelled some two hundred and fifty miles, and estimated that there would be a further sixty or seventy miles to the coastal corner of the country and the border shared with friendly Séjumé.

Séjumé was one of the last outposts of France's diminishing empire. Its capital, Ste. Pierre, was an astounding slice of "la vie Parisienne" set in the humid clutches of Africa's tropics. Ste. Pierre was a favourite holiday resort for many of West Africa's expatriates who found themselves with a few days of local leave - not enough for a "home" visit, but far enough away from everyday surroundings to afford a welcome change of scenery. Henri Gaudet, an unencumbered bachelor, had been to Ste. Pierre several times, and it was at his insistence that the five had directed their vehicle towards what they hoped would be the general direction of this promised haven. They had no other plans, anyway, so why not? But first they had to get there.

Henri swung the limousine as far into the bush as he could, out of sight from the searching eyes of pursuers, and its occupants covered it with leaves and branches. They began to inch their way through the forest on foot, still hoping that the direction they had chosen would be the right one for freedom.

The forest, Derek had often been told, was not necessarily the hot, foetid and dangerous place which most people like to believe. Nor was it so thick and tangled as to make it impenetrable - after all, his predecessors used to go on trek through it in the days when "on trek" meant cutting through the undergrowth, long before the advent of roads, cars or trains. Rather, the forest was a miracle of beauty where immense trees thrust their leafy summits upwards for hundreds of feet in search of sunlight. The forest was where the shorter growths, incapable of competing with their high-reaching neighbours, crept and crawled and twisted up and around the trunks of the tall trees to find the same life-sustaining rays.

Derek and his companions were far from interested in or overwhelmed by the natural beauty of the phenomena as they penetrated deeper into the gloom, but more concerned with finding a way through it. It was dark and shadowy. Pinpoints of light filtering through a million leaves far above gave the scene an eerie, greenish tinge. The centuries-old carpet of dead leaves, soft as a down quilt, gave off an earthy scent. All around were the huge trees, straddling on great, curling buttress roots, towering upwards until their foliage merged into the green roof of the forest. Between them were the young trees, thin and tender growths which had just shaken themselves free from the cradle of leaf mould. They stood in the everlasting shade of their parents, as though preparing themselves for the inevitable effort of reaching upwards in their own rights towards the sun.

Threading aimlessly between the thick trunks could be seen faint paths, the highways of the forest, which its inhabitants had stamped out over the decades. In some places where a giant tree had toppled, still being supported pointlessly by its neighbour as its roots crumbled, the overhead foliage was broken, and patches of blue sky glowed like far off lanterns through the dark tatter of leaves. The sun slanted down through these holes, turning the leaves where it touched them to gold, and throwing a web of misty sunbeams through which the butterflies flittered. There was not much other active life to be seen, unless one went searching for it in the right places. There was proof enough, though, that life was teemingly abundant, by the incessant rasping noise of cicadas, crickets and frogs. Unseen monkeys chattered overhead as they stalked the five humans, while birds kept up a symphony of hidden hoots and shrieks.

It was Derek's first real up-close encounter with one of West Africa's great rain forests, other than the times he had tried to observe them while driving through, along questionable roads. At first he was mildly fascinated, but after the first day the novelty wore off. Food was not an immediate problem, although its variety was very restricted. They were able to live on the fruit, the berries and the roots which were in abundance. Henri was an invaluable mine of knowledge, advising and directing what could and what should not be eaten, a by-product of a more down-to-earth lifestyle than that in which any of the others had been involved. All the same, they still had to hope that their intestinal fortitude would be able to cope with anything of a toxic nature. Derek and Jim noticed that Henri was not eating; sweat was pouring out of him as he struggled to pretend that nothing was wrong.

There was no shortage of small game, but they considered that it would be imprudent to risk a shot. Even if the sound of gunfire didn't attract attention, there was a strong possibility that smoke from the cooking would. To say nothing of the inevitable gathering of ever-watchful vultures, who would give away their position faster than lighting a flare. The alternative was to eat whatever they caught in its raw state, and Derek wasn't hungry enough for that option. They were far from nourished in terms of a balanced diet, but they were able to satisfy their immediate hunger needs.

Progress was desperately slow. On a good day, five or six miles was an achievement, and this was only an estimate. They parted every branch, every frond before moving forwards, lest they stumble across one of the patrols which by now were sure to be looking for them. The pressing and ever-present problem, though, was water. Not that there was a shortage of it, since one of the most notable features of the forest was the innumerable tiny streams, shallow and clear, which wandered in intricate and complicated patterns across the floor. They glinted and rippled as they coiled themselves around the smooth, worn boulders, and they hollowed out the earth from under tree roots as they went on into the depths of the forest. They chuckled and chattered over miniature waterfalls and scooped out deep pools in the sandstone where blue and red fish and tiny frogs lived out their short but busy lives.

The Europeans were hesitant to drink at first, and it was sheer desperation which drove them to ease their thirsts from the tempting waters. After years of conditioning themselves to drink only boiled and filtered water in the safety of their own homes, their fear of picking up some dreaded tropical disease was, at first, almost as great as the fear of being recaptured or killed. They had been able so far to avoid dysentery, beri-beri, blackwater fever and a few others, and this was not a good time to start; the alternatives, though, were to surrender or die of thirst. They drank sparingly on the first day. When nothing bad happened they grew bolder, and drank in the warm but clear jungle water until the fears of ingesting undesirable parasites vanished.

The fugitives fought a constant but losing battle against a multitude of insects, particularly mosquitoes. In addition, unseen and unexpectedly voracious nettle-like vegetation left irregular lines of angry, crimson bore-holes on unprotected skin. Any exposed flesh soon became a blotchy mass of irritating red and white lumps, calling out to be scratched but pulsating in agony when they were.

They encountered many snakes, especially in and around the pools of water. Not knowing for sure which were venomous and which were not, they took the prudent measure of treating them all with the greatest of respect. On one occasion they froze into immobility as a plump, squat-looking reptile slithered noiselessly across their path. Henri recognised it instantly as a gaboon viper, one of the world's most deadly. It had obviously recently shed its skin, and presented an intricate and fascinating patchwork of pink, red, beige, silver and bronze. They waited until it had tucked itself safely into the undergrowth before resuming their progress.

The screeching but hidden monkeys were their constant companions, warning the rest of the forest that intruders were in their midst. Long-snouted brown lizards performed their comical and inimitable push-ups before scurrying for safety in the thick tangle of branches. This was nature at its best, wonderful but frightening, innocent but treacherous, primitive but intricate. None of the intruders had before experienced it at such close quarters and with such intensity, not even the worldly-wise Henri.

Uncomfortable as they were, their will to survive kept prodding them forward, knowing that nothing could be worse than falling into the hands of their hunters.

15

The men, traditional protectors, were amazed at Jean's fortitude and physical endurance. She insisted repeatedly that she would neither expect nor welcome any special privileges simply because of her sex. Her energy seemed to be boundless.

"When is the arrogant male species going to accept that women really do have a stronger physical constitution than men? Someday we'll not only be equal in this world, we'll be....."

She couldn't think of a word with enough emphasis to finish her prediction. She didn't want to say "superior", but that was what she meant.

James Barrett was particularly impressed. His lifestyle had been very male-dominated, firstly at all-boys schools, then with the army, and more recently the classic colonial brotherhood which he enjoyed. At least, he told himself that he enjoyed it, since he had never had the inclination or opportunity to change it. True to the tradition of his day, Jim held the conventional view of women as being very much the weaker sex, to be afforded due courtesy and respect but not much else. He had never met anyone quite like Jean before. He had heard about them and read about them, especially in America, but never actually come into close contact with one. She was awakening something in him – it was an awareness that this long held concept of women wasn't quite correct. There might, after all, have been something missing from his otherwise orderly lifestyle.

James Barrett was a self-contained man, a well-organised bachelor, with very many acquaintances but no-one who had ever been close enough to call him "friend". Derek, for instance, didn't care for him very much, but tolerated his logic and precision. He found the bank manager to be arrogant in a cold and impersonal way, intolerant of weaknesses in others and not prepared to compromise. Not that James didn't have weaknesses of his own, but he preferred not to recognise them. For instance, his evident stand-offishness was seen by some to be in itself a weakness, but James looked upon it as a facet of his superior upbringing. Even his undisguised liking for Scotch he carried well; he had many times been seen to drink too much, but unlike most people, he didn't allow a degree of intoxication to loosen his tongue. His attitude tightened under the influence of liquor and he became more unfeeling, more sarcastic, more critical. He never let these occasional bouts interfere with his job, either.

"When it gets to a point where a fellow can't be on seat at 7.30 each morning with a clear head, that's the time to start getting a grip. Otherwise it's no-one else's damned business."

He had a professed dislike for children and domestic animals, and little patience with anything without an obvious and meaningful function.

"That's probably why he never married", some gossips said.

"No woman would have him, the conceited pig."

Others put forward an alternative theory why he hadn't married. This was proven to be unfounded after reports, unsubstantiated, of an incident with the secretary sent by Head Office to re-organise the typing pool.

At his job James was meticulous, observing all the rules and discipline of a bank manager and overseeing a well-organised and well-run branch and, later, region. As such, he enjoyed a certain high prestige level in the community and inspired confidence among staff and clients alike. No-one would hesitate to approach him to discuss a financial matter, or ask for monetary advice, no matter how personal, knowing that they would receive the best available counsel. It was also comforting to know that James was the essence of discretion, and confidentiality was guaranteed.

James P. Barrett had been born 40 years ago in Sussex, the only child of a wealthy gentleman-farmer. His upbringing was correct, genteel and imbued with all the niceties of the upper middle class of the day. He met the right people on the right occasions, and went to the best schools at which the son of a country gentleman would be found. He passed through Harrow and Cambridge with distinctions in almost everything to which he applied himself, but it was obvious from the start that he had neither the inclination towards nor interest in farming.

James applied to the Foreign Office and was accepted without question as a Consular Trainee, by virtue of his academic record and obviously "suitable" background. He found after a short time, however, that he was no more cut out to be a diplomat than he was a farmer, and he abandoned this career almost before it had started.

It was suggested by a banker friend of Barrett senior that James might like to "have a look at the banking industry", and an offer was made to find him a position in the overseas branch of

African and Asian, or "A. & A.", as it was known on Threadneedle Street. James proved to have an aptitude for banking, much to his father's relief, and it was not long before he began to climb the promotion ladder. Just as he was reaching an acceptable level of respectability, the beckoning finger of patriotism dressed him in a khaki uniform and sent him to fight against Rommel's forces in North Africa.

James was seconded to a Military Intelligence unit where his logic, clarity of vision and high degree of precise efficiency helped to save the lives of many fighting men. When the war ended he held the rank of captain. He was persuaded to stay in uniform for a further two years in order to help with the "mopping-up" of Nazi fugitives. When he finally returned to civilian life in 1947 he did so with an immaculate record of service. It was a very creditable performance for someone who had only just passed his twenty-sixth birthday.

Unlike Derek, Alan and most others, James did not choose West Africa as his work arena. Moresia was where A. & A. had sent him on resuming his career, and in the thirteen years he had been there he had progressed steadily to his present position of regional manager for all Western Kumanga. This made him jointly fourth from the top on the seniority scale of the whole country, and there was no doubt that someday, in the Bank's vast network of interests, he would reach general manager status.

James had always been very particular about his appearance, even as an undergraduate. His present rank made it imperative that whether socially or on business, his attire would always be impeccable. He knew that behind his back his staff referred to him as “Jim Dandy”, an antiquated and hackneyed title, but one which appealed to the Africans’ sense of mischievous humour. It certainly applied to James, most of the time. He didn’t look much like a dandy now, though, in his torn and blood-stained bush jacket. However, he seemed to have adapted to the circumstances, as indeed they all had. After all, it was now a matter of survival. All the same, Derek couldn't help but admire James for his sense of poise and fortitude, given the situation into which he had been dropped.

Africa's night smell is a dry, nose-pinching mixture of wood smoke, mouldering protein and the all-embracing odour of open, stagnant drains, which line every town street and serve as the catch-all for everything not wanted. In the bush, where Mother Nature disposes of her waste in a much more genteel and effective manner, the drain odour is replaced by rotting vegetation, nature's own fertiliser, which looks after itself and causes offence to no-one. Africa's smell takes a little getting used to, but gradually becomes an inseparable part of Africa itself. Africa, whose memories can instantly be revived by just one whiff; Africa, whose travellers can be transported back immediately on contact with any one of the nose-tingling ingredients which make up the backdrop. It is a smell which proclaims the continent's experience of centuries of near-primitive human habitation.

The darkness of the night overtook the fugitives at the end of each day, as though it had been trying to catch up with them. On the third evening, tired, dispirited and patch-worked with scratches and bites, they scouted around for a suitable clearing in which to settle down and grab whatever sleep would come. To stumble around in the murky blackness would be dangerous as well as pointless. The forest by night was a very different place from the forest by day. Eyes gleaming down from the tree-tops above told them that everything was awake and watchful, and the undergrowth seemed to be alive with squeaks and rustles. Dead twigs fell and crumbled, sounding like ghostly footsteps, and over-ripe fruit plopped and splattered on the forest floor around them. They could hear the cicadas, who never sleep; the occasional screech of a bird would echo throughout the trees, making the nervous humans jump, as though it were a personal warning that they should not be there. The hyrax would start its piercing whistle, working itself into a powerful crescendo. Then it would stop suddenly and mysteriously, as if cut with a sharp knife, leaving the air quivering with the memory of the cry. Birds called out to each other with an incalculable variety of sounds, from the creak of an old barn door to the trill of a piccolo, to a sparkling cascade of rich, harmonic tones. Who knows if their cries were ever answered? Or were they just a means of expressing what was in their tiny minds?

Surrounding these symphonies of nature was an awesome shroud of deep silence, extending back to the very beginning of time itself, and impressing on the human minds that this absolute wilderness was the antithesis of their civilised world.

Derek wondered if the others were as scared as he was. Perhaps scared was not quite the right word - apprehensive was more like it. Or perhaps "frightenedly apprehensive"? Derek smiled to himself at the word games his confused mind was playing. He and his friends had been thrust, by no fault of their own, into a situation never remotely contemplated by anyone. And all because they were foreigners in a nationalistic land whose child-like government was bent on exercising its so-called rights, regardless of the consequences.

To add to the complication was the question of Jean. Had she come to him that night in Qedar for a specific reason, or was she simply in need of fulfilment? What would she think if he went to her now and tried to carry on where they had left off? What would the others think?

These were some of the questions which plagued him and sent

much-needed sleep further away as he wrestled with his conscience. He stood up and ambled over to where Jean was keeping watch, a rifle cradled loosely in her arms.

"I can't sleep. My mind is going round in circles, and I wondered if..."

"Well you won't sleep if you walk about. Try lying down."

It was a rebuttal, plain and simple. Derek went back to his spot.

Frogs seemed to be everywhere, croaking and barking from the rocks by the pools and streams. There was a circle of blue-blackness all around, broken only by the occasional flicker of Alan Rushton's matches as he worked his way through what was left of Nsenji's cigarettes. During these brief flares the leaves and grasses took on an ethereal bluish-green tinge, and the monstrous curving roots of the giant trees looked like horrible tentacles ready to grab at any living thing close by. The air became heavy and damp with dew, although the rainy season was long past. Derek couldn't help thinking what it must be like at the bottom of the ocean, where no real light had ever penetrated over millions of years. It was creepy, mysterious. It was fascinating to a degree, but by this time Derek was in no mood to feel any sense of awe.

Derek seemed to feel the drums before he heard them. The vibration penetrated the sub-conscious level of his light doze and told him that the trees, the bushes and even the ground were shaking. Then he was wide awake, and sat upright.

"Do you hear that?," gasped Alan as he loped towards him. "I think they're coming this way."

James and Jean were already awake and scrambling to their feet. Henri was a little more reluctant, but eventually dragged himself after the others as they drew further back into the bushes, well away from the clearing. Derek could hear the sound of the drums clearly now, haunting, rhythmical, proponents of something foreboding, or even sinister.

"Definitely getting louder. Seems like a parade of some kind. Perhaps we should go further back..."

Jim's words were drowned as the chanting began, and then they could see flickering pinpoints of light coming through the trees. They moved back a few more yards out of the path of the procession and waited, tense and tingling as it drew closer. The chant became louder. Then it was upon them, passing no more than thirty feet from their hiding place. Derek estimated that there were about 50 African males, all singing and dancing to the intricate rhythm of the tattoo created by the drummers.

At the head of the procession was a tall, plump man wearing a full length robe covered with ornate and intricate designs. On his head was a crown of brightly coloured feathers, seemingly iridescent in the torchlight. He carried a staff which looked as though it could have been ivory, and matched his necklace of curved teeth. There was no disputing his high rank. Immediately behind him were four attendants, the drummers and the torch bearers. Then came the others, white streaks down their faces and limbs. They were dragging a reluctant and loudly bleating goat, which had only one eye. In place of the other was a bloody hole with a carved, bone-handled knife protruding.

Weaving in and out of the marchers with amazing agility was the ju-ju man - a small, wrinkled figure whose head and face were obscured by an ebony mask, hideously carved and coloured, with goat horns embedded in the top. The ju-ju man wore amulets and anklets of bone which rattled as he danced, and he waved around what looked to Derek like a human shin bone, brandishing it under the noses of everyone except the chief. It was a frightening sight. It bore a remarkable resemblance, though, to some of the accounts which Derek had read during his Head Office training days, accounts of old, primitive rituals which had supposedly been stamped out. Except that in those accounts the victim was not a goat, but a person.

Curiosity took the upper hand, and the five Europeans followed the procession at a discreet distance. They were led to a clearing in the forest where the Africans, still dancing and chanting, arranged themselves in a rough semi-circle around a pile of stones which had been carefully erected under an overhanging bough. There were dark brownish stains on the stones and surrounding leafy ground, and strange but ominous markings on nearby tree trunks.

The chief seated himself on a tree stump and barked out an order, on which the drums stopped and the dancers threw themselves down on the ground. The goat was dragged before the chief, who struck it on the head five times with this ivory staff. This increased the animal's bleating, almost drowning out the incantation which the ju-ju man started and was echoed by the tribesmen. Eventually there was a curt nod from the chief, and the drums began a different, more feverish beat. A gourd was produced, and after the chief had taken a prolonged gulp, each tribesman drank deeply before resuming dancing to the hypnotic beat of the drums.

"Time for the palm wine," whispered Alan. "I wondered where that would come into it."

"Quiet, you idiot! Unless you want to take the place of the goat."

A second gourd began to go around, then a third. The only one not drinking was the ju-ju man, who was supervising the stringing up of the goat by its hind legs over the branch, so that its head was only inches above the stone altar. As the palm wine flowed, the beat of the drums became faster, the dancing more frantic and the chanting louder, mixed with shrieks and wails as a ritual fever took control of the participants. The ju-ju man leaped about the group, then cavorted around the altar, then gyrated before the chief, his shin bone stick describing intricate patterns in the night air.

The pulse continued to increase, faster, louder, on and on, until it seemed that the dancers couldn't possibly keep up such a furious pace any longer, and must surely collapse from exhaustion. Suddenly the chief stood up and spread his arms out wide. The music stopped instantly, as did the dancing and shrieking, leaving the only sound coming from the suspended goat. The hidden onlookers had a good idea what the next step would be, but the fascination of it all held their eyes firmly fixed on the scene.

The chief took from one of his attendants a long, gleaming machete. The drums began a slow, quiet, sombre message, gradually increasing in volume and intensity as the chief walked towards the altar, the machete lifting higher at each step. He barked something to the ju-ju man, who began gabbling to the tree tops, arms outstretched.

Derek stole a glance at his companions. Alan had half-turned away from the scene, but couldn't resist glancing back. Jean had put a hand up to her mouth as if to stifle a scream, but kept on watching. Jim's face was expressionless, apart a slight tightening around his mouth. Henri was silently mouthing something and slowly shaking his head, sweat soaking the collar of his shirt.

The drums reached a high point, the ju-ju man turned to face the crowd, and the chief's machete came down. Derek wondered if he could stop himself from throwing up. The sharp blade struck the goat in the soft flesh of the throat, and was drawn across three times. Blood began to spurt out like an angry red geyser, splattering the chief, the ju-ju man and the altar. The drums changed their rhythm, and the tribesmen rushed forwards, arms outstretched, to rub their hands in the gushing blood which flowed down over the stones of the altar and to the ground beneath. Derek's stomach heaved as he saw some of them licking their hands, and even jostling to place a tongue under the spewing throat of the unfortunate animal.

Derek turned round as he heard a gagging sound behind him and saw Henri doubled up and retching. Jean was trying to lead him further into the bush. They all knew what the consequences of being discovered would be. Not that Henri's small sounds could be heard against the orgy going on in the clearing, but it was better to be safe.

When the flow of blood faltered to a trickle, the chief threw down the machete, raised his arms wide and shouted. The shout was taken up by the tribesmen, and the rhythm of the drums changed again. The chief walked slowly back the way he had come, followed by his attendants, the ju-ju man and the drummers. The rest of the tribesmen finished off what was left of the palm wine and went back along the path their leader had taken. The clamour and torchlight faded into the distance, leaving the five Europeans very shaken and very queasy, in silent contemplation of the drama which they had just witnessed. The goat was left hanging, and two of the tribesmen took up sentry-like positions to guard it from the vultures.

"My God," was all that Jim could find to say.

"Pardon," mumbled a very shaky Henri. "Je suis mal, très mal."

There had been many stories passed around about happenings like this, but no-one had ever actually witnessed them at first hand, or even known any European who had. Much of it was thought to be hearsay, or, at best, highly embellished as it went from bar top to bar top. Now they knew differently. They had been as close as anyone could be without actually being a part of the grizzly event. But it was not something they relished sharing with anyone.

The snapping of a twig close behind made Derek and Jim turn around, to find themselves face to face with an astonished African. He was swaying gently under the control of the palm wine, the whiteness of his teeth and eyeballs showing dully amid the blackness all around him. He turned and began to run, uttering a yell which turned to a grunt as Derek brought him down with a rugby tackle he hadn't used since his school days.

Before Derek could do anything to clamp the man's mouth, Jim's large hands locked around the black throat, choking off any further attempts to warn his fellow tribesmen. The man's struggles gradually slowed then ceased, but the pressure from Jim's hands didn't.

"That's enough, Jim. Leave him now. He's unconscious. He's not going anywhere for a while."

Jim shook his head from side to side and continued squeezing, staring intently at the bulging eyes below him.

"Jim, give it up."

Derek tugged at Jim's wrists but was unable to loosen their grip. Alan jumped forward to help, and by dragging on one arm each they were able to lift Jim's hands from his victim, who lay still and inert. Jean stepped forward and felt for a carotid pulse, then raised her head slowly.

"He's dead."

There was a strange look on her face, a look of awe, of disbelief and what seemed like admiration.

"My God, you've killed him."

Jim met her gaze without flinching.

"It was him or us. And, quite frankly, I'm sick of it's always being us. Yes, I killed him. He's not the first man I've killed. And at least, we're still safe – he won't be telling anyone where we are."

He glared around the group, as though daring anyone to challenge his reasoning. This was a different side of Jim that Derek was seeing. He was still cold and logical, true, but once again he had shown that he could also be ruthless, determined and lethal if the occasion demanded. It was emotion of a different kind.

Wordlessly they dragged the lifeless body a hundred yards or so into the bush, well away from the path, and covered it with leaves and twigs. With luck, it wouldn't be found until they were many miles away from this area. Perhaps not until the next ritual, by which time there wouldn't be much left but bones.

Derek looked at Jim squarely.

"I'm not sure that was entirely necessary."

"It was."

Jean said nothing, and slipped her arm through Jim's as they edged back to where Henri was resting his head on his arm against a tree.

They moved away from this evil place and tried to grab some more sleep. It was a long time before the night noises of the forest were filtered out by slumber.

16

On the fourth day, having slept badly after their gruesome experience, the travellers began to feel the effects of their unaccustomed exposure to Africa's fierce elements. Henri was in the worst shape, sweating profusely and complaining of feeling feverish. Jean did not need to be a trained and experienced nurse to notice the glazed look, the pronounced tremble, the heavy, stumbling gait. This was more than travel fatigue and under-nourishment. This was serious. This was malaria.

Finally, Henri could go no further. He lay down and Jean knelt by his side, mopping his brow with a grubby handkerchief proffered by Jim. It was already bloodstained from dabbing his many bites, but it was all they had.

"I can not go," Henri muttered. "I must rest. You must go on, and I will catch up with you bientôt."

"Like hell," was Alan's immediate response. "We'll carry you, if we have to. 'Course, a small crane would help..."

This brought a smile to Henri's face.

"Mes amis! You are too kind. But I will be fine after I have rested."

They all knew this wasn't true. This was a severe blow. Apart from being unable to offer anything in the way of medical aid, it would be impossible to make good speed with a sick man to handle. Especially one as heavy as Henri. They were weak with starvation and barely able to keep going themselves, without the burden of someone Henri's size to carry. On the other hand, to leave him behind was unthinkable. That could only result in a slow and painful death at the mercy of the elements and forest predators.

Derek knew from his own experience that a mind tortured by malaria is a mind in terror, a mind trapped in infinite nightmare. Not the customary nightmare which ends in sweat-drenched relief, but the endless nightmare of delirium from which there is no escape.

The grotesque and tortuous nightmares of malaria cannot be imagined, cannot be simulated, cannot be created, even, by a normal, healthy brain. Malaria follows a relentless cycle of attack, starting with icy chills accompanied by an all-consuming thirst. This is followed by a burning, desert-like fever, with body temperatures so high that brain damage is an ever-present danger. Then comes the deluge of sweat, when every pore exudes fluid, so much fluid that the body becomes desiccated and powerless, every movement and gesture being a supreme, energy-draining effort. At the point when the fleeting respite of semi-consciousness offers hope of remission, the chills come back and the cycle resumes. During the whole process the nightmares continue, relentless, tormenting, unremitting, leaving the subject helpless, defenceless and pathetic.

In the old days they used to think that malaria was something in the tropical air which reacted unfavourably with the white man's respiratory system. After all, the very name was "mal-air". Whatever they thought, it was certainly a contributor to the west coast of Africa's being referred to as the "white man's grave". And so it was to many. And yet, sophisticated as modern medicine was in combating the disease, there was still no foolproof way of preventing it. All one could do was to take the daily tablet and hope for the best. None of them had taken a tablet for several days; it was depressing to think that they could all go down with the disease.

An average malarial bout would be 72 hours, but Derek had seen cases lasting for as long as two weeks, or, as in his own case, as short as 36 hours. Yes, this was a serious setback. Of all the members of their little group, Henri Gaudet was the one about whom Derek knew the least. In the snobbish atmosphere of the European Club, those who worked with their hands rather than their brains were looked down on as being definitely proletariat. Henri was such a person. He was, after all, little more than a glorified truck driver. Although his spoken English was quite good, it was obviously acquired more by use than by learning. To many people he lacked the polish which might make him "acceptable" in the Club's social hierarchy.

There was quite a large French-speaking expatriate community in Ugbeshu, and over the decades they had developed their own social club. This was where they preferred to gather, to dance, to drink, to pass their leisure time, and to hell with the toffee-nosed snobs at the "other" club, especially the English. The outcome was that very few of the "other" club members had taken the time to get to know people like Henri. Had they done so, they would have found, as Derek had during the past few days, a warm, sincere and totally compatible individual whose desire was to be of no trouble to his companions, even offering to sacrifice himself so that they could maintain a modicum of speed. Henri was OK, and they wouldn't dream of leaving him behind.

After a couple of hours' rest they decided to press on. Taking Henri under each arm, Derek and Alan half carried, half dragged him at a stumbling, bumbling gait, well aware that their former cautious approach was a thing of the past. They staggered on slowly, painfully, for four hours or so, aware that they had covered no more than about half a mile, then sank down gratefully for a rest. They couldn't hope to get very far at this rate. Unless some sort of help could be found soon, one or more of them would become food for the vultures which were already starting to circle around above the tree. But what? How?

Alan's face was gaunt and drawn, and he fumbled in his shirt pocket for Nsenji's cigarette case. It was empty. He flung it into the bush, and began to curse and swear like a man demented.

"Oh, shut up!" Jim's urgent voice slashed through the humid air like a whip. "You're starting to annoy me".

Alan stopped his monologue and glanced at Jean.

"Sorry,"

"Oh, don't mind me. I've heard most of it before anyway. Probably used some of it myself at times."

I bet you have, thought Derek, then he closed his eyes.

Jean was on his mind for much of the time. It was idiotic, he told himself. It was childish, just like the schoolboy crush he had on the very first girl he had ever kissed when he was fourteen. He began to imagine, as he had back in those innocent days, what it would be like to have her around all the time, exclusively his. It was preposterous, and he scolded himself for even allowing the thought into his mind. He was a happily married man. He wondered, though, how many other men had entertained the same fantasies about Jean, how many had rejected the thought, as he surely must;

how many had been coldly turned away?

He opened his eyes to find Jean looking at him. She looked straight into his eyes as though looking into him, reading his mind, taunting him. She was a cool one, that. Cool but passionate, friendly but aloof, suggestive but unreachable. Why had she come into his room that night? Why his? Was it just to tease him? Derek couldn't read her at all.

Everything fell silent. The monkeys vanished, the birds flew into the high branches and even the insect noise seemed to stop. The runaways looked at each other anxiously. Derek stood up, gripping his rifle firmly.

"There's someone there."

He heard a sound in the bush behind him and swung around, his finger on the trigger. He relaxed as he saw that the noise came from a boy, no more than ten years old, and completely naked. The boy held his arms out in front of him.

"No shoot!"

Derek lowered the rifle.

"My farder him say friend. Make you put down gun an' him come."

The Europeans looked at each other in bewilderment. Henri struggled to a sitting position, leaning heavily on a tree trunk.

"What?"

The boy spoke again.

"Please, sah, my farder wan help you, but no fitti come in while gun him dey for you hand. Him sen me say put down."

Through the gloom of the clearing Derek could see the silhouette of a man holding a machete. There were several others behind him. The man waved.

Derek waved back then looked at Jim, who nodded, then carefully placed his rifle on the ground. Derek put his gun down, and motioned Alan to do likewise. Alan was reluctant at first, but after opening then closing his mouth he followed suite.

The Africans stepped forwards cautiously into the clearing, tense for any sudden threatening movement on the part of the white strangers. There were about twenty of them, dressed in a variety of garb from full flowing robes to a mere loin cloth. They were all armed with a club, a machete or a spear, and they all had a blank, expressionless face.

The white men stood very still as the Africans surrounded them, staring and frowning, and muttering to each other in a tongue Derek could not recognise. Jean went back to caring for Henri, who had lowered himself back on to his bed of leaves.

"Sannu! Mene me sunan wannan wuri? Ka na jin turanci?"

Derek addressed them in the only native language he had ever been able to master. The possibility that these forest dwellers would speak Hausa was remote, but it was all he could think of at the time.

The Africans became motionless and silent, as though trying to ponder the ever-mystifying actions of the White Man. Derek opened his mouth to speak again, but was silenced by a shake of the head by Jim.

A tall, powerful-looking man came forward from the rear of the group. He was dressed in a sparkling white shirt and shorts, and carried no weapon. Derek was surprised to see that he wore shoes. The others moved aside to let him pass.

"You'll excuse me if I don't reply in Hausa - I never did pick it up. But I did work hard at my English, though, so perhaps we can use that? I'm sure you'd be more comfortable."

He laughed, his tones falling like pearls from his immaculate teeth. He put out his right hand towards the gaping Europeans.

"Father Simon. I'm from the mission near here. We heard you were in the area, so I was sent to bring you in. A bit like the good shepherd I'm supposed to be?"

At this he went into a peal of laughter, which was echoed by some of the tribesmen, as he shook hands with each of the fugitives. His face hardened, though, when he saw Henri. He clapped his hands and the tribesmen produced a crude stretcher made of two rough-hewn poles lashed together with palm fronds. At the Father's barked order Henri was carefully and labouriously loaded on to it. Derek noticed that some of the other tribesmen were gingerly picking up the rifles, as if afraid they might go off at their touch. A grinning young man in a faded and torn bush jacket unloaded each weapon in turn, with a flair which said that he, at least, knew what he was doing.

Father Simon looked around and gave a curt instruction to the stretcher bearers, who carried Henri, weaving and wobbling, off into the forest.

"And now if you will please follow me?"

It wasn't so much of an invitation as a command.

"By the way, do forgive me for sending a boy to do a man's work, so to speak. I find that people are less likely to shoot a child, even desperate people such as yourselves. And he **did** volunteer."

They looked at each other, then Jim shrugged and stepped forwards. The others took this as the signal to follow. They were stunned, but too exhausted to argue. They followed meekly, unable to think of what to say to the obliging so-called priest. He sensed their mood.

"Cheer up - you're among friends. Just thank The Lord that we found you before the soldiers did, or you'd be feeding the worms by now."

He chuckled at this, then stopped to pick something up out of the bush. It was Nsenji's gold cigarette case. It gleamed as a ray of sunlight caught its polished surface, reminding Derek, rather fancifully he thought, of the proverbial ray of hope which is always supposed to appear. Perhaps this was it. The priest offered the object to Alan.

"Yours, I think. At least, you were the one who threw it."

In a daze Alan accepted it and put it into his shirt pocket. It was empty and useless, but some day he might use it. Unless he gave up the habit again.

After about two hundred yards they came to a rough track in the undergrowth, which widened into a well-trodden path. It became apparent that they were being taken towards a village, judging by the steadily increasing clamour. Not, Derek hoped, the one from where the sacrifice party had brought the unfortunate goat.

After about fifteen more minutes the labouring, grunting Africans, almost staggering under the weight of the helpless Henri, came to a stop. There was a hurried discussion with the priest, then the stretcher party stood back to let the others pass.

"Come," the priest invited, and they trudged on for another hundred yards or so, when the tree line stopped abruptly. There before them was the most breathtaking and welcome sight they had ever seen, and had all but given up hope of ever seeing again. In their tired and weakened condition all they could do was stare, numbed by the shock of the vision, and hoping that it was not just a mirage.

The travellers looked out over a well-cultivated vegetable garden laid out in immaculate rows, and being tended by hordes of women and children. Sloping down gently for about a hundred yards to a clear, narrow stream, every square foot of the fertile land was being put to good, productive use. On the opposite bank of the stream they could see a panorama of well-kept flower beds, neatly-arranged bushes and colourful trees whose branches hung heavy with ripening fruit. A carefully manicured lawn joined together these oases of colour, and surrounded two fading white buildings with a faintly Moorish look. Only the reddish hue of laterite creeping up the lower walls distinguished them from some which Derek had seen on travel posters.

The smaller of the buildings was of modest proportions, built of stone or concrete blocks and faced with plaster. The walls were topped by ventilation gaps, looking to Derek like dark, mysterious, probing eyes examining the visitors as they gazed. All the brightly-painted shutters of the many windows were wide open, and a rusting corrugated iron roof projected out far beyond the walls, offering protection from the tropical rains.

There was an open veranda running along the two sides of the house visible from their viewpoint. It was shaded by two creepers, one with blue convolvulus-like flowers, and the other with giant, white snapdragon-like heads with wide petals and yellow centres. Surrounding the house were many, many tall trees. Derek recognised mahogany, kapok, silk-cotton and oil palm, including a huge one from whose splendid head long leaves fell for some fifteen feet. There was one enormous cotton tree in the centre of the flower garden around which a seat had been built, plus a number of young and unbuttressed trees, their tiny leaves making a tracery against the deep blue of the sky.

To the side of the house, and joined only by a covered walk-way, was what looked like a church built of the same materials. The strangers stared in dumbfounded silence at the dull, solitary bell housed in a tall, wide tower rising from the roof of the church. This was topped by a shining copper cross, ablaze with the rays of the late afternoon sun.

Derek, awestruck, read out loud the inscription arranged in a semi-circle over the cavernous church door.

"The Holy Order of Saint Anthony."

Alan took up the smaller wording beneath.

"Lefya Mission."

In a daze, and unable to believe that this really could be true, Derek and his companions were gently coaxed down the path towards the stream, where a wooden foot-bridge united the two sides of this incredible spectacle. They mechanically acknowledged the cheerful greetings waved and shouted at them by the women working in the gardens. Some of the children, naked and laughing, ran up to them to get a closer look, and even tried to touch them as they passed.

Derek pinched himself to make sure that he wasn't dreaming or even hallucinating. They were destitute, at the point of despair and completely lost, mentally as well as physically; it had to be more than mere chance which had delivered them to a House of God.

As they crossed the footbridge and started up the slope towards the house, a bronzed and grey-haired figure descended the steps of the pillared veranda and hurried to greet them. He was dressed in a faded blue shirt and khaki shorts, and had sandals on his feet. He held out both hands to them.

"Welcome, welcome to Saint Anthony's. I am Father Sullivan. Father Paul to my friends, and these people are all my friends."

He waved his arm loosely around the compound.

"It is indeed a merciful God who has led you in this direction. But then I'm sure He's been watching over you all the way."

He shook hands with each of them in turn as they introduced themselves. The priest spoke rapidly in a native tongue to the tribesmen, ending with what Derek judged to be a questioning tone.

The Africans replied with sharp exclamations, nodding their heads vigorously, then laid down the rifles on the veranda and promptly returned the way they had come, smiling and nodding as they passed.

"I was just telling them that they shouldn't breathe a word of this to anyone outside the village, just as a precaution."

He knows, thought Derek. He knows who we are and why we are here.

By this time it seemed as though the entire village, especially those whom Derek had seen working in the gardens, had congregated at the foot of the veranda steps. The plump, gaily-dressed women shrieked and giggled among themselves, while their piccins daringly ran up the steps then retreated, as though curious yet scared of the unsavoury-looking oyibos who has appeared in their midst. Fr. Paul spoke to them tersely in what seemed to be the same language he had used on the men, and they began to retreat and go back to work. One of the women darted up the steps and touched Jean on the breast, not really able to believe that she was actually a woman. Fr. Paul shouted something to her and waved his arms, but Jean smiled benevolently, not seeming to mind the intrusion. The woman cried something unintelligible, and this set off a wave of cheering in the crowd, as though to indicate that Jean had their support, a declaration of feminine kinship. Jean waved back, and a bond was made between them. It was a bond which Jean would renew many times over the coming week, a bond which would ultimately secure the safety of the ailing Henri Gaudet.

The newcomers followed Fr. Paul up the steps towards the house, still unable to believe that they had found a haven of refuge. They noticed that Fr. Simon had disappeared with the party carrying Henri. They hesitated at the top of the steps, being acutely aware of their dishevelled state, and not wanting to stain the gleaming terrazzo floor, but Fr. Paul waved them inside. Their clothes were torn and ragged, ripped almost to shreds by the twigs and thorns through which they had been obliged to scramble. The threads which were still left about their tortured bodies were blood-stained and grimy with a reddish paste of dust and sweat. The men had not shaved for five days, and Jean's tied back golden hair was a dull, lifeless sepia shade, resembling the end of a frayed rope. They were all covered in bites, scratches and cuts, some of which were still oozing blood and others showing signs of infection. Jim wore a coronet of dark brown around his balding dome where a deep gash from an overhanging and unseen branch had crossed and re-opened a previous wound.

They were indeed a sorry and disgusting sight, and began to explain how they came to be in such a condition. The priest was not yet ready to listen. He clucked and fussed around them, calling for water, ointments and bandages. He and Jean began to bathe the worst of their sores.

"All in good time," he repeated with a hint of Irish brogue. "First we must fix you up with somewhere to rest. Emmanuel, please take Madam to the spare room, the one at the end of the hall, and show her where the bathroom is."

Jean finished off tending to Jim's head wound, then followed the steward upstairs.

"Please come with me, gentlemen."

Fr. Paul led the men across the veranda to the back of the residence, where a stilt house was almost hidden in the trees.

"I'll put you in the guest house. It's very primitive, I'm afraid; used to be the old mission until we got the new place built. We don't get many visitors, certainly not four at a time, and it's not worth the trouble and expense of fixing it up. I think you'll find everything you need to sort yourselves out, though, and I'll have some clean clothes sent in to you. Make yourselves at home. Dinner in an hour or so. I'll meet you on the veranda. Now, if you will excuse me?"

Then he strode away briskly, waving as he went.

The guest-house was truly a relic from the past. It was a stilt house of the style favoured by early traders, pre-war government administrators and missionaries. Derek had seen many such buildings, some of them still in use after seventy years. The elevation not only kept the inhabitants safe from the river's seasonal swell, but also made the most of the cool evening breezes which skimmed the tree tops. Foot-long lizards scampered out of their way and disappeared into the walls as the men climbed the stairs.

The foundations of the residence took the form of eight concrete slabs supporting rusty iron girders which rose for some twelve feet to hold up the floor joists. From here the ironwork surrendered to the much more economical and plentiful timber, of which the rest of the house was built as far as the rusty, corrugated iron roof. The exterior walls of the single storey residence were made of thin wooden slats, looking like permanently open louvres and running horizontally the full length of each wall. Through the cracks in the floor they could see the ground below.

They found a large, rectangular sitting room, furnished with the customary wood-frame chairs, and a faded rug in the centre of the worn floorboards. One end of the room contained a cracked dining table and four time-worn chairs. The thick layer of dust confirmed that this room had not been used for a long, long time. There were three small bedrooms, each housing an iron bedstead, a lumpy flock mattress and a chair similar to those in the sitting room. Everything in the place was old, decrepit and musty. It smelled of Old Africa.

Derek, despite his years in West Africa, could scarcely believe the condition of the bathroom. He had seen some primitive facilities in his time, especially when touring in the deep bush, but nothing to compare with this. Not even in the oldest and remotest of stations.

The focus of attention was, of course, the bath tub. Not just for its condition, but also for its positioning, half way along and two feet away from the far wall. It was a typical old, cast iron coffin with carved legs. It had once had a white enamelled interior, but this was now a curious piebald design where decades of brown staining and chips in the surface had been left unattended. The single water pipe was six inches from the ground, a convenient tripping-up height, where it emerged from a rough hole in the side wall. The pipe did not end after delivering its contents to the bath, but took a sharp upwards turn and disappeared through the middle of the ceiling. It re-appeared three feet away and zoomed down at a crazy angle into the ancient water heater where it exploded in a welter of copper, brass and lead in a nightmarish welding job. This ended its run.

The boiler, Derek later learned, was a fairly recent addition to the system, having been donated and installed only forty years ago. It didn't work. There was no spout to let the water out, and Derek could see a blackened hole in the wall where, he assumed, the butane cylinder had once stood.

The rest of the bathroom was a maze of pipes and drains conveying water, in theory at least, to and from the cracked wash basin, the toilet and the bidet, all of which were stained brown with the dirt and rust of ages. It was a nauseating sight.

Despite its disgusting appearance, though, it performed the required function, and as the priest had indicated they found soap, towels, razors and everything else they needed to clean away the sweat, grime and memories of over four days in the jungle. They shared out the assortment of clothes which Father Paul had left in one of the bedrooms, and it was only 45 minutes later that they appeared on the veranda, clean and refreshed. There was no sign of the priest or of Jean. But then Derek had been married long enough to know from experience that it was asking a lot to expect a woman to be ready in the space of an hour, even at the best of times. Considering her starting condition, it could be a while before they saw Jean.

They sat back on the wicker chairs and looked out across the tranquil scene. The activity in the vegetable garden had ceased as the sun, far, far away, slipped down into the forest. Beyond the tree line the smoke from a hundred cooking fires made dark smudges against the horizon. An occasional laugh rang out from the boys' quarters, a semi-detached life but dependent on the big house for its existence.

The familiar figure of a beaming, white-uniformed steward appeared with three glasses of beer.

"Cool", Emmanuel told them. "Not cold proppa, because fridge only get kerosene power, not make t'ings cold good like 'lectric fridge. I keep tell farder we go get 'lectric like my brodder where work for forestry mastah, but him say cost too much for gen'ratah - no fit pay for. So I go make gen'ratah some time wid old car engine".

And he probably could too, thought Derek. The ingenuity of the so-called illiterate African peasants never failed to amaze him. The idea of making a functional electric generator from an old car engine was preposterous to the European mind. Yet he had seen many such apparent miracles performed, and he had no doubt that it would be accomplished, sooner or later.

The visitors smiled and sipped the beverage gratefully.

"Best tasting beer I've ever had in my whole life", Derek told Emmanuel, not without some truth, and to the obvious delight of the steward, who went away smiling and nodding.

The master-servant relationship is as old as evolution itself. There have always been those who command and those commanded, although progressively down the civilisations these relationships have changed in substance and description. Such is the case with Europe's involvement in Africa. Derek, only mechanically aware of his companions' chatter, found himself contemplating the subject.

Up until very recent times it had been clear and predictable. The European explorer, conqueror, coloniser, was the undisputed master, and the Africans in his service were known, referred to and summoned simply as "boy". This was no longer the case. Various constitutional moves had termed the White Man as "employer" or "manager", and the African now commanded the greater self-respect of being called "employee", or "steward", or whatever was his calling. There were even some instances, particularly in government circles, where the roles were reversed, and many prominent and influential Africans insisted that their white subordinates address them as "sir".

A far, far cry from the wicked, immoral and guilt-ridden days of the slave-trading holocaust.

Slavery was still prevalent, as was inevitable among tribal kinships. Officially it was banned by government decree, but total subservience to elders and superiors is the very essence of Africa's tribal-based lifestyle. Not the White Man's problem now, Derek told himself.

Father Sullivan eventually appeared from around the side of the house. He was now attired in the customary white linen cassock of a Catholic priest in the tropics. He was followed by Jean somewhat hesitantly, who was dressed in a red chequered shirt, tails tied at the waist, and a very large pair of khaki shorts held up by a piece of rope. There was a twinkle in the priest's eye.

"The best we could do", he explained, pointing to Jean. "We certainly don't cater to ladies in distress. Or any other dress, if it comes to that".

He chuckled to himself at the pun he had just made.

"Now, I believe dinner is ready. Bring your drinks with you, by all means."

They followed him into the house, and were joined by Father Simon. Father Simon answered the question which was on everyone's lips before they could ask it.

"Just a touch of malaria. Nothing too serious - I've seen worse. The next few days will be rough for your friend, but he'll come out of it soon. The fever is still severe, and his temperature is high, but time will be the best healer."

He smiled around the group as he sat down at the table, his gleaming teeth matching the whiteness of his cassock.

"I fear he is a little too old and out of shape to be playing in the forest."

"Father Sullivan", began James after everyone had taken a seat at the cracked but polished table. He was interrupted by a wave of the priest's hand.

"Everyone calls me 'Father Paul'. The Sullivan part is only used when I sign papers and receive mail." The scorched skin on his face wrinkled into a deep smile.

"Father Paul", resumed James. "I feel that we owe you an explanation. It appears that you have saved our lives, more-or-less".

Father Paul waved again.

"More likely that The Lord has been on your side this day. But why don't we eat first, then you can tell me about it after dinner? Although I expect I know the gist of it already". He glanced around their puzzled faces. "The drums, you know. The bush telegraph.

Even in this modern age, the drums are still an important and largely accurate means of spreading news. But let's eat."

This was their first cooked meal in five days, and they attacked it greedily. They neither knew nor cared what they ate, and Derek cleared his plate twice. It was an excellent meal, but he had been so hungry at the start of it that he hadn't given much thought to the skill of the cook until it was all finished.

"A wonderful dinner, Father. Thank you so much. I can't remember when I last enjoyed a meal so much".

There was a chorus of consent from the others, and they moved away from the table to enjoy a cup of steaming and aromatic coffee. All except Father Simon, that is, who excused himself to check on his new patient. When they had settled themselves in the crude but comfortable armchairs they began to tell their story.

They started with the night of the arrest, each person putting in a detail or two as a thought came to mind. The sequence of events was unfolded to the priest, who kept nodding at certain points, as if to indicate that he was already aware of the occurrence. Although Derek had never held or even been exposed to any Catholic sentiments, he couldn't help wondering if this was what it was like to be in the confessional. The difference was that this time they had already performed the penance.

The priest listened intently until the twilight turned into total blackness, by which time the story tellers had reached the point of their arrival at the Mission.

Father Paul shook his head and offered up a prayer for those who had suffered an untimely death, ending it with "and may the Good Lord take care of them and forgive them for all their faults, whatever the motive." He then glanced at the big clock on the wall and stood up.

"A truly remarkable story, and of course it's far from being over yet. You're welcome to stay here for as long as you think fit, but I must warn you that Government soldiers won't be very far behind. As for your sick friend, he has no choice. I'm told that it will be well over a week before he has enough strength to travel, so if we get word of soldiers nearby, you'll have to leave him behind. He's in good hands, though. Apart from Father Simon, who is proficient in first aid, we have among our little flock an ex-army medical orderly, and malaria is no stranger to us. Oh, and I mustn't forget the expertise of Miss Sheldon, here, while she's available".

It was the first time Derek had heard Jean's other name. Jean Sheldon.

Father Paul spoke out again.

You must excuse me now. It's time for the evening Mass. You are welcome to join us, if you feel so inclined, although I assume that none of you is a Catholic?"

It was more of a statement than a question.

He glanced sharply at his guests.

"Or alternatively, I'm sure you will sleep well."

Then he left them, and they saw him pass the window and walk towards his little church.

The visitors fell silent, looking around, looking at their feet, at the ceiling, anywhere but at each other.

"Well?" Jean stood up. "What about it? Don't you think we have something to be thankful for?"

Derek slowly raised himself from his seat.

"I-er-suppose we do. I'll come with you."

They left James and Alan sprawled in the easy chairs, but before they had reached the doors of the church, Derek heard the double pad of feet behind them. He felt an unexplainable twinge of disappointment. They waited until the other two had caught up with them, then entered the church. The small building was crammed with Africans, their heads bowed in simple piety.

"Now I know how a sardine feels", muttered Alan, as he squeezed himself into a pew next to Derek.

"Sshh! You're in a church, not a pub".

Jean's rebuke was cutting and effective, and Alan sulkily bowed his head along with the others.

Derek was hardly aware of what was going on during the ceremony, performing the appropriate actions of tribute with the rest of the congregation in a semi-trance. He wasn't a particularly religious man, but did feel a little overcome by the wonderment of their reprieve. He silently reproached himself severely for going through life without ever really taking time out to give thanks. Of course, he was also squashed into the pew very tightly next to Jean....

They didn't see the priest again that evening. They were drained, mentally and physically, and each fell into a deep, peaceful sleep.

17

Derek awoke the next morning when the African sun was already well into its ascent. The shuttered windows threw thin horizontal bars of light across the floor and up on to the bed. As the fuzzy absurdities of slumber dropped away, he realised that he was alone in the room. Well, why shouldn't he be? He pushed back the mosquito net and walked slowly towards the window. As he opened the shutters a flood of brilliance poured in, causing him to blink and turn away. When his eyes had become accustomed to the dazzling brightness, he looked out on the scene below. The gardens were once again a hive of activity as the villagers maintained the interminable battle against Nature's encroachment. Damp cobwebs spangled the lawn surrounding the house, and the exotic scents from extravagant tropical blossoms reached up to his nostrils.

He could see James and Alan sitting in lawn chairs under the immense shade of an oil-bean tree. They saw him framed in the window and waved. A sharp knock on the bedroom door made him turn around in time to see a smiling steward enter with a tea tray. It reminded him of his bachelor days. In a household not accustomed to the presence of females the steward would rarely wait for the customary "come in" before entering, and he had an uncanny knack of knowing when Mastah was awake.

"Farder him say ask what you like for breakfast, sah."

"Whatever's going, Emmanuel. I leave it to you and cook. I'm sure it will be good, whatever it is."

Emmanuel smiled his way out. Derek contemplated whether he should take the tea and join his friends outside, but decided against it and sat down on one of the wicker chairs.

He sipped the tea slowly and cast his mind back to the previous week when the nightmare had started. He had been arrested, beaten and imprisoned. He had been held captive in a hotel and told that he must work for the Kumangan Government, to do whatever they instructed within the framework of his commercial powers. And that was without, he realised with a shudder, any real guarantee of being released unharmed when they had no further use for him. He had witnessed, and in fact been a party to, a deliberate, cold-blooded murder, flown out of the country in a tiny aircraft which had of necessity landed in a seemingly neutral country. He had been further detained, and told that he was to be sent back to face retribution for his crimes. He had again escaped, and experienced another murder. He realised just how much of this action had been due to the efforts of the ever-active Axel Svensen, and sent up a silent prayer for his salvation, according to Father Paul's wish.

That was enough to satisfy any man's desire for excitement, but it wasn't all. He had seen two of his colleagues horribly killed, and had driven away in a stolen car. He had spent close to five days in the jungle, totally unprepared for such an ordeal, been involved in a third killing, and just when it seemed hopeless to keep going, he had stumbled across this Utopia, where kind people were taking care of him. It had been an exhausting, frustrating week, and it was little wonder that he felt drained.

Although much of the tension of the last few days had already begun to ebb away, he was not yet ready to relax totally. He was safe at the moment, but it was like being in the eye of a hurricane - there was more to come before he could say that the ordeal was over. The longer they stayed at the Mission, the greater would be the risk of discovery and recapture. It would also mean plunging his hosts into great danger, should their whereabouts become known. It was all right for Father Paul to say that he and his followers were above suspicion, that his influence and reputation would protect him from trouble with the authorities, but every man has his price. Somewhere among the villagers, someone would succumb to Government pressure or promise, and Father Paul would have to do a lot of praying and persuading to keep himself out of trouble. Obviously, Henri Gaudet wouldn't be in a position to travel for a while, and that posed another problem.

And then there was Jean. Jean had come into his life to add a further complication, to change it and throw a cloud over it. He had never shown any interest in other women until last week, until she came to him, to torment him, to involve him in a guilt which he did not need. Try as he might, Derek couldn't push the memory of that night in Qedar out of his mind. It was the night he had succumbed to the most basic of human urges. Jean was getting to him like no other woman had ever got to him, except for Debbie. He wondered where she was sleeping, and if they would ever again....

He stopped the thought right there, and stood up. He finished his tea and ambled into the bathroom, where he washed and shaved unhurriedly. They would probably stay for a few days, relaxing and recovering, trying to build up their strength before planning the next step.

He went downstairs and was met by James and Alan, who were coming in for breakfast.

"Sleeping the sleep of the sinful, eh?", asked Alan.

"What do you mean by that?"

Derek felt a rush of guilt, and hoped that it didn't show. Had somebody been talking?

"Well, nothing really. It's just an expression, you know..."

Jean entered the room, and the three men looked towards her. She looked radiant.

"Sleep well?", asked James.

"Like a log. Best night's sleep I've had for a long time."

She stole a sly, smirking glance at Derek, who turned his head away in embarrassment.

Over breakfast they discussed their plight and tried to formulate some sort of plan for their next move. They were well aware of the risk to which they were putting the Mission and the priests by staying. Father Paul had insisted that the villagers of his flock were truly devout, and would not be inclined to divulge that there were four fugitives in their midst. But Derek, James and Alan had all been in the world of business long enough not to trust everyone at face value, priest or not. They were grateful for the respite, but keen to press on. At the end of the meal, they had resolved to wait for two or three days. This would give them chance to fully recover, and to check on Gaudet's progress.

The following days passed peacefully and uneventfully, during which time they learned much about the mission, its occupants and the surrounding countryside. It was a rough, tough, unglamourous part of the world where Nature had been in control since time began. She still was, in fact, apart form the efforts of a handful of people such as the priests. They were completely surrounded by forest, and the mission was accessible only by a few hand-hewn tracks plus one semi-serviceable laterite road, which became impassable to vehicles during the rains.

The stream which ran through the compound emptied itself a quarter of a mile away into a small lagoon known as Igba Pool. The Pool, as it was simply known, had formed at the bend of a small river, barely more than a stream itself, and was crystal clear and shallow, with a small but secluded sandy beach dappled by the sunlight filtering in through the leaves of the tall trees. It was a haven of relaxation, and the visitors made the most of the opportunity to swim and laze, allowing the distressing events of the past few days to seep away.

The rivulet was fast-flowing but not deep, inviting its guests to be carried along by the current until their feet touched one of the many submerged sandbars. They could then follow a well-trodden path through the bush back to the lagoon. Although it was only a couple of hundred yards or so, they were hot and sweating when they arrived back at the Pool, and ready once again for the delightfully refreshing waters.

They were never completely alone. The presence of a stranger anywhere in Africa's backwoods, especially one with a white skin, immediately attracted a horde of black piccins, laughing and giggling. They stared endlessly at the strangers, more out of curiosity than rudeness. Derek did find himself lying very close to Jean on a couple of occasions, but such was their perpetual audience that all they could do was talk, albeit intimately.

The four strangers were looked upon with some suspicion at first by the villagers, particularly in view of their ghastly state during their first encounter in the bush. After a couple of days, however, the happy, carefree Africans began to treat them with respect and even affection when it became obvious that they were Father Paul's friends and guests. Jean was especially admired, since some of the villagers had never before seen a white woman at close quarters. To Derek, who had spent all his West Coast career dealing with profit-motivated market people, this was a delightful and refreshing encounter. This was the true African native, who had a deep respect for Nature, and lived the simple traditional life of his ancestors.

The focus of life among Africans is the family, or rather the extended family. Unlike some cultures, Africans do not dispose of their old and infirm when their usefulness in the community comes to an end. Rather, the aged are revered and respected, their experience and worldly wisdom valued and utilised by the young. It is not uncommon to see a wrinkled old crone taking charge of a brood of youngsters so that the mother might attend to her chores unhampered, or even join her husband in the fields.

Children are truly regarded as the resource of the future, and a man is measured by the number of offspring he can produce. This is particularly true in the case of male children, whose strength can be counted on to help ease the toil of existence as they grow older. Alternatively, a clan, or perhaps a whole village, will contribute to the education of a promising youngster, knowing that when the protégé becomes a successful professional or businessman, he will, in turn, help to support his benefactors financially for the rest of his life.

Africans adore children. It is not uncommon to come across a white child who prefers the company of a steward, a nursemaid or even a garden-boy over adult members of his own race. Despite crushing poverty, extensive mal-nutrition and below-adequate health standards brought about by squalid conditions, African families are close, protective and for the most part happy. There are exceptions, of course. Some individuals, reaching a level of sophistication where they emulate their white colleagues, begin to look disdainfully at tribal lifestyles, and make no secret of their contempt for traditional values. This attitude, like the firearms and venereal diseases brought in by the early European adventurers, is an insidious but unavoidable fact of life, which is part of that influence called "civilisation".

Derek often recalled with amusement an incident which had occurred a number of years ago when he was a department manager. He learned that his chief storekeeper had just become a father for the third time. After extending his congratulations to the proud parent on the birth of another son, he expressed his wishes that there would be many more such joyous occasions. The response was surprising.

"No, sah, no more piccin."

At a loss to understand this unusual and morose reaction, Derek asked why there would be no more piccins.

"Because, sah, I hear say on radio dis morning dat every fourth child born in de world be Chinese. An' I no want Chinese baby."

All members of the same family, the same clan and even the same tribe, are brothers. It took Derek a while to get used to hearing his traders and staff refer to someone with a totally different name as "my brother". He tried to picture a lawyer and a bus driver who had grown up in the same suburb of Birmingham referring to one another as "my brother". Perhaps the white races still had a lot to learn.

Derek and James spent many hours chatting with Father Paul

on all manner of topics, but mainly on the politics of Africa. The task of converting the natives from paganism, animism and other traditional cults had started over a hundred years ago. It had been a slow, grinding process, but the missionaries, and specifically The Order of Saint Anthony, could be proud of its efforts. The peace and tranquillity of the surroundings led Derek and James, inevitably perhaps, to reflect on the remarkable record of missionary work which had been undertaken in the past while the very foundations of modern Africa were being laid. It struck them as an incredible story of Christian vitality, creativity and commitment. From whatever sub-faith or tradition these early men (and women, occasionally) came, their contribution in terms of development and human relationships cannot be measured. The Church in Africa today owes everything to that period of immense effort and self-sacrifice.

The much-maligned "missionary invasion", with all its compromises and limitations, managed to do some exceedingly useful work. It began when conquest and colonialism had all but destroyed the traditional social systems, and it served to provide the positive and creative elements in the community. It has long been felt, but rarely admitted, that the early colonial powers in and around West Africa uphold an immense sense of guilt for their very considerable part in the slave trade of the seventeenth and eighteenth centuries. This is recognised as perhaps the greatest imposed period of human misery and degradation in all of history. Although it is an undisputed fact that slavery had been part of Africa's tradition for many centuries before the advent of the White Man, the very concept of slavery itself is in direct opposition to the basic dogmas of Christianity. It is thought, in some moral quarters, that the enthusiasm, the devotion and ultimately the success of the Christian Missionary movement has helped to atone in some ways for these early crimes against mankind, and perhaps lifted some of the guilt.

Whatever the extent of the theorising, there is no doubt that without the unbelievable hardships suffered by the missionaries of God on those early days of Africa's awakening, modern Africa would be missing one of the most vital and important ingredients of its present life-style.

This was significantly evident at Lefya where, apart from the ever-present and ever-powerful juju which still raised its ugly head on occasions, the surrounding villages in the parish had come to accept Christianity. Father Paul was worshipped almost as much as The Lord Himself.

Derek had come across the power of ju-ju many times, as they all had, and it gave him an uneasy feeling. James Barrett had, in fact, been the victim of one such episode, and although his Christian upbringing would not permit him to subscribe in any way to supernatural beliefs outside of the Church's own dictates, the incident had left him very puzzled and somewhat hesitant to condemn the superstitious practice outright. Like most sane-minded and clear-thinking Europeans, James had at first scoffed at the idea of witchcraft in any degree, but now he wasn't quite so sceptical.

One of his functions as a bank manager was to advance money to farmers and agriculture dealers to help with the vital cocoa and palm oil crops. One such operator had secured from James the princely sum of ten thousand pounds, but instead of applying it to his business, as intended, he diverted most of it to other "undisclosed" uses. James followed the prescribed bank procedures in a vain attempt to recover the advance, and eventually called in a senior loans executive from Head Office to handle the somewhat sensitive matter. The Loans Director made the position quite clear. The transgressor must pay up within a given period of time, or face court proceedings, which would not only enforce repayment, but would also cause the dealer a great amount of embarrassment, and reflect on his prestige within the community. Having finally elicited a promise from the reluctant dealer to comply with the Bank's demands, James and his visitor went off to dine at the Club, a process which ran into several hours.

On their return to James's bungalow later that evening, they found an array of sticks, stones, feathers, bones and blood smears adorning the veranda - unmistakable evidence of a powerful ju-ju. They shrugged off the threat as a primitive means of trying to scare them into changing their position, and in fact treated the matter with some amusement.

The following day, as James was about to take his guest to the airport, his car would not start. Nothing seemed to be out of order mechanically, but the engine just refused to fire. The executive took a taxi to the airport, vowing never again to return to Ugbeshu.

For the following two weeks, until James went on leave, there was nothing which he or the experts could do to make the car run. James had intended selling it anyway, since he had planned to pick up a new home delivery one while on vacation, so he left instructions for it to be sold off at the best price it would bring. When he came back, he was amazed to find that when the purchaser had handed over his money and changed the ownership registration, the car had sprung into life, as if by magic. Perhaps it ***was*** magic, he found himself guiltily wondering.

At any rate, the car was still running up to a couple of weeks ago, and being driven by no less a person than the unrepentant cocoa dealer himself.

Father Paul had been in Africa for almost forty of his sixty-nine years, and had, in fact, been in charge of the Mission for the past twenty-five. During this time he had become almost as familiar with the local languages and customs as he was with his own, but his faith never wavered.

Paul Patrick Sullivan had been born into a large, impoverished family in the heart of Liverpool's slum area. His father had emigrated from Ireland as a young man with the after-effects of the potato famine burned deeply into his memory, in search of a decent life, away from the poverty and misery of his childhood. He never found it. The only work open to him, as a coarse, illiterate peasant, was at the dockside, whenever he was lucky enough find a crew which was short-handed. He met and married a good, sensible Catholic girl who was not too proud to earn a few extra shillings by taking in washing for the more affluent. Between them they struggled for twenty-five years to raise their nine children according to the teachings of the Church, until the weary and faded woman, old before her years, could work no longer, and went to join her Creator for eternity. Heartbroken at the loss of his wife, Sean Sullivan turned to the whisky bottle for consolation, and his body was fished out of the River Mersey a few weeks later.

Paul's four elder brothers went to fight for England's cause in the Great War, and never returned. It has always been a deep moment of pride in an Irish family to see one of their sons enter the priesthood, and Paul's only regret was that there were few of them left to witness the event.

After his ordination he immediately volunteered for missionary service in the emerging areas of the Dark Continent, and was sent to the fledgling mission in Lefya. He had been home several times, but could not, on those occasions, identify with what used to be "home". The slum areas of Liverpool, as with most urban centres, had been cleared, and replaced by newer, high-reaching slums made from concrete. His holidays were depressingly boring, and he could hardly wait for them to end when he could return to his real home in the hot, humid forests of Africa.

As he told his guests, they saw very few white faces in that part of the country. In fact, apart from the occasions when they travelled the fifty miles or so to Zekwi for supplies which they were unable to grow or make, they were quite on their own. They preferred it that way, although they were always prepared to extend a sincere welcome to anyone who happened along. This they had just demonstrated. They ministered to the whims of their flock in every conceivable fashion. Looking after the spiritual needs was but a small part of their lives, as Derek and his friends observed during their stay. They had to be teachers, physicians, farmers, counsellors, tutors, judges and law-enforcers. They had to direct, advise, encourage, demonstrate, decide, supervise and above all understand anything and everything with which the people in their parish were involved. All of this they performed with kindness, generosity, goodwill and patience in an environment which would have severely strained the faith of the Apostles themselves.

Father Simon, they learned, was in his mid-thirties, and had been singled out many years earlier by Father Paul as being a highly intelligent, receptive and emotionally sincere youth, with an uncanny perception of the plight of his fellow Africans in their struggle to accept "modern" ways. He had adapted readily and devotedly to the doctrines of the Roman Catholic Church, and it had not come as any surprise to the priests when he had asked for an opportunity to take Holy Orders. It had been a painstaking, uphill struggle, but after many years of study and self-sacrifice, including a two-year spell in a Nigerian seminary, Simon Agembo Ngora had been ordained as a fully-fledged priest. He had requested an immediate assignment to the mission at his native Lefya, a move which Father Paul heartily endorsed and pulled strings at the highest level to secure. The source of his medical knowledge was a mystery to everyone. It was assumed that he had picked it up while in Nigeria, with a bit of instinctive but unauthorised native medicine thrown in. Whatever the origin and the practices, there was no doubt that he seemed to be able to cure people.

Father Simon was idolised by the villagers. He had the tenderness of an angel, the compassion of a saint, and the understanding of one who had grown up in the immediate area. He was, as Father Paul pointed out, the Mission's greatest asset, undeniable evidence of the Church's commitment to Africa and Africans. It was expected that eventually Simon Ngora would become one of Bujavi's first black bishops - an appointment which would give Father Paul more satisfaction than anything else he might achieve in his already notable ministry.

Sometimes the village children would offer to take the visitors for a walk through the dense forest, which was obviously their playground. They would scamper through the trees ahead of their new white-skinned friends like birds, stopping occasionally to allow the less agile adults to catch up. They would hop gleefully over fallen logs, which were waiting for what was left of their termite-ridden carcasses to rot into oblivion. All the time their chatter, unintelligible to anyone but themselves, proved to Derek that they were part of Nature itself. Derek experienced the curious sensation of living in the present and the past at the same time, as though a moving picture had been stopped at a single frame with the pattern of millennia frozen for him to perceive.

The forest lives by no rules or laws except its own. Life among the plants flourishes in what appears to the orderliness of the human mind to be a state of utter confusion. Leaves fall and nurture the soil, paving the way for more buds, more flowering, more breeding and ultimately more shedding, all of which seems to be occurring simultaneously. A whole season can pass in one day, yet there is no spring and no autumn. The forest is a giant greenhouse, offering the perpetual heat and moisture necessary to stimulate plant life. Tree roots crawl along the ground like serpents, or rise high in the air like flying buttresses intent on pushing the top-most branches into the freedom of the open sky. The "law of the jungle" is a term often used to describe the cruel self-serving elements of Man's behaviour, and was aptly applied to Derek's commercial cut-throat world. Yet no human would dare to emulate the ferocity, the self-preservation, the means-to survival which the jungle must practice in order to stay in existence.

Father Paul was a mine of informed knowledge. Despite all the years which his guests had spent in Africa, it was refreshing for them to talk to this fascinating man on subjects to which they had hardly given a thought.

"Our doctors and scientists," the priest pointed out one evening after dinner, "are to be commended for the advances they have made in saving and prolonging lives in undeveloped parts of the world such as this, particularly in terms of child mortality. But the consequences pose a new and different sort of threat, which so far has scarcely been addressed."

"Consider it this way. If all goes well, every surviving infant will need to consume, during its life, somewhere around twenty-two tons of staples, be it rice, maize, millet, wheat or whatever. In addition, he'll need the meat from several large animals such as cows, deer or bullocks, hundreds of chickens and three tons of fish. To supplement this, he will expect to eat an indeterminable amount of vegetables, fruit and other extras, to say nothing of his anticipated water consumption. This means that over the next two generations the food requirement for Africa, Asia, South America and other regions will double. This is before we can even start to add in the descendants of those we've saved."

"Where will all this extra food come from? Which land will grow it? Who will be able to afford to pay for its cultivation? Eight out of ten Africans are already undernourished, and I shudder to think what the situation will be like in a hundred years' time."

"If you starve city people, they riot. If you starve country people, they die. The erosion of the peasants' political power compares with that of the soil beneath their feet. So to whom should the politicians listen? Who keeps them in power? Food crops don't receive Government subsidies. The food will just get eaten and be of no economic value to the country. No, my friends, the subsidies go to the cash crops such as cocoa, tobacco, cotton, palm oil, and so on. For these are the ones which can earn their worth on the export market. Food crops can't."

"This continent's agricultural situation is in a mess because its original principles were forged by foreigners, keen to pull whatever benefits they could out of Africa while the going was good. Well, the going is not so good now they've left, but do they care? Will they come back and feed the people they've mislead? Will they pay to retrain the farmers, to teach them how to grow food the local people can eat, instead of what they can ship overseas? I don't think so!"

"As I said, doctors and scientists are doing a wonderful job of preserving and prolonging life, but, God forgive me for saying so, I can't help wondering whether interfering with Nature will be for the eventual good of Mankind or prove, in the long run, to be a total catastrophe."

It was a deep, philosophical topic, and one on which Father Paul obviously had strong views. They could offer no answer, nor did they even try.

Derek's respect for the devotion of the missionaries who gave their entire lives to Africa increased by a hundred fold. He had always regarded them, in his busy commercial affairs, as something of a joke - a relic from the last century, out of touch with the real world, and totally obsolete in their contribution to the modern world. This was an opinion which he now abandoned as he came face to face with the real sincerity, the real purpose of a missionary's devotion.

It wasn't all work, though, as Father Paul and Father Simon related to them. There were occasions, rare occasions, when the four priests at the mission would find themselves together in the evening after Mass, with nothing of an urgent nature to claim their time. Then they would shed their habits, both physical and mental, and sit around together as though they were in a prestigious London men's club, reading old newspapers, discussing world affairs, playing Monopoly, drinking whisky, and even telling jokes. It was valuable down-time, total relaxation, and seemed to refresh them for the next day's tasks.

These moments of leisure were treasured, but it would be wrong to say that it was their only enjoyment. The very nature of the work itself was both enjoyment and fulfilment. Derek and his companions were not to have the opportunity of experiencing such a "night off", since the other two priests were away on a re-stocking expedition, which they combined with a tour of the villages in the parish. The priests had a radio transmitter at the mission, but it was rarely used. So deep were they in the jungle that their ability to transmit, and even to receive, was greatly hampered. Apart from which, re-charging the battery was a complicated process involving an ingenious bicycle-powered charging contraption, no doubt contrived by the ingenious Emmanuel. It was with extreme reluctance and after much soul searching that Father Paul consented to the attaching of a copper rod to the top of the magnificent cross to act as an antenna.

"Only in the interests of common sense and very much against my moral views of the sanctity of God's house." But it was, after all, the only high structure to be of any use as a radio mast.

So far as Father Paul could remember, the radio had not been used more than a dozen times, all of them being emergencies. Still, it was comforting to know that it was there if needed. Over the past few days, though, it had been manned continuously in the hope of picking up any news regarding the search for the fugitives.

Their stay coincided with a "second burial". This was a celebration of great joy for the relatives and friends of the deceased, all of whom contributed food, palm-wine, money, or just plain help in an all-out effort to send the dead person to join his ancestors in style. The first burial, the actual interment of the corpse immediately after death, was a mournful and sad affair, usually attended by the sacrifice of goats or fowl and a great deal of weeping and wailing. After a period of mourning, not usually more than a year, the second burial was a release to everyone. The deceased was released from his "waiting period" before acceptance into the distinguished company of his forefathers, and the mourners were released from their dutiful vigil. It was in complete contrast to the first burial, being more of a festive occasion. There were bands, parades, dancing, feasting and overwhelming happy relief.

"Until just a few years ago," Father Paul told his British guests, "an indispensable part of the first burial ceremony was human sacrifice. Depending on the rank or wealth of the deceased, as many as 100 slave wives would either be killed outright, or have their arms and legs broken, then they would be laid at the bottom of the grave as a sort of lining. After the burial the guests would have a huge banquet of human flesh, and hope that they would be given the skull of one of the victims as a souvenir. It was a long, uphill battle to stop that practice, but we won in the end."

Jean couldn't help a shudder as she listened. Thank God she was a European and not an African, living now and not in those days.

The white guests marvelled at the energy with which the Africans tended the gardens and made the most of what the fertile land could offer. There was no shortage of food, or its variety. The staple diet was still gari, yams and plantains, but with an abundance of meat. Apart from bush-pig, duiker and guinea-fowl and a host of other creatures which roamed wild for the taking, the mission kept its own stocks of chickens, turkeys and goats. The chickens were a ludicrous blue colour.

"They dye them with indigo to discourage hawks from making off with them," explained Father Paul when questioned. The priests were able, from time to time, to purchase a cow from the nomads who scraped a living by driving herds of emaciated Zebu cattle from the north to southern markets.

"And that's all we can expect in the way of beef," the priest told his visitors.

"Trypanosomiasis."

Father Simon looked around the blank faces.

"Other wise known as sleeping sickness. Carried by the tsetse fly. Affects most equine and bovine life in these parts. These sorry-looking specimens you see around here are the result of a genetic experiment. It was found that by breeding Zebu with Ndama cattle the blood parasite, for some reason, couldn't flourish as it does in other species."

Assorted fruits were served with every meal. Mango, paw-paw, banana, citrus and even strawberries were served - sometimes separately and sometimes in the wonderful and familiar "jungle juice" assortment. A special delicacy was said to be a portion of certain snakes, but this was a treat which the Europeans declined.

At least, as far as they knew – there were so many new and different tastes offered to their palates that for much of the time they had no idea what they were eating.

Six days passed in all, six days of relaxation, talking over the situation and recovering from their jungle ordeal. At the back of Derek's mind all the time was the knowledge that it couldn't last much longer. Pleasant and restful as the interlude was, sooner or later they would have to make plans to move on, before their pursuers eventually got wind of their whereabouts.

They found the evenings to be the most fascinating, as they sat on the veranda at dusk and talked with - or, more usually, listened to - Father Paul. Sometimes they would take a slow stroll around the gardens, and even the village beyond. They could see the glow of a candle or home-made paraffin lamp by the door of every village dwelling, looking from a distance like stars which had come down to earth, bringing comfort and light to help the inhabitants through the long, black night. At close quarters it seemed as though the village itself was aglow, but gently, as Nature would prefer.

Derek fully expected (or was it hoped?) that Jean would show some further signs of her interest in him. Beyond their many and deep conversations, however, there was nothing. Was she waiting for him to make the first move this time? Come to think of it, James seemed to be paying her more attention than he used to. But then it could just be that James hadn't had many dealings with women, and this could be a new experience for him.

Derek shook himself mentally. This is absurd, he told his reflection in the mirror. We have far more important things to think about than a twinge of imaginary jealousy, however justified it might be.

On the morning of the seventh day, as the visitors were lazing on the veranda and chatting with Father Paul, the peaceful serenity was shattered by an agitated voice coming from the very depths of the bush itself.

"Fa' Paul! Fa' Paul! Mgba edeji nkadu! Fa' Paul!"

Father Paul stopped talking and stood up with an anxious look on his face. A half-naked youth burst out of the trees, ran through the garden, across the foot-bridge and up to the veranda, where he flung himself exhaustedly at the priest's feet. He was gasping and croaking, but so furious and fast were his words that even Father Paul couldn't understand him.

The priest made the boy sit on a chair to recover his breath and composure, and spoke to him slowly but firmly in a native tongue.

The youth nodded and spoke with urgency, arms waving and eyes rolling as he relayed what was obviously a message of extreme importance. When he had finished speaking, Father Paul turned solemnly to his guests.

"This is Jaju. He lives in the next village, about four miles from here. The headman sent him with a warning. This morning they heard the drums saying that government troops have found the car. They're spreading a search net in all directions. So far they haven't picked up your trail, but it's only a matter of time before they do. You must leave immediately."

Derek knew it had to come, sooner or later. In a way it was a relief. They were well rested, and the sooner they left, the less would be the chances of involving their kindly hosts in cruel retribution. But what about Henri? He was up and about, but still too weak to face the forest again just yet. This was where Father Paul again displayed his courage and selflessness. When the searchers arrived, if they ever did, the Frenchman would be secluded in the chapel, masquerading as a visiting priest confined to prayer - they would think of a reason why. Many of the hunters would be

Catholics; even the Muslims among them would respect the sanctity of a Holy man at prayer, infidel or not. Derek and James didn't like the idea, but it was the only one available. If anyone could pull it off, Father Paul could.

When this ploy had been worked out, they set about provisioning themselves with water and as much food as they could carry. They armed themselves with ropes, knives and machetes, then sat down with Father Paul to work out a route which would be the most likely to gain them their freedom, and a rough map was drawn. They decided against taking the stolen rifles. There was very little ammunition left anyway, and it was unlikely that they would have enough fire-power to be able to shoot their way out of a tight situation, should one be encountered. The guns would be more of a hindrance than a help. Alan and one of Fr. Paul's trusted flock buried them in a deep pit below the compost heap.

It was time for farewells. Jean was reluctant to go while Henri still needed her professional attention, but agreed that her presence would be nothing but an embarrassment to the priests if the soldiers should happen to come. He appeared to be in good hands, anyway.

The visitors were profuse with gratitude, which the priests brushed off as being "God's deliverance". They bowed their heads while Father Paul asked for Divine help in setting them free from their burdens, and he hugged each one in turn. They vowed to repay the Mission someday for its kindness, although had no inkling of how they were going to be able to do so.

Then the travellers were ready once again for the reclusive forest. They picked up their belongings, and trudged off into the gloomy, chattering shelter of the rain forest.

18

They pushed their way once again through the undergrowth, the now familiar if forbidding jungle, but this time they were more prepared in mind and spirit for what they had to face. They had left the mission just after lunch when the sun was at its zenith, and the village was taking that most civilised aspect of supposedly uncivilised areas, the siesta. It was now two weeks since their first internment, but it seemed like a lifetime. Acting on the directions given to them by Father Paul, their plan was to strike out for the border between Bujavi and Séjumé, but not, this time, in the direction of Zekwi, which had been their original intention when they had driven off in the stolen car. According to Father Paul's map they were to take a dog-leg route to a point where the River Zakurdi separated the two countries. How they would cross the river had not yet been decided, but that was a problem they would deal with when it arose.

"Like crossing our bridge when we've made one," Alan had joked in his usual flippant way.

After a steady trudge of four hours, which were uneventful apart from the flow of optimistic conversation, they stopped for a meal and a welcome rest. Then they were on their way again until darkness began to surround them, and they had to surrender themselves to the whims of the African night. They slept little and badly in shifts of a few hours each, Jean insisting on taking her turn on sentry watch as well as the men. The night passed without incident, and they welcomed the dawn with the attitude of those who had been spared to see another sunrise.

During the second day they came to the road which Father Paul had told them would help speed their progress. To call it a road was stretching the bounds of credibility a bit. It was scarcely more than one truck's width, built by the United States during their oil search days to act as a supply route from Zekwe harbour to their drill sites. The past dozen or so years had seen the surface deteriorate to its present pitiful state, as federal and regional authorities argued as to whose responsibility it was to repair it. No-one conceded or accepted this responsibility, and it was even suggested that they should ask the Americans to come back and fix up "their" road.

Despite its condition, which was now more laterite than tarmac, it was infinitely easier than forcing a path through the jungle. Or at least it would have been, were it not for the occasional vehicles which bumped and rolled along it, forcing the travellers to take cover.

The original building of the road had been quite a feat of engineering. It had been cut through the jungle, thick and tangled, as a giant thresher would cut through a wheat field. Every few hundred yards Derek and his companions would have to traverse a narrow bridge, sometimes wooden, sometimes stone, sometimes a rusting Bailey bridge. These bridges spanned the many creeks and tributaries of the great rivers which were the traditional life lines of the hinterland. The rivulets ranged in width from few feet of lazy, shallow and crystal-clear waters to a hundred feet of seething, fast-flowing reddish-brown, carrying the branches and forest debris collected on their journeys.

As the travellers passed across each bridge they could see the thatch and ironwork of village huts huddled along the banks of the stream, and the innumerable canoes moving effortlessly through the water. Some of the crude houses were built on poles away from the lapping surge of the current. There was one very wide creek with a single track iron bridge spanning it. Against the network of rusty metal on one side sat the decrepit hulk of a bus, its front completely stoved in and buckled beyond repair, looking like a metallic monster frozen into immobility. They knew from experience that the inanimate carcass of the once-proud vehicle would stay there for ever, or until some negligent driver would smash into it at high speed and propel the rotting ruin into the waters below.

Derek had long ago ceased to marvel at the condition of the commercial vehicles which plied the roads of West Africa. They defied the laws of technology by keeping going, and the laws of averages by keeping apart from each other as much as they did. These were the new life-blood of modern Africa's travel system. They were the main form of transportation, and sometime the only one, for both freight and passengers alike. A so-called mammy-wagon was basically a truck chassis with a wooden body built on to it, and equipped with hard, uncomfortable seats. It was common to see the passengers sharing the seats with goats, chickens and even pigs, while luggage and bicycles would be lashed to the top or sides. Since they invariably carried three times the load for which they were designed, they made inter-city transport relatively cheap but dangerous.

The front, sides and rear of these vehicles were adorned with highly optimistic Biblical statements in an effort to ensure safe passage by Divine guidance. Phrases such as "In God we trust", "The Lord is my Shepherd", and "God will protect me" were typical. Derek sincerely hoped that God would, since the drivers certainly had little regard for the rules of safety. The longest slogan Derek had ever seen emblazoned on a wagon was "He who wishes the downfall of his neighbour will never succeed in his undertaking". Unless, of course, he happens to be the driver of the vehicle.

These mobile, crowded death-traps would hurtle down the centre of the road at break-neck speeds, challenging all who dared to stand in their way. It was not uncommon to see them playing "chicken" with their own kind coming in the opposite direction, to the obvious delight of those on the winning side. It was truly amazing that accidents were so few in number. But when one did occur, it was a veritable massacre.

The corpse of a bus or wagon which hadn't won the challenge lay adjacent to most bridges, washed clean by the perennial fury of the rainy season. The hulk could sit by the roadside or in the ditch for ever as a symbol of God's temporary displeasure with mankind, or with just that particular driver. But never as a warning to others.

Occasionally the police would make spot checks, usually to ensure that passenger loads were not being exceeded, which they usually were. The outcome depended on the comparative wealth of the owner of the vehicles so subjected. One of the perquisites of the traffic policeman's job was to demand and receive a "head tax", in exchange for the proverbial blind eye.

Although it might seem to the casual observer that drivers on West African roads were insanely oblivious to the possibility of collision with each other, Derek knew that it was quite a different story where pedestrians were involved. Although drivers didn't appear to reduce their speed or increase their vigilance when approaching or passing through a village, they seemed to have an uncanny instinct for avoiding any life form, human or animal, which may inadvertently stray into their path. This was largely due to the widely known consequences of injuring, or worse still, killing, the cherished member of a village clan.

Derek had once hit a cow while driving through a remote village. He was prepared to stop and survey the damage, but was exhorted by his frantic driver, taking a temporary respite from his duties, to "keep going, sah. Keep going, very fast." Derek reluctantly heeded the warning, later to learn that had he stopped, as he originally intended, his very life would have been in danger from the villagers whose valuable commodity he had struck. The rule was, "if you hit something or somebody, don't stop - make a report to the nearest police station, and hope that the officer doesn't owe any allegiance to that particular village." Otherwise, the driver could be forced to a stop, and subjected to the cruellest of retribution. If not put to death outright by the enraged family of the victim, he would most certainly be horribly maimed or disfigured. He would probably never recover the will to drive again, even if he were still physically able. Derek heared stories of drivers being beaten, dismembered, blinded and even de-genitalised for running over or into a villager on a bush road. The advice to keep on driving was very sound.

Movement along the road was in no way limited to motorised traffic. In fact, the bicycle was by far the most popular means of short-distance transportation, and a man could be ranked by the number and quality of the machines he owned. They would carry incredible loads. It could be simply a case of beer, or several four-gallon drums of palm oil. It could be a full-size door or a pair of live goats. It could even be several people hitching a ride at the same time, complete with all their loads. The bicycle was the poor man's commercial vehicle.

Then there were the walkers. Women from villages scraped out of the forest walked in stately, chattering files to collect water, each with a calabash or kerosene tin on her head, slopping dribbles of the precious liquid down her blouse and lappa. The women were not the only walkers. Sometimes a man would come by balancing a tray on his head. On the tray could be four of five calabashes of palm wine, frothing its way up and out of the narrow necks and causing rivulets of foam to run down the yellow containers and on to the tray, despite the carrier's peculiar knees-bent shuffle which was supposed to minimise jarring. What a pleasure, thought Derek, to live in a land where wine can be found literally growing on the trees! Perhaps that contributed to the African peasant's perpetual state of happiness?

At first, the travellers would dodge behind a tree at the slightest sight or sound of movement, but after a while the exercise became futile. Whether they were seen or not didn't seem to matter any more. They were too close to victory now to waste time hiding when they could be making progress.

There was one incident during this stage of their journey which caused a certain amount of anxiety while it lasted, but they were able to laugh about it afterwards. As they were making their way in single file along the road, keeping a wary eye open for unfriendly activity, a dusty, toothless old man sprang out from behind a tree and waved his arms at them menacingly. He was tall, well built and completely naked, apart from a pair of shorts which he wore around his neck. From his tangled, curly hair down to the pink edges of his cracked feet he was covered in reddish dust, in which his trickling sweat had made black streaks.

The four Europeans pulled up sharply, almost bumping into each other, as the prancing figure waved his arms and ranted at them.

"Amugu-mugu! Amugu-mugu!"

A wave of stale, sickly palm wine breath engulfed the shaken travellers as the man thrust his head closer to them, eyes bloodshot and bleary, lips flecked with white saliva.

"Amugu-mugu! Amugu-mugu!"

Then the man stopped his antics and his shouting as his eyes focused on Jean. He took a step closer and began to manipulate parts of his body in obscene but unmistakable gestures. Jean backed away and James placed himself squarely between her and the ugly, leering spectre. A low, lascivious "amugu-mugu" escaped the man's distorted mouth as he tried to push past James, hands raised and cupped. James stood firm, blocking the man's path. Although they couldn't understand the words, the meaning was plain enough.

At that moment a small girl, wearing a cloth wrapped around her body and knotted behind her head, ran across the road and tugged at the maniac's arm. She implored him by her actions and shrill voice to come away, but to no avail. The lunatic continued to convey his desires, to the obvious amusement of the small crowd which had begun to gather. A grinning onlooker turned to Derek.

"Am sorry, sah. Him crazy an' drunk. Den call am "mugu-mugu". E brain go rotten for palm wine since long. Him not make trobble, jus' talk, but him crazy an' him arways drunk. Him say want oyibo woman, but no trobble. Him crazy. You give him money an' him go away."

"We have no money," spluttered Derek, more angry than

scared. "Ba kudin. Tell him no money, savvy?"

"Yessah, savvy. We go take am now-now. Sorry, sah. Sorry madam."

There was a small commotion as a plump, hefty woman pushed her way through the growing crowd, an angry gleam in her eye. She grabbed the raving wretch by one arm and by his shaggy hair, tugging at him and screeching in a high-pitched, almost hysterical voice. When this failed to have any effect, she picked up a stick and laid into him, putting all the force of her considerable body weight into every blow.

The unfortunate man tried to protect the different parts of his body from the hail of blows, and staggered away in the direction his attacker indicated, like a cow being herded into pasture. The crowd went wild, jibing and jeering as the victim and assailant disappeared into the bush, still yelling at one another. When he could control his mirth, the man who had spoken to Derek turned back, as though he felt compelled to explain.

"E wife, take am home. She make am plenty palaver, for him be crazy drunk. An for want nother woman, ay, ay, ay..." He went away shaking the fingers of his right hand in the peculiar African gesture of wonderment.

Still greatly amused by the entertainment, the crowd began to disperse, leaving the Europeans to take a deep breath and shakily resume their trek. Alan was the one to open up the conversation.

"That was a bit scary. Did you notice the…..Oh, never mind"

Jean turned to him.

"What? I ***did*** notice that you didn't do much to help."

"How would you..."

James stepped in.

"Cut it out, both of you. What is scary to me is that we've now been seen by God knows how many people. Doesn't it occur to you that they might find it a bit odd to see four white people walking along this road? I mean, white people just don't walk about in these parts. Don't you think that they might just mention it to someone, sooner or later, and that the authorities will cotton on and send a patrol after us like a shot? And it won't be a friendly patrol, either."

This had occurred to Derek, and he subconsciously increased his pace, hoping to be as far away from this place, wherever it was, when the news got out and the patrols picked up their trail.

"Anyway, thank you", Jean said, as she slipped her arm through that of James.

The gesture didn't go unnoticed by Derek. He wished that he had been the one who had offered her protection from the crazy man instead of James.

They walked on in silence.

They were able to cover an estimated fifteen miles before night fell on the second day. This left them, they calculated, a further sixteen or seventeen before they reached the final obstacle - the half-mile wide river which separated Bujavi from Séjumé and safety. They should have no trouble in covering this distance on the following day, provided that they could keep their pursuers well behind them.

After another uncomfortable night sleeping as always in shifts, they resumed their trudge on the third day. Their spirits were high as they realised that this could well be the last day they would have to spend in the forest. There had been neither sight nor sound of any patrols since leaving the mission. Their stride was jubilant and strong, despite the fact that they knew they would soon have to leave the road which had made their passage so much easier, and they would have to push once again through the bush for the last few miles.

By mid-afternoon they came to a wide, fast-moving stream which Father Paul had marked on his crude map as the point where they must plunge back into the bushy undergrowth. With their food almost gone, they had to resort once again to supplementing their nourishment with whatever the land and trees had to offer. They were helped in a small way by a honey guide which seemed to take a fancy to them. The honey guide is a drab little bird of the African forest which Derek had heard about but never before had the opportunity to see at close quarters. It has a knack of finding caches of honey, which it is more than willing to share. It flew ahead of them, waited for them to catch up, then flew some more, as if urging them to follow. Eventually, the bird gently guided his human followers to a nest of honey, and sat patiently on a tree branch while they opened up the nest. There were no bees inside, as Derek had expected. Folklore, he recalled, required that a substantial piece of honeycomb has to be left for the little bird, failing which the next time he sees you in the forest he will guide you not to a honey nest, but something very unpleasant, such as a hungry leopard.

The stream provided them with a welcome opportunity to refill their water containers, and after a few minutes' rest they pressed on, with mounting optimism. They were too close to triumph now to feel anything but resolute. By sundown, on the third day, they found what they were looking for - the mighty River Zakurdi.

They moved as close to the river bank as they dared without leaving the covering protection of the trees. There was now less than half a mile between them and the open arms of a friendly regime where they would be among sympathizers, instead of vengeful pursuers. But this stretch of terrain was more difficult, more challenging than any yet encountered, and one which would not be covered easily.

This thought was uppermost in the minds of each one of them as they stared at and across the surging current of this great waterway, as though inspiration might spring from it. They walked slowly and thoughtfully through the trees parallel with the river's flow, making the most of the sun's dying rays before they would be forced to settle themselves for the night.

After a few hundred yards the trees by the river bank gave way to a bed of granite, in which the eddying waters of millennia had hollowed out a confusion of pools and miniature waterfalls. Here and there the currents had worn grooves in the rock, separating themselves into a multitude of little streams which danced and flirted along the diversions until they eventually channelled themselves back into the main flow. On its landward side the ninety-foot wide slab of rock was fringed by fine sand, glowing amber in the weak and dying rays of the sun. They could see two pairs of fiery eyes shining in the sand. As they crept closer they made out the shadowy forms of two broad-snouted crocodiles, about eighteen inches long, of the type very familiar in West Africa's rivers and streams. The reptiles raised their heads alertly as the intruders approached, then scurried frantically across the rock platform and into the water, where they glided away to safety.

The four travellers crossed the slab of rock and entered the forest on the other side, where they found an enormous tree raised high on its stilt-like roots. This would be their resting place for what they hoped would be their final night of forest living. They arranged themselves as best they could to take whatever sleep would come to them during the hours of darkness, having no definite plan of how the final obstacle was to be overcome.

It was coming to an end, thought Derek, as he tried to grab at the sleep which kept eluding him. Their days of detention, of humiliation, of near-starvation, of upraised hopes and overwhelming despair, they were almost at an end. There was only this uninviting water between them and the freedom they had been seeking for the past three weeks.

A motor boat chugged by on the river, its headlight glaring and sweeping the trees on each side. It could be a patrol boat looking for us, thought Derek. With a twinge of excitement he stumbled across the thought that it might be rescuers from the other side, but it would be very foolish to anticipate wrongly and call out to them. He noticed in the light from the boat that the two crocodiles had returned to their sandy lair.

None of them could sleep beyond a brief, light doze. They heard the snarl of a leopard, and Derek's mind raced back to a report he had once read, left behind by the District Officer of Ugbeshu a couple of decades ago when the "leopard cult" was in its heyday throughout parts of West Africa's coastal forests. It told of a large number of people who were apparently falling prey to roaming leopards. The mystifying element was that they were all mutilated in much the same way. In some instances leopard pad marks were found near the body, but not in all. Then the police discovered a cache of bamboo poles tipped with sharp steel spikes, and the emergence of leopard cults turned the supposed "accidents" into a full-scale murder investigation.

At first, proof was next to impossible to find. It was widely believed among villagers that under certain conditions, men could turn themselves into leopards - a sort of African version of the werewolf story - and that certain ju-ju men had the medicine to do just that. When forensic science established that the flesh scrapings on the arms and head of some victims were done by steel and not claws, it became clear beyond doubt that leopards were not the culprits. A large "leopard force" of police eventually and slowly tracked down the perpetrators of the killings, mainly as a result of help from reluctant and terrified informers. The activities of the cult ground to a halt as its ringleaders were denounced and hanged, and the activity was formally outlawed.

There were still some leopards roaming the forests, some which still attacked humans if the circumstances were right. Most of their victims, though, were cattle and goats. It was unlikely that Derek and his friends were in any danger, but at that hour of the night, imagination combines with weariness to play tricks of fantasy on the mind.

They desperately needed to refresh themselves for the final stages of their flight, but it was a long time before sleep finally overtook any of them. It had been suggested at one stage that they should take advantage of the darkness to make their next move, but this was eventually rejected. It was hard enough to make progress when they could see where they were going, but to blunder about in the darkness would be foolish. Moreover, they didn't yet know what their next move was going to be, let alone press on with it.

Derek drifted into the unreal world of semi-fantasy, where conscious thought mixes with unfettered dreams, so that one really doesn't know what's actually happening, what's being imagined and what's subconscious wishful thinking.

He was brought back to full wakefulness by a sudden shout. Not loud, more like a vocal gasp, but enough to push back the frontiers of sleep. He jumped up in time to see Jean lift up her knee swiftly and forcefully, catching Alan squarely in the groin. Alan let go of her and doubled up on the ground, coughing and groaning, his hands pushed down between his legs.

"Bastard!", snarled Jean. "Try anything like that again and I'll cut a piece off you. And you know which piece it'll be,"

She had a knife in her right hand.

"What's going on?", asked James, rising to his feet.

"This creep decided it was time to force the issue. He's been coming on to me for the past few days and can't take the hint. I think he's got it now".

There was silence as Jean resumed her watch-night duty and Alan crawled back to his resting place. The other two lay down again, unable to think of anything suitable to say. Our Miss Sheldon certainly knows how to take care of herself, thought Derek. Alan won't try anything like that again.

Dawn eventually came, and all the colours of the spectrum were poised to herald the advent of their master, the almighty sun. At last he glided over the African world in a fiery half-circle of red flames, then levered himself into the sky by pushing on the tree-tops. He brushed the white light of the moon before him, and into immediate obsolescence. A new day was born unto the world.

After tossing and turning and pacing about between snatches of restless sleep, the men tried to clear their minds and concentrate on a plan of action. They were fully awake by the time the sun had lifted all the night shadows from the forest.

Jean alone seemed to have had no difficulty in sleeping since the end of her watch.

"Any ideas?", she asked pleasantly, as though planning a day in the park.

The others didn't answer her, as they sat staring across the expanse of water which was their only obstacle to freedom. To have come so far, to be able to see their objective in the shady distance, and yet to be unable to reach it gave them a disconcerting feeling - so near yet so far.

"Let's look at all the possibilities", suggested James in his usual logical manner, as though he were discussing some impending financial transaction in the comfort of his air-conditioned office back in Ugbeshu.

They threw in their ideas, considering very carefully all the alternatives open to them, before rejecting most as impracticable. To swim would be extremely hazardous, if not impossible. Even the best of swimmers would have a hard time fighting the strong undercurrents, and they were far from that. To attract the attention of one of the boats which were already active on the river could also be dangerous. They might just be delivering themselves to a patrol boat already looking for them. Nor could they trust the occupants of the canoes, and anyway they didn't have anything in the way of a "dash" to offer. They knew that the nearest bridge was almost at Zekwi itself. Even if they were lucky enough to reach it, their chances of being able to cross unchallenged were slim. Besides which, that was another tedious 35 miles away. No, they would have to think again. There had to be a way.

"Canoe!", suggested Alan. "Let's take a canoe."

""What do you suppose......do mean steal one?" asked Jean testily.

"No!" retorted Alan with a sneer on his face. "We ask the nice gentlemen if they would oblige by giving us one. To celebrate our escape". He snorted. "Of course we steal it! How else would we get one? You….." He was going to add "you stupid bitch" or something similar, but stopped himself at the last minute.

Jean fell silent, and James's lifted his head slowly.

"By God, I think you might have it. Here's what I suggest."

It was eventually agreed that their best recourse, in fact their only viable recourse, would be to make their way along the river bank until they came upon one of the many villages which owe their lifestyles to the waters of the river. There was a good chance that somewhere there would be an unguarded canoe which they could steal without being discovered. Not immediately, anyway. All they would need would be a few minutes to paddle themselves out of sight.

They were hungry and grimy, but far from dejected as they sipped carefully at their diminishing supply of water. It was, after all, only half a mile which separated them from the freedom they had been seeking, but it was a greater challenge than any they had yet faced.

They crept along for two hours, keeping an ever-wary eye open for morning wanderers. Monkeys and birds became their constant companions again, and mosquitoes continued to plague the unprotected parts of their skin. Derek glanced anxiously from time to time at Alan, hoping that the physical and emotional strain would not bring on another near-breakdown under the pressure. But Alan looked strong and determined, completely in control of himself. Perhaps the knee in the groin had smartened him up a bit.

By mid-morning they came to their third village. The first two hadn't presented the right opportunity. One had no available canoes, or at least none they could see from the cover of the bush, and the second was a hive of activity by the water's edge. It would have been far too dangerous to attempt an act of larceny.

This one was more promising. There was a large clearing fringed by a cluster of huts, their circular roofs rising to a point above the mud walls. Their hopes dimmed a little when they saw the Bujavi flag hanging limp atop the only solid-looking building set apart from the native dwellings. This could only mean that it was a government office of some sort, and wherever there was a government office there was sure to be officials with a telephone. Perhaps even a couple of policemen. Whether the phone was in working condition or not was another question, but they dare not risk being spotted and reported. The structure was made of unfinished concrete block, and topped by the inevitable corrugated iron roof. Its lower walls were adorned by the usual reddish-brown smear of laterite which the years had thrown against them, and the louvred windows were broken and hanging loose.

As the four crept closer, they were able to make out the faded lettering over the door proclaiming, in an apologetic sort of way, that this was the Federal Tax Department - District Sub-office. It was in English only. Typically, in a country where hundreds of tribes each spoke its own language, the only universal language to which the government could turn had to be English. Or French, depending on its background. There was no other real universal language in Bujavi – at least, not a written one. Its national boundaries had been imposed in reverse. When the European powers held their famous Berlin Conference during the previous century to share out African possessions, no-one claimed Bujavi, which finished up with its borders edging on to adjacent territories. It was a bit like three suburban householders each building a fence, leaving the one in the middle with no need to do so.

There was one bright hope, at least. A Tax Office was hardly likely to have soldiers, or even police, stationed within its confines.

There was a faint murmur of activity coming from beyond the clearing, and a young official, dressed as always in a khaki uniform, was stretching himself in the doorway of the Tax Office. The Europeans waited until several of the office staff left the building on their way to a lunch break and siesta, the last one locking the door, then they moved closer to the edge of the clearing. Alan pointed excitedly to a point beyond where two canoes were drawn up on the reedy beach. This was the break they had been praying for. There was still the problem, though, of crossing the clearing without being seen. Assuming that this could be accomplished, Derek calculated that the building itself would shield them from the village. And, more importantly, from the owners of the canoes.

In subdued but eager voices they debated for a few minutes whether to walk confidently and brazenly across the clearing, or to make run for it. If they attracted someone's attention they might not have enough time to reach the water's edge before the alarm was raised, so the cautious approach was probably the best. To be captured now, having come so far, would be the epitome of disappointment, to say nothing of the near certainty of death.

"One of us should go round the back and see what it looks like from the other side," suggested Alan.

"Round the back of what?"

Jean's tone did not hide the scorn she felt.

"I think you're really losing it."

"No", contradicted James. "There might be something in that. If we go round the back of the village through the bush we'll be on the other side of the clearing and nearer to the water. We won't be seen from the village."

"But that could take ages. They'll be back from their chop by then."

A silence engulfed them as they digested this latest idea.

"Maybe we won't have to", said Jean as she wriggled away to the right. "Be right back."

The men protested and started to follow, but she waved them back. They watched breathlessly as she worked her way through the undergrowth to where several kaftans were drying in the sun. She grabbed four of them, still slightly damp, and wriggled her way back, picking up a braided cap as a bonus.

"Perfect disguises. Put them on."

Without giving any thought to the possibility of tumbo flies, which have a nasty habit of laying their eggs under human skin whenever the opportunity arise, they all pulled the fading robes over their torn and dirty clothes. The loose-fitting garment hid Jean's shapely figure, and she stuffed her hair under the cap.

"Now we go bush proppa".

She put on an impish grin, and even included Alan in her dazzling smile.

"Derek, you look like Ebenezer Scrooge", said James as Derek stood up to see if the garment covered his knees. "All you're short of is a candle".

"Well, you don't exactly look like a Saville Row model yourself."

James found some black mud and slapped it on his face and arms, then as an afterthought, tried to cover up his greying temples.

"Never thought I'd see the day when I'd try to pass for black."

"Yes, but where did you leave your banjo?"

Derek and Alan were unable to control their feelings. James Barrett - Jim Dandy, to be seen in this condition. A month ago it would have been unthinkable.

They followed Jims's example with the mud, then stood up to inspect each other. From a distance they would pass for Africans, provided they were not challenged face to face.

"Ready?"

"Ready."

They took a deep breath and were on the point of sauntering into the clearing when a shout from behind made them freeze. More shouts were heard, then the wail of a female voice, joined by more and more, until the clamour built up into a crescendo of agitated yelling at a high volume. The Europeans-turned-temporary-Africans looked at each other in alarm and disappointment, then crept backwards into the bush, crouching as low as they could without losing their vantage point.

They heard a crashing in the undergrowth beside them, and a young, wild-eyed African youth passed within a few feet of them and burst into the clearing, running as though his life depended on it.

It probably does, thought Derek, if this is what I think it is. His suspicion was confirmed as a horde of villagers rushed past their hiding place without a glance to either side, and took up the pursuit across the clearing. Two of the men were dragging a screaming, struggling girl, very reluctant and very naked.

"A bit of hanky-panky going on, it seems," muttered Alan. "And caught in the act, so to speak."

"Shhh!" James frowned a silencing glance at Alan, but it didn't take the leer off his face.

No wonder the lad is running, thought Derek, as the youth plunged into the bush on the far side of the clearing. Especially if it's the chief's daughter he's been enjoying.

Or worse still, one of his wives.

Derek knew from stories he'd heard that adultery was a serious matter in some tribes, and that the punishment could be severe. Not officially, of course. There was no law against it in a judicial sense, but native law and custom has its own remedies for what Alan referred to as "hanky-panky". He recalled reading once about what used to happen in the old days where adultery with chief's wife was discovered. First of all, the wife was beheaded, which was an instant cure to her wayward tendencies, but her lover had no such quick and painless death.

One account told of the unfortunate culprit being led naked from village to village throughout the chiefdom by means of a thorny creeper threaded through his nostrils. Each headman would perform a certain ritual, according to local tradition. It started with having knives pushed into the man's flesh, but not so deep that they would damage any internal organs. Then, as the procession progressed, the victim would have his ears cut off, his shin-bones scraped bare, his arms hacked off at the elbows and his eyelids removed. At any time he could be commanded to dance to the frenzied beat of the drums, failing which a slab of flesh would be cut from his buttocks or his back, or his genitals would be harshly removed. Finally, when it looked as though the man was at last about to die, the executioner would request the chief's permission to cut off the wretch's head. If this were not granted, the next step was to chop off a leg, but still command the unfortunate to keep dancing on his remaining limb. This usually finished the act, since as soon as the man fell to the ground, which was inevitably soon, he would be clubbed to death.

Derek hoped that the youth would escape. Not that this sort of treatment would be handed out in this day and age, but the least the young man could expect would be an impromptu operation which would prevent him from ever committing the same sin again.

When the confusion had died down, James edged forwards, then stood up.

"Come on - this is probably the only chance we'll get."

He strode forward, and the others followed him, fighting down the urge to run and get it over with. When they were a little over half way, a dog barked behind them, making Jean visibly jump.

"Steady", commanded James. "Keep going."

The dog bounded forwards, barking fiercely, his canine instincts telling him that these were intruders. They did their best to ignore it, and carried on with their agonizing stroll, as though they had every right to be there. A shout from somewhere in the rear brought a thump to Derek's heart, and he expected the worst. The dog reluctantly but obediently ceased its aggression and ran back to its master, but not without a menacing snarl to warn the four interlopers to keep away from the settlement.

With a wave of relief they reached the riverwards side of the Tax Office, then stopped dead in their tracks at the sight of an elderly, grey-bearded villager sitting silently at the river's edge and staring out across the water. He had been invisible from the other side of the clearing, his green agbada merging in chameleon fashion with the tall weeds.

At Jean's stifled gasp he turned his head on its scraggy neck in their direction, his bloodshot eyes trying to focus on the four strange figures no more than twenty feet away. An empty calabash lay at his side, and the sickly-sweet odour of palm wine reached their nostrils. His mouth fell open and he started to rise.

With the speed of a cobra Alan sprang forward, knife in hand, and pushed the blade with an expertise he never knew he possessed between the old man's ribs before a sound could be uttered.

The others stood there transfixed, their eyes wide, their mouths agape, as Alan withdrew the blade and gently laid the lifeless body in the undergrowth. Another death.

"Sorry. That's all I could think of to stop him raising the alarm."

Derek gulped very hard, and words stuck in his throat. Jean turned away, pretending she hadn't been affected. James didn't even flinch. Probably saw a lot of that in his army days, Derek thought. That's why he didn't hesitate to kill the man at the rest-house or in the bush.

"You did the right thing, lad."

Alan turned to the canoes and cut the tethering ropes, leaving a red smear as both sides of the blade were wiped clean. After removing the paddle, he pushed one of them with a mighty heave into the fast current, to be carried downstream.

The other one he held while his companions pushed it into the water, and they scrambled aboard.

Derek and Alan began paddling furiously away from the river bank and into the surging waters.

They had begun the final stage of their journey.

19

The sun paled and faded as hitherto unnoticed storm clouds, the size of continents, crept across the deep blue of the afternoon sky. On both sides of the river the curtains of vegetation grew darker and more forbidding as the pinpricks of sunlight were snapped off. The fierce winds which usually herald the approach of a tropical storm whipped the troubled waters into an even greater frenzy as Derek and Alan tried to propel the canoe away from hostile land. The first sheet of lightening seemed to drop from the heavens into the water around them, and a battery of thunder shook the treetops. Raindrops as big as bottle caps began to pelt the canoe and its occupants, then a giant unseen hand unzipped the bulging canopy of cloud. The rain became a vertical curtain of water, soaking everything in the path of its descent.

The jungle faded in a mist of evaporation which carried with it the curious if familiar smell of sodden earth and decaying logs. The whole panorama of sky, forest and water seemed to meld into a single, wild entity, as if to reinforce Nature's unquestioned supremacy, warning those who ventured therein to approach with caution and respect.

Although he had never tried it, Derek had always imagined canoeing to be a simple matter. He had been ferried by canoe many times in the past when his duties had taken him touring his district. He had seen boats twice the size of this one laden with cloth bales, bicycles, goats and even motorbikes being deftly propelled by a single paddler. He had never once given any thought to the expertise required. They made it look so easy, these African river men. Derek was now beginning to appreciate the skill and dexterity of these paddle-pushers, a skill and dexterity which he couldn't even hope to emulate.

Derek and Alan were able, by a superhuman co-ordinated effort, to widen the gap between them and the hostile territory behind them, but the opposite bank didn't seem to be coming any closer. The wind, blowing up-river from the ocean, did not make their progress any easier. By the time Derek judged them to be about a quarter of the way across, they had been taken more than twice that distance downstream. This didn't really matter, though, as long as they were able to maintain the energy required to paddle the full width of the river eventually. He hoped that the midstream current wouldn't prove to be any stronger and sweep them away completely.

As he paddled, Derek couldn't help but reflect on the days when this kind of transportation was the only option open to those intent on travelling in West Africa. Apart, of course, from foot-slogging through the bush. It wasn't all that long ago, either, by European standards - it was only within the last 30 years or so that motorised transport had been possible. Odd to think that when these parts were being opened up by way of navigable rivers, the older nations of the world had already been moving people and goods by road and rail for quite a while. They were even experimenting with air travel. A different world.

What were they like, those early explorers, merchants, administrators? What was it that made them leave the comfort of London, Paris, Lisbon, Brussels, and drew them to the "White Man's Grave"? There were fanatics, certainly, like David Livingstone and Henry Stanley; there were businessmen like George Goldie and Cecil Rhodes. There were adventurers such as Mungo Park and missionaries like Albert Schweitzer and - well, like Father Paul, for instance. But what about the ordinary men, the Colonial Officers, the Chartered Company clerks, the soldiers, the merchants' representatives who volunteered to come out and help "settle" the lands shared out at the Berlin Conference of 1884?

Heaven knows, life was frustrating enough in the 1950's and 1960's when all, or at least most, of the conveniences of man's ingenuity were available. What must it have been like 60 or 70 or 100 years ago? They certainly must have been made of much sterner stuff in those days.

He was brought back to the present as a shout rang out across the water from behind them, and Jim turned around to see an agitated figure waving at them excitedly from the clearing which they had just left.

"No doubt the owner of this fine vessel. Get ready for some fireworks."

It was only a minute or two later that a horde of villagers, attracted by the man's antics, milled around by the water's edge shouting, jabbering and waving at them in the rain to come back. Derek and Alan threw all they had into their paddling, not caring that they were moving twice the distance downstream than across.

Then the shooting began.

"It's O.K.," chirped Alan. "The bad guys are always rotten shots."

He cried out in pain as a bullet ripped through his upper arm, knocking him to the bottom of the boat and almost tipping them into the foaming waters. Jean shook her blond hair free and used the cap to try to stem the blood flowing from Alan's arm. His eyes opened as he tried to smile.

"Except in real life, of course."

Jim grabbed at the paddle which had slid from Alan's hand, but wasn't quick enough. The frothing current carried it out of reach into the angry cauldron.

This left Derek as the only source of power for the little craft, and he redoubled his efforts. They weren't exactly a sitting target as they bobbed about in the water, but they were nonetheless defenceless against the barking rifles. This thought gave him yet an extra surge of energy; everyone's life depended on him now. He allowed the canoe to turn with the river's flow, while still paddling furiously. Although this manoeuvre would give the gunners a larger target at which to aim, the current would carry them out of range far more quickly than trying to fight across it.

The rain made the paddle slippery. The mud they had used for camouflage streaked down their faces and arms, giving them a curious zebra-like appearance. Derek hoped that the intensity of the storm would drive the gunners in search of shelter. The wind howling through the trees had little effect on the river, though, since it was already a seething, frothing witches' brew in its normal state.

A bullet zinged past his ear, and a second one struck the canoe below the water line. Gradually the splashes in the water lessened and eventually stopped. Derek stole a glance over his shoulder. They had rounded a bend in the river and could no longer see the clearing. He knew that already someone would have found the old man's body. Thank the Lord that Alan had had the presence of mind to cut loose the other canoe. They hadn't seen any sort of motorised craft around, and he hoped that the officials wouldn't magically produce one. If that happened, they would soon be overtaken. And killed, without doubt.

Derek also saw James on his knees furiously jabbing with his finger at the bullet hole through which water was spurting. Despite the seriousness of their predicament, he saw the funny side of it and began to laugh, allowing the boat to drift with the current.

"Sorry I can't find you a plumber right at this moment," he threw over his shoulder at the comic-book appearance of the once-immaculate bank manager. Dirty, mud-spattered and bleeding from a cut on his wrist, James looked like a carpenter's apprentice who had just put a nail through a water pipe. The ill-fitting kaftan didn't do much to improve his appearance.

"I'm glad you think it's funny," was the gruff reply from James as he finally managed to wedge his little finger in the hole.

Derek's laughter grew louder and eventually brought a smile to the face of the proponent. Soon they were both roaring heartily. The scene was not really so funny, but the feeling of relief so overwhelmed them that their pent-up tensions and anxieties began first to ooze away, then were released in a rush of guffawing. Despite the searing pain in his arm, Alan struggled to a sitting position and soon found himself unable to resist the infectious if inappropriate laughter. Jean remained unmoved and continued to dab at the wound with strips torn from the hem of her kaftan.

"Twice round the lake, then home for tea." Alan yelled in a maniac voice.

"Keep still," commanded Jean, who was unable to see any humour at all in the situation. "How the hell can I attend to this while you're wriggling about like a naughty, hysterical kid? It's a gunshot wound, for God's sake! And you two aren't helping, acting like silly schoolboys. What's so funny?"

This made them bellow even more, an extra load of fuel to the fires of uncontrollable mirth.

"Idiots!"

Gradually they gained control of themselves and Derek picked up the paddle.

"Home, James," ordered Alan, still chuckling.

"Aye, aye, sir," replied Derek. "Except that James isn't driving. I am. James is otherwise occupied in the bilge department."

This set them all off again, and even Jean couldn't repress a smile. It had been a long time since they had had anything to laugh at, and it was a while before a level of sobriety was eventually reached.

The rain stopped as suddenly as it had started. The wind dropped, the clouds drifted away in search of other mischief and the cheerful face of the sun once again smiled through. Their sodden clothes began to steam, as did the very jungle itself. They soon dried off.

Derek glanced over his shoulder again, and his heart fell almost to his knees. What he had feared most of all was now happening. The boat behind them was little more than a blur in the choppy waters, but unmistakably coming closer. He could hear the engine now, and dipped his paddle into the water with renewed and somewhat futile energy.

A splutter of machine gun fire cut through the air, but they were still too far away from their pursuers to be within target range. But it was a warning, though. As he gritted his teeth and fought with the current he became aware of another commotion ahead of them, and a small but powerful-looking motor launch displaying the Tricolor emerged from the reedy bank on his right. It was much closer than the pursuers, and Derek could see four white-uniformed figures in its bow. Three of them were pointing rifles in his direction.

Alan had seen them, too.

"Here comes the cavalry. Right on cue, in the bloody nick of time!"

It was all Jean could do to prevent him from standing up. Derek relaxed and once again allowed the canoe to drift.

A loud-hailer burst into voice as a sun-bronzed white man emerged from the cabin of the launch.

"Attention! You 'ave entered French territory. Leave at once or you will be arrested. If you resist we shoot".

The message was repeated in French, as if to reinforce its content. Then it was repeated, presumably, Derek imagined, in a Bujavi dialect, by one of the African crew members. The response from the Bujavi craft was another burst of machine-gun fire, this time coming perilously close to the bobbing canoe.

"Great God, we're right in the middle of this", Alan screamed as he flattened himself as best he could at the bottom of the boat.

"If the bad guys don't get us, the good ones will."

Jean fell on top of him as the rifles on the French boat barked out simultaneously, more of a warning than anything else.

"At last", Alan smirked, "you do want me, after all. And to think that..."

His mirth was cut short by a sharp slap on the face.

"Don't get any ideas, you slug. I just don't want to get shot, that's all. It's certainly not your body I'm interested in."

The canoe was obviously in the direct line of fire between the two armed craft, and the French boat turned and sped out towards the middle of the river, releasing another volley at the trespassers, who were now a clear target. One of the pursuers threw up his arms and fell overboard, dropping his gun. The loud-hailer crackled again.

"I repeat. You are in French territory. Go back now."

Another boat appeared from the Séjumé side, this time a much larger one, and Derek could see two men crouched behind an Oerlikon 20mm canon at its bow. After another long and defiant burst of fire, the Bujavi boat turned and fled, leaving the inert body of its fallen crew member to the crocodiles. Obviously, a handful of foreign fugitives were not worth a diplomatic faux-pas. The launch drew closer and the French official waved a friendly greeting, as the larger boat cruised the river in case the enemy tried a new tactic. It would also pick up the Bujavi casualty. If he survived, he would be patched up and sent home. He was guilty of nothing but obeying orders.

Alan and Jean straightened themselves up to a sitting position while Jim carefully and painfully withdrew his finger from the bullet hole which had been its home for so long. Water immediately started to gurgle in, covering his feet. The fugitives threw off their robes and shouted excitedly at their approaching rescuers.

"Never, in my whole life, have I been so anxious to be arrested." Jim said it for them all.

In a matter of moments eager hands were lifting them from the water-logged canoe. There was a flurry of hand-shaking, cheek-kissing and back slapping by the French-speaking white man, then the impact of it hit them - they had made it. After weeks of stress, of anxiety, of hopelessness they had made it!

As the French boat lurched its way landward they glanced unremorsefully behind them. The ordeal was finally over. Goodbye jungle, goodbye prisons, goodbye injustice and ingratitude. With a faint twinge of regret, which soon passed, they saw the crude canoe - their lifesaver - slowly disappear beneath the rushing waters. The gunboat, having chased away the bandits and picked up the injured sailor, circled the remains of the canoe once, then chugged away down river. Then the four turned towards the bow of their new craft and looked back no more.

They had made it!

After almost three weeks of terror and anxiety, Derek, Jim, Alan and Jean scarcely dared to believe that they were safe and free. Or, at least, they assumed they were, since there had been no indication so far to the contrary. They were with friendly people who were smiling and shaking hands, kissing their cheeks in the French way and helping them and making them feel welcome. These people were not shooting at them or pushing them at gunpoint; they were not ridiculing or threatening them or forcing them to hide in the forests.

The four walked with the Captain of the launch along the wooden pier from which the boat had set out a short while before. They didn't have to hide or creep along like hunted animals; they didn't have to keep glancing behind them to see if they were being watched or followed or hunted. They walked, with as much dignity as their dishevelled state would permit, to a small bungalow which proudly flew the Tricolor, mid-way along a semi-circular gravel drive.

A casually-clad white man emerged from the bungalow to greet them. The Captain saluted, spoke briefly in French so rapidly that Derek couldn't understand, and offered his hand to the people he had just rescued.

"Bonne chance. Go wid God."

He turned and went back to the boat.

"Merci beaucoup, Gaston," the civilian official said in an

unnecessarily loud voice.

He introduced himself as Jacques.

"Bien venue, madame et messieurs, to my 'ome. Really it is the local office of the Département des Forêts, but while I live 'ere I call it my 'ome."

His English was hesitant and uncertain, but grammatically correct. A lot better than our French, I bet, Derek thought. Jacques smiled at them and ushered them along the driveway to the house. The white-uniformed Africans waved from the pier.

"There is some transport on 'is way to take you to Ste. Pierre," Jacques told his guests. "It will take yet two 'ours more, so until then you must eat and wash and rest. Alphonse!"

At this a young African in steward's whites appeared.

"Some chop for my guests. Vite! On veut manger! But first," he said, turning back to his visitors, "a little cognac, peut-être, to, 'ow shall we say, settle the nerve?"

It occurred to Derek that Jacques must have very bad nerves, since the portions of cognac poured and handed round were far from little.

Derek and Jim began to gabble their thanks, their gratitude, their indebtedness for the timely rescue, but Jacques waved them to silence.

"Tah! C'est rien! It is nothing. In this place we 'ave to 'elp each other, oiu? It is not a credit to me, though, because we are all warned that you come. It was just a matter of waiting and watching up and down the river for where you appear. Then the drums tell my staff that you are close by, and we are 'appy that our Coast Guard amis did not hesitate to put their boats at my disposal. We have been waiting for two days now."

While he was speaking he withdrew a first aid box from the drawer of a huge mahogany desk. Jean took it from him.

"I'll do it. I'm a nurse," she said rather tartly, and began to clean Alan's wound. "It's not too bad; probably damaged the muscle, but missed the bone."

They all wanted to ask the question, but it was James, as usual, who found the words. But not until he had downed the cognac in one gulp and held up his glass to Alphonse for more.

"How did you know we were coming in the first place, and how did you know whereabouts on the river we would be?"

His second cognac disappeared and Alphonse, after a glance from Jacques, placed the bottle near to him.

The others nodded vigorously at the questions as if to emphasize the importance. Jacques smiled approvingly as Jean deftly snipped off the loose end of a bandage.

"Ah, that Père Paul, 'he is some man, yes? Somehow 'e sends out a message to all our confrères on this side of the river. 'e tells us the plans you 'ave, where you want to go. So we just have to wait. The puzzle is 'ow can he do all this without letting the Bujavis know? Je ne sais pas!"

At this last statement he threw his hands up in the air in an absurd gesture of helplessness and incomprehension. Derek saw the action more as Jewish than French, but couldn't help sharing in the wonder. As Jacques had rightly said, that Father Paul really was "some man".

They sipped their cognac (except for Jim, who seemed to be treating it like water) and listened to the talkative Jacques tell of his life. He told about his young years in Paris, his service in the Free French during the war, his posting to Africa and his present assignment as District Forestry Officer for the French Colonial Service in Séjumé. He had a wife somewhere back in France, a city girl who could not reconcile to the loneliness of the African jungle, and had left him after only six months of marriage. Something like the present episode was an exhilarating interruption of an otherwise dull and monotonous lifestyle. Little wonder he had taken to "settling the nerve" in such a fashion. Derek realised that occasions when Jacques would have anyone of his own race or colour with whom to converse would indeed be few and far between. This was a heaven-sent distraction.

Jacques didn't seem to be interested in the adventures of his four guests, apart from thanking God that he, personally, had been the one who was able to rescue them. After several attempts, they gave up trying, and, in between making use of the basic bathroom facilities, let Jacques ramble on.

The one-way conversation was finally interrupted by Alphonse.

"Chop ready".

The meal was simple and not very appetising, but under the circumstances very much appreciated. When they had finished eating and were enjoying a deliciously aromatic imported coffee, the crunch of tires on the gravel outside told them that their transportation had arrived.

Jacques rushed out to greet the newcomers, and returned with a small, plump and mustachioed man whom he introduced as M. Renault, the personal representative of the Prefect. To Derek he personified the impression he had always held of Hercule Poirot, the famous fictional Belgian detective, but he kept his thoughts to himself.

The rescue must be regarded as high-profile for the Prefect to send someone important to collect them. And with an armed Jeep escort!

M. Renault had apparently used this as an excuse to leave a "très drôle" diplomatic reception. He went through the usual formalities of welcome, etc., thanked Jacques for his not inconsiderable part in the rescue, and invited the four duly impressed travellers to ride in his air-conditioned Citröen, complete with Government flag and escort, for the final stage of the journey to Ste. Pierre.

"About three hour. Au revoir, Jacques, et merci beaucoup."

M. Renault explained to his new companions that they were technically illegal immigrants. Not for the first time, Derek reflected, but this time the formalities should be easy to straighten out. M. Renault clucked and tutted as he learned of their three-week adventure, but assured them that everything would be taken care of as quickly as possible, and that he would use whatever influence he had with the Central Government to speed up their departure.

"L'indépendance, it is all they talk about. Next year we, too, will see the same thing, malheureusement. But how will they manage without us to guide them? They want to be free, to throw out everything we have worked to achieve, then they ask for more money to keep the régime going. How can they do it? C'est impossible."

Derek knew what would happen - it would be the same as the Moresia situation, the Gold Coast situation, the Congo situation, or any other African independence. But he kept his silence, leaving the Poirot look-alike bemoaning the folly of sending such unprepared children into an adult world.

M. Renault did not stop talking. In contrast to the deep-thinking and uncommunicative Henri Gaudet, Derek found M. Renault and his subordinate, Jacques, to be victims of an apparent effusive compulsion to talk. He tuned out the Frenchman's prattle, and his attention strayed beyond the confines of the limousine as it sped effortlessly towards the capital.

M. Renault interrupted the flow of his conversation as the car slowed down to squeeze past the remains of a semi-trailer lying upside down across half of the road.

"It is typical of the disregard. It probably carried no insurance. I expect the owners have already gone for bush. Trying to get it moved is like..."

He didn't finish the sentence but threw up his arms in the same gesture which Jacques had used, then returned to his previous topic of conversation, whatever that had been. Derek wasn't sure; Derek wasn't listening.

Derek realised that the forest was becoming less dense, and eventually he could see only a fringe of oil palms bordering the road. The other giants of the forest had probably been mercilessly cut down as the city became hazily closer. Derek began to smell the characteristic odour of slums as the suburbs gradually surrounded them. It was an odour which he had come to love but despise, cherish but abhor, accept but reject. It was the odour of festering rubbish, of open latrines, of tribal cooking; it was the odour of decaying food, of sweaty bodies, of spilled diesel fuel and of the ever-present palm wine. It was the odour of poverty, of disease, and of ignorance. It was the odour of the new Africa, the Africa which he had helped to create. It was an Africa which was powerless to stop the old life turning over to the westernised and totally unsuitable new life. It was an Africa which saw the mass movement of rural populations to the urban areas in search of the dream, the slick, sophisticated, new African way of life which movies and T/V told them was there. They didn't consider that there might be no jobs for them in the cities, but once there it was too late to turn back.

They reached Ste. Pierre and were taken to the Hôtel de France, which, apart from its somewhat unoriginal name, held a five-star rating. M. Renault handed them over to a slim, slightly effeminate young man who was introduced as the Foreign Affairs Secretary, although they never did catch his name. For the first time in the whole three weeks they had been together they each had their own room, their own bathroom and all the luxury a French colonial hotel could offer. And it was all at the expense of their hosts, who couldn't do enough to ensure their comfort. There would be certain restrictions, of course, until the British Consulate could arrange the necessary papers to allow them to go home, but it would be for "a very short time only", they were told.

They enjoyed a sumptuous dinner, during which the Secretary, who told them to call him Raoul, skilfully kept the conversation away from their exploits.

"For diplomatic reasons," he mysteriously told them, although Derek couldn't figure out why. After the meal, Raoul left them to themselves, and a weariness he hadn't experienced for a long time crept over Derek. He excused himself and went to his room. Despite his tiredness he couldn't sleep. His brain was too active, too wound up, too confused about what he wanted to do but shouldn't. Finally he made up his mind, pulled on his pyjama trousers and crept down the deserted corridor. He hesitated for about fifteen seconds, then tapped gently on Jean's door.

He thought he heard a low murmuring coming from the other side of the door, but couldn't be sure. The door opened fractionally and in the light from the corridor he saw Jean, clad only in a man's shirt.

"May I come in?" His voice was squeaky, whining and almost pleading.

"Derek. What...? It's not really convenient, not right now."

She stole a glance over her shoulder, and that was what gave it all away. Derek pushed the door further open and stepped over the threshold. Propped up on one elbow on the bed was James Barrett, with a look on his face which turned from annoyance to sheepishness.

"Why, er, Derek. This is a bit of, er..."

He waived his free arm in a gesture of "c'est la vie". Derek looked from one to the other, then without a word he turned and strode out of the room. He heard the door close softly after him and the same low murmur, which faded as he strode back to his room. He felt cheated. He shouldn't really. Jean had a perfect right to entertain anyone she wished. And anyway, James had more right to be there than him, being a bachelor.

He went into his bedroom and released the catch on the door.

Damn. Damn. He'd made an absolute fool of himself. He felt like crawling away and not being seen again by either of them. Well, at least it had settled the matter of Jean for once and for all. He had become just one more scalp on her belt. As had James, apparently.

During the following thirty-six hours the red tape of government was displayed in all its glory. The Consul did advise them, though, that all "interested" parties in Britain had been notified of their deliverance, and that they were free to telephone their relatives. If, that is, they were lucky enough to get through. Derek knew from experience that this would be an exercise in futility. A "booking" of at last three days' notice was usually required to secure a call to anywhere in Europe from West Africa. But, nevertheless, he made the effort. He wasn't really too concerned that it was quite unsuccessful, since the media would have already told the world of their escape by now.

The Kumangan government made the expected strong representation to Séjumé for the extradition of what they described as "the callous murderers who were attempting to evade justice by sheltering under the wing of an unsuspecting neighbour nation". When it became apparent that their request would be ignored, the "unsuspecting neighbour nation" became a "discriminating colonial conspirator" almost overnight.

The extradition requests by Kumanga were presented in person by none other than Tony Agamoru, who was being held directly responsible for the original escape of his prisoners. Tony knew that his political career couldn't afford another blunder, especially one of this calibre. In addition to his official consular duties, he was using the visit to look after himself, and had secretly made provision to take "voluntary exile" if the present mission were to fail, which it likely would. He still had many friends in London, and it would be no problem to lose himself for a while until everything blew over. Or until his influential family could grease the right palms. Anyway, it wouldn't be the first time a member of his immediate circle had been forced to make a hasty but expedient retreat. It was with a wide smile and well-remembered familiarity that he joined the Derek and his friends in the secured wing of the airport, much to their amazement and concern. They didn't know until the last minute that he would be travelling with them. He acted as though nothing had happened between them, as though they were still ordering drinks in Ugbeshu Club, still friends. The others weren't so accommodating, though. Their recent memories were still very real and very painful. They totally ignored their former captor.

Eventually the Caravelle lifted its passengers from African soil. The slight pain in Alan's arm, now tightly bound and in a sling, couldn't detract from his jubilation, the jubilation which they all shared. As the jungle panorama slid away beneath them, Derek felt a strange mixed sensation of nostalgia, relief and apprehension. He peered down through the plane's window, staring at the diminishing vista of what had been his home, his career, his aspirations.

Africa is the only continent without a history. It wasn't that the peoples of Africa didn't make history, but just that they seemed to devour it as they went along. It had been as inevitable as the march of time itself that eventually Africa would come to light, would come to life, but it took the nations of the Western world to discover it. Before that Africa knew nothing of itself. It was like an adolescent orphan who never knew its parents, and had no means of finding out anything about them. Or about itself, either. Africa today is like a society without a purpose, thanks largely to the efforts of the Europeans who dragged it protesting and struggling into the twentieth century, and forced upon it a set of values totally alien to its traditional outlook. The West rushed upon Africa like a troublesome, uncaring tidal wave, stirring up the deposit of centuries, and then receded without leaving even a rudimentary foundation of any use to the African way of life.

Africa was forced into democracy without enlightenment, into bureaucracy without honesty and into nationhood without unity. There was no regard for tribal affinities when the physical borders were drawn, leaving most countries of Africa wide open for inevitable conflict – conflict born of centuries of tribal differences.

Certainly the West's material goods were welcomed, and eagerly, but its ideas were received with rather more hesitation. Some were accepted, certainly; others, though, such as taxation, monogamy, and tribal tolerance, were infinitely displeasing to the African mind. As such, they were abused, rejected or, at best, complied with in token only.

Africa is full of enigmas which only time can solve. The European conquerors might be very surprised or even shocked to discover in a hundred years' time what has been kept and what has been discarded, or twisted totally out of shape. Africa will make its own history from now on, but at its own pace and in its own fashion.

Derek's philosophical musings evaporated as a smartly-dressed stewardess asked him what he would like to drink. The four Britons loosened their seat belts, lowered their chair backs and relaxed, totally, for the first time in a long, long while. They all wondered, privately and in their own way, if they would be able to resist the beckoning call of foreign lands in what was left of their working lives. Especially Africa.

20

The homecoming was unlike any other which Derek had ever experienced in all his years of travel with CAC. He was accustomed to being deposited at the BOAC terminal, where the traveller from West Africa was easily distinguishable by the crumpled appearance of his only suit, or the obviously outdated fashions which had been in vogue at the start of the tour. This time, though, it was a little different. They had changed planes in Frankfurt, and met up with others who had escaped via different routes. To the practised eyes of the Customs and Immigration officials they were still "colonials" returning for a spell of home leave before going back to wave the somewhat tattered flag, but to the assembled greeters they were celebrities. The difference this time was the circumstances surrounding their arrival. It was unusual, emotional, and very reminiscent of those prisoner of war newsreels Derek had seen many years before.

James was greeted by no less a figure than the bank's Home Office General Manager. Since the death of his parent in a motor accident five years previously, James had not had any close family to meet him and rejoice. His return was congratulatory and formal, in a typically English gentleman's fashion. There was, however, an uncharacteristic faltering in James' voice as he thanked his superior for turning out, and assured him that he was "perfectly alright", and ready for his next assignment. Derek was a witness to this businesslike confrontation. James would probably be given some high place in head Office. Or, alternatively, he might be offered a plum posting to the Far East - the dream of every employee in A. & A.'s diverse interests.

Customs and Immigration formalities were waived, and they were escorted past the long lines of returning business and holiday passengers. There were reporters everywhere, asking questions and popping flash bulbs. The Kumanga Affair was still sufficiently fresh in the public's mind to warrant a "new angle" to the story. Although there had been others before them who had made it back, they were ones and twos, but this was the largest group. Besides which, their expected arrival was announced in advance, rather than being discovered after the fact. They were besieged by reporters and spent the first half hour answering questions and being photographed.

Derek didn't talk to Jean again. She slipped away during the confusion, after talking briefly with a couple of female journalists who were anxious for her story - something about being the only woman among so many men in her group. He couldn't be certain, but Derek got the impression that a tall, red-headed, artsy young man was directing her escape. Perhaps it was better that way, Derek thought. Her continued presence would only complicate things and it would be better to forget. Her impact on his life was pushed out of his mind as he spotted Gordon and Debbie elbowing their way through the throng.

Eventually, formalities concluded, the survivors were allowed to wander out into the cool, welcoming air of a London they had thought many times they might never see again. It was a glorious moment, and already the insidious memories of the past three weeks were beginning to blur.

To anyone who has undergone a lengthy stay overseas, especially in places half a world away, the first few hours of returning home are exciting and exhilarating, but the feeling tends to be short-lived. Derek was not surprised to find that the intoxicating joy which accompanied his repatriation began to evaporate rapidly during the following days. The overwhelming surge of excitement which he and his family had experienced at his return to freedom gave way to anti-climax, and he felt himself falling into a deep melancholy.

After this renewed flush of sensationalism, the Kumanga Affair began to fade into history for good. Even Derek's relatives and close friends didn't appear to be very interested in his exploits. Close, that is, as friends can be when four thousand miles separate them. They were very polite with their congratulations; they were glad to see him safe and sound, of course, but what could one expect if one chooses to go and live in uncivilised parts of the world? Derek should have known from past experience that no-one really cares about the rest of the world. This time, though, he thought it might have been different, given the circumstances. But then, he reflected, events at home, however trivial, are of much more concern when they affect peoples' day to day humdrum life.

Derek was due for two months of vacation, which he began after a couple of days' intensive de-briefing by CAC's top management. They appeared to be more concerned about their assets and business interests than the disposition of the personnel caught up in the Kumanga fiasco. One of the directors offered Derek the use of his villa on the island of Majorca, and Derek took his family on what was intended to be four weeks of relaxation therapy - an effort to laze away his tensions and forget about West Africa for a while.

The holiday had the opposite effect. Derek became moody and listless. He was glad to be out the recent mess, of course, but couldn't help a certain feeling of uncertainty and lack of fulfilment in his life. He couldn't think rationally. The warmth of the Mediterranean sun, contrasting sharply with London's chilly dampness, only helped to sharpen his memories of the good times he had seen in the tropics. It evoked a mixed feeling of regret and nostalgia.

Debbie became more perturbed as the days went by. The children were quick to realise that their daddy, given back to them after they had almost lost hope, was a changed person. To them, he was still the sincere, logical selfless rock of respected stability, who had always known the right things to do and say, and had guided his family with dependable confidence. But there was more, this time - a pensive, unreachable, unfathomable individual, sometimes irritable, sometimes annoyingly complacent, who moped about the villa in a detached and disinterested fashion.

Derek knew that he was acting absurdly. He knew that his attitude, his whole countenance, was very much out of keeping with the Derek Scott everyone had come to know and respect over the years. He couldn't help it, or even summon the willpower to fight it, to snap out of the deep mood and give his family the Derek they wanted and had prayed for over the past few weeks. Things would never be quite the same again, and he was glad when the holiday ended and they trooped in a very disheartened fashion back to London and reality.

In recognition of his years of service, his seniority and unquestioned loyalty, CAC found Derek a prestigious position at its London headquarters. He wasn't too keen on the idea, but it would at least keep his mind occupied and put a halt to the mental rot which was beginning to creep into his life.

"We need more people with your knowledge and experience", Smitty told Derek on his first day at the office, "to help with the training of the young men and women who are eager to go out and carry the Company's new image to developing countries. Education is one thing, but a word or two from those who have been there is worth all the books they can read."

New image? Derek could see a political implication here, internal as well as international. Multi-national corporations such as CAC would go to any lengths to maintain their prestige, not to mention their profit margins. Developing countries? That was a new description. What happened to "under-developed" or "dependent territories"? And ***women,*** too? This was something Derek found hard to reconcile. It was all right, he supposed, to send women out as nurses and teachers and such, but as trading managers? Roughing it in the smelly markets, and haggling with illiterate traders in the Sabon Gari? He couldn't help wondering how old Charlie Woods would have reacted to having a woman as his counterpart. Or perhaps as his boss?

Derek was given an office, a desk, a secretary and the title of "Overseas Human Resources Consultant". He was given a key to the executive washroom, a permanent seat in the management dining room, but very little work to do. He was asked to speak occasionally at training seminars, to interview management candidates and hold intimate question-and-answer sessions with young hopefuls who wanted to know "what it's really like in Africa". He was tempted to tell them that it was not one fraction as good as it was when he was a Coast trainee, but it probably wouldn't detract from their enthusiasm to change the world, but that was an opinion and not part of his job mandate.

The dull, monotonous routine of office life in the City was hard for Derek to take after so many years of Africa's unpredictable challenges. He soon started to become restless, and it showed. Unknown to Debbie he began to make discreet enquiries into the type and extent of the new postings opening up as part of CAC's "new image" in what was now being referred to as the Third World. He had equally surreptitiously been assured that as soon as he felt that he would like to go, Smitty would be happy to accommodate him. He hadn't mentioned it so far, in view of Derek's recent unpleasant experiences, but if Derek wanted another tour overseas, he could have it for the asking. Derek couldn't bring himself to tell his wife that he was unhappy in his new position. The horror of his flight from Kumanga had clouded, and he began to yearn for the excitement, the non-conformity, the challenges, the self-fulfilment which living in exotic places has to offer.

Debbie was happy with the way things had turned out. Here at last was what she had been dreaming about for many years - the chance of a "normal" existence. They were buying their own house, instead of renting; she would furnish and decorate it the way she wanted, instead of tolerating Company provided accommodation; she would go shopping in the new malls which were going up, instead of being driven to the tiny and ill-stocked Company retail outlet. She did miss the domestic help, of course; it was nice to have someone else to clear the table, to wash the dishes, to serve the coffee while all she had to do was to sit down and entertain her guests. But at least she would now be in charge of her own kitchen where she could arrange things in an orderly, uncluttered manner. And, moreover, be able to find them, without the frustration of wondering where other people had stored her few treasured possessions. There were all kinds of things which other people take as a matter of course which she could now do. She could be a "normal" housewife.

Alan Rushton, had been offered a good position in the CAC home office, but had turned it down. Being just as unsettled as Derek, had decided, on a whim, to enter university in the hope of acquiring the minimal degree which now seemed necessary in order to qualify for even the most menial of administrative jobs. Another ego trip, probably, thought Derek. Half way through the first year Alan ran out of enthusiasm (and money, probably), gave up and emigrated to Canada. Alone, Derek learned - Nancy had refused to go; the break was final. Derek never heard from either of them again.

After a long, relaxing vacation James Barrett was offered, as expected, an executive position in Threadneedle Street, the bank's head office. Having no close relatives in Britain, and in fact no ties at all with the old country other than his employers, he declined the offer and requested a further overseas posting. The last letter he had sent Derek was from Hong Kong, where he was taking over as General Manager. James would probably sit in the Managing Director's chair some day.

Of Jean there was no further trace. Derek often thought about instigating some sort of search, but always backed out at the last minute. It could do nothing but harm, anyway.

There was a brief letter from Henri Gaudet, thanking Derek, James, Alan and Jean for their support. Or, as he put it "for saving my life in the bush". The soldiers had never come to Lefya, having been tipped off that the fugitives had departed. Another of Father

Paul's ruses, perhaps? Henri was now doing the same job as before, but in Gabon, a thousand miles from Kumanga. He had also renewed his faith in the Catholic Church. He was happy

Derek insisted on contacting Jeremy Wilson's parents personally. They appreciated the gesture and laid no blame anywhere for what had happened to their son; they didn't even blame the governments of Kumanga of Bujavi. The guilt was very much on their side, or at least his father's, but hindsight is always painful. It just hadn't worked out as planned, that's all. God's will.

Axel Svensen would never be forgotten. They all owed a lot to the seemingly reckless actions of the fearless Scandinavian, actions which in retrospect played a large part in their eventual escape. It was too bad that such a powerful force of humanity had to die. But then, Derek reflected, it was probably how Axel himself would have wanted it. The Swede would never have wished to pass away in peaceful senility in some old peoples' home.

Derek, like Gordon, had never been one for committing his thoughts to paper. He never kept a diary, and was a reluctant letter writer. He spent so much time writing and dictating business reports that writing for pleasure just did not appeal to him. However, since time now hung heavily on his hands, he felt that he couldn't let his experiences go undocumented. He began to bring his thoughts together and made rough notes about his life, his career, his escapades, his fears, his opinions and his philosophies. Above all, he collated his recollections of Africa, from his first tour so many years ago to the more recent tribulations. He doubted if he would ever be able to put them together in an organised fashion, and certainly never interest a publisher; only famous people or literary geniuses have that privilege. But still, it would give him the satisfaction of bringing out the mental chaos which had been building up inside him since he left Kumanga. His thoughts were mainly about the ruthless ingratitude of peoples, of countries, of whole nations who do not appreciate the help they had been given, the start in life, the direction and training towards their eventual maturity. It would, of course, be centred around the Kumanga Affair, but would need much, much more to make it viable.

Derek felt more troubled and unstable now than he ever had done during the ordeal of fleeing for his life. That episode had a purpose, but now he had no purpose. Semi-retirement held no meaning. He was pleased to be with his family, of course, but he was missing Africa's enchantment. Obviously he could never go back to Kumanga, or to any place which had an extradition agreement, at least until the government changed. Under its "new image" program, though, CAC had branched out into Eastern and Central Africa, as well as some Caribbean countries and Asia. Most of the staff members being sent out to these newer stations were young and inexperienced, and the Company needed seasoned veterans to keep affairs in good order.

It was a little disconcerting to see that many of the recruits were asking to be let out of their contracts well before their tenure was up. They were disillusioned with what they found in the "developing" world, and not prepared to make the necessary adjustments and sacrifices. CAC needed people with maturity and experience to try and put a stop to these defections.

"Spoiled young college kids", was the frequent comment around the office, mainly from tough, wise, veteran Old Coasters. "Don't know the meaning of pioneer spirit. Expect to walk into some place like Malum Fashi or Ikot Ekpene and find it like Torquay. Think it's all glamour and holiday. Now if they'd been in the Gold Coast thirty years ago...."

Derek knew that if he asked he could land a responsible job in Kenya, Rhodesia, Uganda or even South Africa, where the Company had been looking for a foothold for years. This "new image" thing might just open the door to many more opportunities. He may even be considered for a General Manager position if he pushed for it. If he really wanted it. Dammit, he really ***did*** want it! But Debbie didn't, having just found her idea of heaven right here in England, and there was where the problem lay. Best not to say anything, at least, not yet. But he shouldn't leave it for ***too*** long, though, at the rate at which the Colonies were disappearing.

He kept dismissing the thought, but it seemed to keep returning, probing at him, teasing him.

But Derek couldn't help recalling the words spoken to him on his first tour by a sun-baked Old Coaster:

"Once you have seen Africa, you will forever hear her calling you back....."

EPILOGUE

Gordon Blake closed the book softly, Derek's picture staring out at him from the back of the jacket. Derek did go back to Africa, eventually. Nowhere near Kumanga, of course, but as General Manager of the Anglo-Rhodesia Development Corporation, which was CAC's joint holding in that country. The Company prospered under his command, despite the restrictions of Ian Smith's U.D.I.

Debbie had not gone with him, at least not at first. There had been a bitter quarrel, which had almost destroyed their marriage. In an effort to keep their relationship from falling apart completely, Debbie had reluctantly joined him for a few months of each tour, but it was never the same – not like the glory days of Moresia. They grew further apart emotionally, and it was a sad, bitter and disillusioned Debbie who finally gave Derek the ultimatum after six years of this aimless existence - give it up now or lose me and your children for ever. Derek gave in and took his pension, having completed well over the required amount of overseas service . It was time to go, anyway. That upstart Mugabe was slowly gaining support, making plans which would surely draw the country into chaos. The last thing Derek wanted to go through was another Kumanga!

Boredom became his greatest problem, especially when his book was finished and published. He knew he could never write another - he had put his all into this one.

But then Gordon knew all about boredom.

The wind had dropped completely, and the night was clear and calm. Gordon Blake closed his eyes. West Africa was very different now. Everything was different; the whole world was changing, leaving him behind, as it had left millions of others behind during its long history. Was that why he caught himself guiltily hoping that he wouldn't have to cope with it much longer?

Perhaps.

He lit another cigar, and watched the smoke curl upwards, no longer drawn by the draught from the fireplace. Life is like a cigar; it sparks into life, burns brightly at its prime, then sputters and dies. He wasn't quite ready to sputter just yet; he would keep going for as long as his spark remained.

Like the cigar.